the counterfeit CONVERT

Also by Linda Chadwick

Second Chances

the
counterfeit
CONVERT

Linda Chadwick

Bonneville Books
Springville, Utah

This is a work of fiction. The characters, names, incidents, places, and dialogue are products of the author's imagination, and are not to be construed as real.

ISBN 13: 978-1-59955-417-4

Published by Bonneville Books, an imprint of Cedar Fort, Inc., 2373 W. 700 S., Springville, UT 84663

Distributed by Cedar Fort, Inc., www.cedarfort.com

LIBRARY OF CONGRESS CATALOGING-IN-PUBLICATION DATA

Chadwick, Linda, 1969-
  The counterfeit convert / Linda Chadwick.
    p. cm.
  ISBN 978-1-59955-417-4 (acid-free paper)
  1. Mormons--Fiction. 2. Impostors and imposture--Fiction. 3. Dating
(Social customs)--Fiction. 4. New York (N.Y.)--Fiction. I. Title.

  PS3603.H3325H53 2010
  813'.6--dc22

  2010010731

Cover design by Angela D. Olsen
Cover design © 2010 by Lyle Mortimer
Edited and typeset by Megan E. Welton

Printed in the United States of America

10 9 8 7 6 5 4 3 2 1

Printed on acid-free paper

To my mother, Marilyn Paulsen,
for teaching me compassion and charity
through her example.

Also, to my husband, Lynn Chadwick,
for supporting me, encouraging me,
and for buying me my own laptop.

Acknowledgments

Thanks to Amy Carpenter for assisting in the editing process. And a special thank you to the Cache Valley Chapter of the League of Utah Writers for your critiques, your constructive criticism, and your support.

ne

As the elevator made its way to the fifteenth floor, Tristan Taylor took a deep breath and straightened his tie. Stepping into the lobby, he noticed the pleasing aroma of apples and cinnamon. The scent seemed to relax his nerves.

Taking a few steps into the room, Tristan saw the receptionist talking on the phone. He waited a few moments for her to finish and then approached the tall oak desk.

"Good afternoon, beautiful," he said. "My name is Tristan Taylor. I have an interview with Mr. Hodges."

The heavyset woman glared up at Tristan. Her tiny, square, red-framed glasses seemed to emphasize her intimidating green eyes. "I believe your appointment was thirty-five minutes ago," she said. "Mr. Hodges is now in a meeting."

Ignoring her unfriendly tone, Tristan cleared his throat and stepped up a little closer. "Yes, well, I'm running a bit behind today. You see, the N train broke down—again—so, if you would be kind enough to let Mr. Hodges know I've arrived . . . I don't mind waiting until he's finished."

"I'm sorry, sir. The interviews are over."

Clenching his teeth, Tristan leaned up against her desk. One side of his forehead began to throb with the pulsating blood that was surging through his veins.

"The interviews are not over, because I haven't had mine yet!" Tristan said.

"Mr. Taylor, Mr. Hodges interviewed twenty-two people for this position today, all of whom were on time. So you tell me, who do you think he's going to hire?"

Reaching over her, Tristan grabbed the phone from her desk and held it out in front of her.

"Call him!"

More than one person had told Tristan that one of his most undesirable traits was that he never seemed to know when to back down. He really never meant to come across as violent or psychopathic, but he soon found himself being escorted out of the building by two badge-wielding American Gladiators with badges who effortlessly tossed him onto the sidewalk. The ever-present crowd of New Yorkers swarmed around him without batting an eye.

"Don't ever show your face around here again," one of them called through the crowd.

"If you know what's good for you," the other said, chuckling, as they walked back into the building.

"They must really love their job," Tristan muttered. He gathered the crumpled remains of his portfolio, got to his feet, and joined the current of pedestrians. Out of the corner of his eye, he noticed a garbage can. He made his way over and tossed the pages in.

Dragging his feet back toward the subway station, Tristan stuffed his hands into his pockets and hung his head. He didn't care about constant shoves from those around him. His only thought was how he'd just blown what may have been his last chance to repair his career.

Dejectedly, Tristan made his way down to the 57th Street subway station. At this time of day, the train was almost empty. Resting his head back against the seat, he took a deep breath and slowly exhaled. He glanced at his reflection in the window as the lights of the tunnel whizzed by, disgusted with the face that stared back at him.

There had been other interviews over the last several months, but they all turned out the same way. There were just too many applicants with more experience. The only color on Tristan's resume was the Redline fiasco following him around like a dark, humiliating shadow. In every interview, it always seemed as though his reputation preceded him.

Being employed by one of the top advertising agencies in Chicago was like a dream come true. Tristan worked hard to make his way up the ladder and was finally given his own account.

Redline Cosmetics wanted a catchy slogan for their new line of lipstick. With some fast talking, and a lot of persuasion, Tristan's ad was soon plastered across magazines and billboards everywhere. But the wave of success he'd been riding soon came splashing down.

The tabloids called his ad sexist and degrading to women. Tristan never thought of it like that. A woman kneeling before her man as he swabbed the lipstick across her lips seemed passionate and alluring. Unfortunately, his employer sided with the press, and Tristan found himself unemployed.

Tristan foolishly had thought New York City would be the start of a better life. But after two months, he still had no job and no money. To make matters worse, he'd dragged his two friends along with him, promising them a better future.

Cole and Austin had been his best friends since the fourth grade when he'd moved to Cleveland, Ohio, from his hometown, Des Moines, Iowa. Cole and Austin were already friends, and Tristan was the new kid on the block.

Letting his mind wander back in time, Tristan remembered the first day they met. Neither Cole nor Austin had wanted anything to do with him. Try as he might, Tristan could not get them to accept him.

Austin had always been the playground bully, and Tristan was determined to change that. One day, the two of them got into an argument over the basketball hoop. Tristan's temper got the best of him, and he landed a punch that sent Austin to the ground.

The other kids formed a circle around them, egging on the fight. Tristan kept his fists tight and his arms up, ready for another round. Austin pulled himself to his feet and wiped some blood from his nose. Tristan thought for sure he was dead when he saw Austin heading toward him. Austin stopped right in front of him, and Tristan gulped down the lump in his throat.

"I'm not afraid of you," Tristan stuttered, feeling his knees shaking beneath him.

Suddenly, Austin smiled. That was the scariest moment of the whole fight. Tristan was sure Austin had gone completely insane. Austin then did something so unexpected it made Tristan flinch. He reached out his hand.

"Truce?" he asked Tristan.

Tristan lowered his arms and let out the breath he'd been holding. He reached out and gave Austin's hand a hard shake. "Truce," he agreed.

Cole, impressed by Tristan's courage—or lack of brains— also accepted him, and the boys formed an inseparable trio. As their friendship grew through the years, so did their loyalty to one another. They moved as a group through high school, college, and eventually to Chicago.

After the Redline fiasco, Tristan sat alone in his empty apartment. As he watched the repo men haul off his stereo system and big-screen television, he knew he had to make a move.

Tristan had always possessed a kind of resilient self-confidence, but when it came to venturing out on his own, he was terrified. So, after a little persuasion and a ton of guilt, he convinced Cole and Austin to accompany him to New York City, promising more money, lots of women, and plenty of excitement.

Instead, the women and the jobs both seemed to be taken. Furthermore, the only excitement they found was riding the subway without getting mugged.

☆ ☆ ☆

Tristan made his way to the tiny apartment he rented with Cole and Austin in Queens—a rundown rat trap above Bubba's Bistro, where Austin worked as lead dishwasher. Though none of them admitted it, Bubba scared the living daylights out of all three of them, but they kept their mouths shut since he let them live above his restaurant at a severely discounted rate.

Walking through the squeaky front door, Tristan slammed it shut behind him. He tossed the car keys on top of the small, round table that was leveled by a thin piece of wood wedged under one leg. He immediately went to the kitchen and dropped two ice cubes from the freezer into a glass. He reached for the bottle of Jack Daniels on the top shelf and poured it over the ice. He gulped down a couple of swallows and was ready to face the firing squad.

Tristan carried his drink into the adjoining living room that wasn't much larger than the tiny kitchen. The living room consisted of a tattered maroon couch with matching love seat, a blue recliner that no longer reclined, and a glass-top coffee table with a small crack down the center.

The apartment reminded Tristan too much of his childhood home and the destitute state he'd hoped to leave behind. Nevertheless, there it was staring back at him—everything from the worn beige carpet to the cracked ceilings.

"Well, what happened?" Cole finally asked.

"The same thing that always happens. I blew it!" Tristan stated. He flopped down on the couch and rested his head. He massaged the right side of his forehead with one hand, feeling a tension headache coming on.

Without delay, Cole was standing in front of him, reacting as well as Tristan expected him to. "Maybe it's time we packed up and went back home," he suggested. He adjusted his thick black glasses to better peer at Tristan with his dark brown eyes.

When Tristan looked up, he instantly recognized the unsettling expression on Cole's face. When the large vein in Cole's forehead stood out, it meant he'd reached his highest level of tolerance.

Cole was the tallest out of the three of them. He stood a good six feet two inches with a small-framed body. His short, spiky brown hair added to his look of intelligence.

Cole's terrible taste in clothing hadn't improved much over the years. It was almost symbolic of his intellect. No matter how hard Tristan had tried to reform Cole's appearance, he'd had little success.

Setting his drink on the coffee table, Tristan returned his glare. "You want us to go back home and admit defeat? No way! I'm not doing it!"

Sure, they were struggling, and the great opportunities the city had to offer weren't exactly knocking on their door, but going back home as a failure was not an option for Tristan.

"Tristan, we have no jobs and no money! Not only that, but we're relying on Austin, and the benevolence of Bubba, to pay the rent!" Cole replied. "Not very reassuring."

"Hey, I resent that," Austin piped up. "Bubba said I could possibly move up to line cook by the end of next week." He stopped chewing on the piece of red licorice in his hand and frowned at the back of Cole's head.

At five-eight, Austin was a little on the heavier side. He proudly sported a small, round belly that he claimed was hereditary. He had teal green eyes, and his sandy-blond hair curled just slightly.

Being the only one out of the three who never went to college, Austin harbored no regrets. He never once worried about what he was supposed to do in life. In fact, after graduating from high school, he was content with scooping ice cream.

"Ooh, line cook! Now we're in the money!" Cole exclaimed, waggling both hands high in the air.

"Hey, I make ten times more than the both of you, seeing as neither of you have jobs!" Austin roared back. He jumped to his feet, ready to defend his honor.

"Come on, guys. Don't argue," Tristan said, trying to interrupt. "There's got to be a solution."

Cole shook his head, and Tristan knew he was annoyed by

his hold-out-hope attitude. Tristan couldn't understand why Cole would want to surrender and go crawling back to his old job—the one he said he hated. After earning a degree in computer programming, he set off to find a challenging career in his field but ended up taking a job with an interior design company. His responsibilities included waiting around until someone had a computer problem they couldn't fix and then sweep in and save the day. It was tedious and relentless. Cole wanted something that would test his skills and reward him with a challenge, so he agreed to make the move with Tristan. But even here in Manhattan, the jobs were scarce and the qualified people were many.

"I'll tell you what," Tristan said. "Let's give it four more weeks. If we haven't found anything . . . well, then I'll go back home," Tristan said, sighing.

"Do you honestly think anything will change in four weeks? I mean, besides Austin's big promotion?"

"I've about had it with you!" Austin shouted. He hurled his chunky torso at Cole with full force and knocked him flat.

They wrestled around on the floor, each one trying to pin the other. Tristan watched calmly, chuckling.

Rising from the couch, Tristan threw himself on top, sending groans of pain into the air. After fifteen minutes of boys-will-be-boys fun, they sat up on the floor, trying to catch their breath.

"All right, Tristan. You win. Four more weeks, and then we go home," Cole panted.

"Great!" Tristan said. "And you know what? Because I have total confidence in our ability to succeed, tonight I'm taking my two best friends out on the town for a fancy dinner."

"Did you forget one small detail? We have no money!" Cole pointed out.

"You may be right about that, but I have something better than money." Tristan grinned as he dug a MasterCard out of his pocket. "I have plastic."

"You know you have to pay that back, right?" Austin stated

in all seriousness. Austin had never been the brightest street-light on the block, but Cole and Tristan had come to appreciate him for who he was. They thought he added humor to an otherwise boring existence.

"Oh, not with this card," Tristan teased. "This card, well, it's special."

"Really? How so?"

"I'm kidding, Austin. Will you just go get ready and let me worry about paying it back?"

As Cole and Austin went to change clothes, Tristan read the want ads. He skimmed down each column, noticing there were jobs in just about every field except what he was looking for.

Throwing the newspaper down on the coffee table, Tristan let out a dispirited groan. However grim the future seemed to be, he wasn't ready to give up. Something had driven him to come to New York, and he was determined to find out why.

TWO

"Table for three," Tristan announced. Roxie's was a little on the extravagant side, but he wanted to prove to Austin and Cole that things were still on the up and up.

"Do you have a reservation, sir?" asked the female hostess.

Tristan realized he should have called ahead, but he wasn't about to back down from a challenge. He casually placed one arm on the tall oak counter and cleared his throat.

"I sure do," he said with a grin. Flirting couldn't hurt his chances of getting a table, so he turned on the charm. "The name is Tristan. Tristan Taylor."

The hostess typed his name into the computer. "Oh, I'm sorry, Mr. Taylor. It doesn't look like you have a reservation tonight."

Cole stepped forward, amused with Tristan's efforts, but his stomach was growling. "Come on, Tristan. Let's go somewhere else."

Tristan waved him off before continuing his quest with the hostess. "Actually, you can call me Tristan, and I see your name is Mandy. I love that name." He focused in on her face, hypnotizing her with his stare. She returned his gaze, taking it all in before blushing like a lovesick schoolgirl. "Wow, you have the most incredible eyes," Tristan said in his most seductive tone of voice. "I'm sure I called ahead. Could you please check your list again?"

The hostess stood speechless for a moment, her mouth gaping open. "I-I suppose your reservation may have gotten lost. I could find you another table if you'd like."

Cole and Austin laughed quietly in the background, intrigued with Tristan's Casanova-like style. With dark brown hair that hung just to the top of his shoulders and thick, dark lashes that enhanced his blue eyes, not to mention the fact that his body was firm and muscular, it didn't take rocket science to understand why women found Tristan irresistible.

Besides having the looks, Tristan also had a certain charm that always got him what he wanted. He was a people magnet, and what was worse, he knew it.

The hostess picked up three menus and escorted them back to a table. She handed each of them a menu and then smiled again at Tristan as she handed him a small white piece of paper with her phone number on it. She gave him a wink and walked away.

"Um . . . Tristan, have you looked at the prices?" Austin said.

"It doesn't matter. We're celebrating."

"Celebrating what? Your enormous credit card debt?" Cole asked.

Tristan opened the menu and swallowed hard. "Do you think this kind of place has a dollar menu?"

"Come on, let's get out of here before the waiter comes over," Cole suggested.

Tristan stood up to leave. As he did, he bumped into a woman who had been walking by the table. The unexpected collision sent her designer bag to the floor, scattering its contents.

"That's just great!" she hissed. The woman wore a modest white dress with brown leather sandals on her feet. She stared at him for a brief moment with agitated green eyes before bending down to collect her belongings.

Tristan immediately dropped to one knee to assist her. "Here, let me help you," he said.

He picked her lipstick up off the floor and held it in his hand.

The small tube gave him a harsh reminder of his mistakes and the past he was trying to escape, causing him to cringe.

The woman reached out and ripped the lipstick from his hand. "I don't need your help, thank you very much," she snapped. She stood up and looked down at Tristan. "Why don't you watch where you're going?"

"Um, I think you ran into me," Tristan said. He rose from the floor so he could face her.

Her long, silky, chestnut brown hair was pulled back into a French braid and held with a yellow ribbon. Her cheeks were flushed. It made Tristan wonder if she was really that upset with him or if it was just overly warm in the restaurant.

"I don't think so! I was just walking by when—"

"What he meant to say was that he's sorry," Cole interrupted. "We were just in a hurry to leave."

Tristan rolled his eyes at Cole. The woman let out a huff as she stepped around Tristan and returned to her table.

"Did she shoot you down, man?" A young, eager waiter appeared beside Tristan with a pen in one hand and a tablet in the other.

"Shoot me down?" Tristan asked

"Yeah, you know, did she blow you off? You were asking her out, right?"

"No, I wasn't. We just bumped into each other. She's not my type."

"Oh, well, that's good. I hate to see nice guys get shot down in their prime," the waiter said. "Now, can I take your order?"

"No," Cole spoke up. "We were just leaving."

"Wait a minute," Tristan said, motioning for Cole to sit back down. "Why would you assume she turned me down for a date?"

"Oh, great," Cole said, sitting back down. "Here we go!" Anyone that had ever questioned Tristan's ability to seduce a woman usually got an earful.

"I didn't mean anything by it. I'm sure you get lots of dates," said the waiter.

"You bet I do!"

"Just not with someone like her."

"What do you mean?"

"Tristan, just let it go," Cole grumbled.

Austin let out a sigh. He realized they would not be leaving any time soon.

"No, I want to know what he meant by that statement." Tristan turned back to the waiter. "What? Is she married?"

"Not exactly."

"Dating someone? Engaged maybe?"

"No, she's single, as far as I know."

"Don't tell me she's a nun, because she doesn't look like any nun I've ever seen," Tristan said, watching her from across the crowded room.

"She's not a nun, but close. She's not exactly the type of woman someone like you would typically date." The waiter looked to his left and then to his right. He leaned over the table to keep his secret limited to the four of them.

"She's one of those, you know, Mormon people," he divulged. "Besides that, her dad was like, this billionaire, and he left all his money to his three daughters over there. They're way out of your league man, even if they do have to get married."

"Wait a minute," Cole interrupted. "How do you know so much about them?"

"They come in here every Thursday night for dinner. They're great tippers, so I usually try and get their table. You know, living on a waiter's income isn't exactly easy. When I worked over at—"

"Just get to the point," Tristan said.

"Oh, well, anyway, I always try to be friendly with people, because, you know, better tips. So they came in one night looking pretty down, and I asked them what was wrong. They went on for ten minutes talking about how their dad had just died and left them all this money. Not only were they upset about losing him, but apparently their cut of the inheritance depends on if they all get married by the time they turn twenty-five."

"So how old are they?" Tristan asked. His curiosity was getting the best of him.

"The two on the right are twins, Megan and Marley. They're only twenty-three, and as far as I know, they're both still on the market. But Rachel, the one that you were talking to, she turns twenty-five in just six months, and she has told me personally that there are no potential candidates."

"It sounds like they're New York's most eligible bachelorettes," Cole said. He really didn't want to know any more.

"You bet they are. But like I said, they're Mormons, so not many men want to get involved with them, if you know what I mean. Besides, they're pretty picky about who they go out with."

Just then, someone from the next table motioned for the waiter, and before Tristan could ask any more questions, he was gone.

"Wow. I can't remember a time before he started telling that story," Cole said. He opened his menu again and looked over the selection. "So, are we going to eat or what?"

"What did he mean by Mormon people?" Tristan asked.

"I know," Austin announced. "It's those people that get that kissing disease."

"That's mono, stupid," Cole clarified. "Just leave it alone Tristan. It's none of our business."

"It might be now." Tristan smiled. "I have an incredible idea. Well, more like a plan."

"No, Tristan! No more plans!" Cole growled.

"Come on, Cole. Just hear me out. What do you have to lose?"

"Oh, let me think. I've already lost my job, my money, and my dignity. What more could you take?"

"Now that just plain hurt. You know I have your best interest at heart."

"Bull! You only think of yourself!"

"Come on, Cole. I want to hear what he has to say," Austin pleaded.

"Fine. Just make it quick so we can enjoy digging deeper

into your credit card debt."

"Okay, here's the situation. They've got more money than they know what to do with, and we have none."

"Well, that's observant," Cole said.

"Yeah, get to the point, Tristan," Austin said.

"My point is, they need to get married right away, and we just happen to be three handsome bachelors. Are you following me?" Tristan asked.

Austin just shook his head in disbelief, his eyes wide while his mouth hung open. Cole glared at Tristan from across the table.

"You're insane!" Cole blurted out. "How much have you had to drink?"

"Look, we've been here two months, and nothing has changed for us. You said it yourself. We still have no jobs and no money. Why not marry these three women, take our part of the inheritance, and live comfortably the rest of our lives?"

"What's the catch?" Austin finally asked.

"Well, like the waiter said, they're probably looking for a Mormon boy to marry. But I figure we can pull that off easy enough. We'll just pretend we're already Mormons. They'll never have to know."

"From what I've heard about these Mormons, you could just marry all three of them and leave us out of it," Cole pointed out.

"Oh man, that's just wrong," Tristan said. "They must have some kind of rules they go by, like not marrying women from the same family. That would just be weird."

"It doesn't matter. We'll never convince them we're Mormons. We don't know anything about them."

"I think it sounds fun," Austin said. "Which one do I get?"

"Come on, Cole, think about it. Do you really want go back to Cleveland to live the rest of your life working at some dead-end job that you'll end up hating? This is our big opportunity. This is the reason I was driven to come here. We need money. We need options. We need those three women."

Cole stayed quiet, watching the girls from across the room. The reluctance written across his face was clear. He looked back over at Tristan and released a heavy sigh.

"What do we need to do?" he asked.

Tristan gave him an impulsive smile. "We need to get to know them and their religion. If we're going to act like Mormons, we need to know everything about them."

"They're leaving!" Austin yelped.

"Shh!" Tristan and Cole both hissed. They watched as the three women walked past their table and out the door.

"Let me handle this," Tristan said.

He rose from his seat and followed behind the three sisters. Tristan watched from a distance while Marley tried hailing a cab. Megan and Marley were almost identical, except for the light-framed glasses that Megan wore and the muscular build of Marley. They both had short, dusty brown hair with a slight red tint and green eyes.

Tristan immediately approached Rachel. She was the one he would focus on. She brought out his competitive nature. She challenged his manhood and threatened his charisma. He would redeem himself, if only for his own peace of mind.

Rachel's complexion was flawless—silky-smooth and radiant. She wore a gold chain around her neck with an emblem resembling a woman, but Tristan wasn't quite sure what it stood for.

"Excuse me, miss." Tristan grinned, exposing the only good thing he ever inherited from his father: his dimples. "I wanted to apologize for the way I acted earlier. It was totally my fault."

Rachel folded her arms and looked in the other direction. Megan and Marley stayed quiet. They watched his every move with skepticism. It was like he was on trial even though he hadn't done anything wrong—at least, not yet.

"Well, anyway, our waiter mentioned that you and your sisters were from the Mormon religion. Is that correct?" asked Tristan.

Whipping her head around, Rachel peered at him, if possible, more suspiciously than her sisters. "Yeah, so what? Are you from some national bureau of religion?" she said.

Smiling at her hostility, Tristan continued. "Not exactly. My name is Tristan Taylor. My two friends and I are also of the Mormon faith."

A cab pulled up to the curb, and Megan and Marley darted into the car without giving Tristan a second thought. He sensed they were annoyed by his presence. He didn't mind. It was Rachel he was interested in, and, to his delight, she didn't follow her sisters into the waiting taxi.

"Is that really the best pick-up line you've got?" she asked. "I mean, really, you look like an intelligent guy. Why don't you try something a little more creative? Like how incredible my eyes are?"

Tristan's jaw dropped in shock, and he stood frozen by her unexpected rejection. Rachel took a step toward the car.

"Better luck next time," she said.

Tristan quickly picked his ego up off the ground and tried to come up with something that would stop her from leaving.

"I'm sorry if you thought I was trying to come on to you," he responded in a soft, velvety voice that would have made most women weak in the knees. Instead, Rachel kept her distance, her face tight and unfriendly.

"Weren't you?"

"On the contrary. I was only trying to find out where you attend church so that we might join your congregation. You see, my friends and I just moved here from Chicago and have found it difficult meeting others of our faith. I was hoping you could help us." He strained his vocal cords to emphasize his desperation.

Out of the blue, her cold, unfeeling eyes lightened. "Oh, I'm sorry about that. It's just sometimes people around here can be so judgmental and cruel when they find out we're LDS. You know what I mean?"

Tristan's brain went into overdrive. *Why is she talking about*

LSD? I thought I heard Mormons were supposed to be incredibly strict about drugs. Clearing his throat, he continued. "Oh, I know exactly what you mean. Being LSD can be very challenging." He poured it on thick, playing into the charade.

Apparently he didn't play well enough, because her suspicion returned, and she took a step back. "Well, anyway, tell me where you live, and maybe I can tell you what ward you're in."

"Oh, well, you see, my friend Austin, he has this thing, well, a phobia actually, about meeting new people. If we could tag along with you and your sisters, it might make the transition a little bit easier for him."

"Um, we live in the Upper East Side and go to the singles ward there."

"That's perfect. The three of us just happen to be single."

"Come on, Rachel. Let's go!" Marley yelled from the cab.

Rachel took out a slip of paper from her purse and jotted down the address of the church building.

"Maybe you'd better put down your number as well, you know, just in case we get lost or something."

After writing down her number, Rachel handed him the paper. As she got into the car, Tristan noticed a fragment of doubt still evident on her face, but Tristan was confident he could get rid of it completely before too long.

★ ★ ★

Tristan went to bed that night feeling more optimistic than he had in months. As he lay there in the dark, he let his mind wander. He thought about his future and what this could mean. With the amount of money Rachel and her sisters had, there was no telling what he could accomplish—anything from starting his own advertising company to traveling the world—the opportunities were endless.

Placing his hands behind his head, Tristan mentally went over the plan. He only had two days to learn everything he could about the Mormons before he and his roommates attended church. After studying the Mormons' beliefs and their way of life, he would then incorporate them into his own way of living. It couldn't be that hard.

The only real challenge seemed to be Rachel. Unlike most women, she resisted his gentleman-like charm and handsome physique. Instead of instantly warming to him, she seemed more annoyed than infatuated.

As Tristan rolled over and nestled deeper into his pillow, Rachel's face flashed through his mind. He could sense she was indeed wary of his intentions. He couldn't blame her. After all, he was lying. Though he'd lied to women before, none of them ever questioned his motives. Perhaps he should have felt a bit guiltier about his deception, but his dreams were closer to becoming a reality than they had been in months.

Although Rachel's hard-core attitude should have been maddening, Tristan actually found it intriguing. In fact, all of her cold cruelty made him that much more determined to succeed. Rachel may be unlike the other women he'd dated, but in the end he would prevail.

Three

When the alarm clock blasted some hideous rock and roll song, Tristan jumped up and pulled on his blue jeans. The day dawned with the start of a new quest—a quest that would hopefully lead to his financial freedom.

After deciding on a nice red and black plaid button-up shirt, Tristan woke Cole and Austin to inform them of his plan. They both grumbled something semi-understandable, which Tristan didn't care to have them repeat, and pulled the covers over their heads. Obviously they weren't as enthused about the whole thing as they were last night. Tristan didn't have time to argue, so he left them home in bed while he ventured out to do some research.

After a half hour on the subway, Tristan took the steps two at a time up to the main entrance of the New York Public Library. After filling out a few forms to prove that he was a city resident, a cute librarian handed Tristan his new library card, allowing him access to thousands upon thousands of volumes.

Logging into the library computer, Tristan found numerous books about the Mormon religion. He jotted down a few titles he thought might be helpful and set off through the maze of shelves.

Tristan found books on the pioneers, early Church history, and several more books on some person named Joseph Smith. Since he knew nothing about the Mormons, he found it difficult to know which book would give him the best information.

Finally, on the very top self, he spotted a large book sticking out from all the others. He pried it from its snug position and read the title more closely: *Mormonism for Dummies*. Perfect. Without hesitation, Tristan headed for the counter to check out his book. As he approached the checkout line, he instantly recognized the girl working behind the enormous stack of returned books. It was Megan!

Oh man! Tristan thought. He quickly ducked down behind the large man standing in front of him. The man glared over his shoulder and then moved away, obviously a little apprehensive of Tristan's odd behavior.

Tristan held the book up in front of his face and moved behind one of the large bookcases. Taking a deep breath, he peeked out around the end. It was Megan all right. Tristan watched her as she picked up a book from the pile and scanned it in. Apparently she was clueless that he was even in the building.

"That was close," Tristan muttered. How would he have explained checking out a book on Mormons? It would have blown everything.

The large man from the line walked past Tristan, shaking his head and eyeing him with suspicion. Tristan just smiled and nodded.

How was he going to get out of the building without being noticed? Coming up with a plan on the fly, Tristan smirked at his own genius and pulled out his cell phone. He waited impatiently until an irritated voice answered.

"This better be important!" Cole howled.

"It is. I need you to call the New York Public Library, main branch, and ask for Megan. When she gets on the phone, keep her busy for about five minutes."

"Dude. Are you on something?"

"No, I'm at the library. I'm trying to check out a book on the Mormons, but Megan from the restaurant last night works here. I can't very well check out the book with her standing right there."

"Why can't you just go to another library?" Cole whined. "Or better yet, just come home, and we'll call the whole thing off."

"Do I need to remind you that last night you agreed to be a part of this plan and are now obligated to help by whatever means necessary?"

"No, you don't need to remind me. I'm well aware of the delusional world you've sucked me into," Cole growled.

"Come on, Cole. I really need your help."

"Fine," Cole grumbled. "Just give me a few minutes to find the number."

"Thanks, man! You saved the day."

"Yeah, whatever!"

Tristan waited behind the shelf and pretended to look at books until Megan was called to the phone. When her back was turned, he swiftly went to the counter and checked out the book. He set off on a fast-paced jog out the door and down the flight of stairs and made his way to the subway station.

✶ ✶ ✶

"Well? Did you get it," Cole asked when Tristan walked through the door.

"Yeah, I got it," he answered.

Cole was sitting on the couch smoking a cigarette and drinking his morning cup of coffee. The scowl on his face and his tone of voice told Tristan he was still perturbed about the early wake-up call.

Cole started smoking in college and was up to a pack or more a day. Tristan warned him that without money, it was going to be next to impossible to support his habit, but Cole didn't seem to care. To curb his craving, he would discreetly dip into the savings account that his parents so graciously supplied. Cole was an only child, and apparently his parents deemed it their responsibility to take care of him for the rest of their lives.

Tristan went to the kitchen and poured himself a cup of coffee and then took a seat on the couch next to Cole. He set the book on the coffee table.

"I thought for sure we were toast when I saw Megan working at the library," said Tristan.

"Let's just hope that book gives us all the information we'll need to pull off this hoax."

"Don't worry, I'll find out what we need to know. Then, once we turn on the charm, the three of them won't know what hit them."

"You seem pretty sure of yourself. But like the waiter said, they're not exactly the kind of women we're used to dating."

Tristan let out a loud huff. "Women are women no matter what religion they are."

"You better be careful, man. She's probably not like the other girls you've been with," Cole warned.

"I could give you the same advice," Tristan said.

Dodging the flying pillow, Tristan went to his room to start reading. He cracked open the book and skimmed through the pages, looking for the major points of the book. He figured he could get the gist of it without actually spending the whole day reading.

He read about Joseph Smith, the founder of the Church, and the vision that revealed the golden plates, which were now the Book of Mormon.

Tristan found that the Mormons believed in a premortal life as well as an afterlife, which were things he'd always wondered about. It answered many of the questions that had been in his mind for years, as well as some he hadn't thought about.

Tristan had gone to church a couple of times with Cole over the years, but religion had never been a significant part of his life. His father was convinced that God didn't exist, and he'd drilled into Tristan from the time he was little that anyone who believed in that kind of nonsense was a fool. After a while, Tristan just dropped it.

Skipping several chapters, he came to a section that left him utterly speechless. He snatched up the book and headed for the living room.

Hesitating for a moment, Tristan watched his two best

friends from the doorway of his bedroom. They were clueless of the bombshell that he was about to drop on them.

Cole was sitting in his chair watching baseball on television. He had a bottle of beer in one hand and a cigarette in the other. Austin had finally pulled himself out of bed and was sitting across the room working on a crossword puzzle and sipping a cup of coffee.

Tristan let out a soft sigh. It was not going to be easy to convince them to change their lifestyles for the greater good.

"Hey, guys? We have a problem," Tristan said. He walked into the living room and began reading straight from the book like it was actual scripture. " 'The Mormons adopt a code of health called the "Word of Wisdom," which prohibits alcohol and hot drinks, such as coffee and tea. Mormons also abstain from smoking or chewing tobacco.' "

Tristan glanced up momentarily to find his friends' pale faces staring back at him. The room suddenly became hot, and Tristan could sense they weren't buying it. He cleared his throat and tried a new approach.

"Well, it also says to use meat sparingly and eat more fruits and grains, which, you know, sounds like a pretty healthy lifestyle," Tristan said with a smile.

"That's too bad for them. They don't know what they're missing," Cole said.

"Yeah, that sounds like a pretty strict religion," said Austin.

"A religion we've got to abide by if we're going to convince these three girls we're really Mormons," Tristan said. He slammed shut the book and sat down next to Cole.

Cole glared at Tristan with stubborn eyes. "No way. I'm not giving up my smokes or my coffee. I'll sacrifice my booze, but not my smokes."

"We're not really converting to this religion," Austin argued. "We can just hide it. Like that time we went to Marshall's eighteenth birthday party. We never told anyone what happened there."

"It's a good thing we didn't," Cole said, laughing.

Cole jumped off the couch and darted across the room to give Austin a quick high-five to seal the memory. When he returned to the couch, Tristan tried again to make them understand.

"Come on, guys, this is hardly the same thing. We've got to live like these Mormons if we're going to pull this off. When the whole thing is over, you can go back to whatever lifestyle you want, but until then—"

"No, Tristan, I'm not doing it," Cole reiterated.

"You both promised to do whatever was necessary."

Austin looked over at Cole, who was shaking his head. The look on his face was that of someone in pain. The vein in his forehead stood out, and his eyebrows crinkled.

"I really have to quit smoking?" Cole asked.

"Think of it this way," Tristan said. "You're breaking a nasty habit while ensuring your financial future at the same time. Isn't that worth the sacrifice?"

"Fine! I'll go buy some nicotine gum tomorrow, but I'm not promising anything."

Tristan picked up Cole's pack of cigarettes and crushed them in his hand. Cole let out a tiny, helpless groan as Tristan threw the ruined pack in the garbage can.

Austin gulped down the last of his coffee as he watched Tristan take the coffee maker and the can of coffee outside to the dumpster, along with their last bottle of whisky from the kitchen cupboard. When he returned, Tristan tried his best to lift their spirits, assuring them this was all for the best.

"We'll see about that tomorrow morning when you're dying for your morning pick-me-up," Cole grumbled.

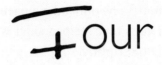our

Tristan reached over and shut off the annoying music that blasted from his alarm clock. "Not yet," he moaned. He closed his eyes and tried drifting back to the dream he so desperately wanted to finish.

Opening one eye, Tristan wearily looked over at the clock. In a panic, he sprang from his bed. His foot caught the covers, and he went flying to the floor. He quickly got to his feet and glanced over at the red numbers on the clock that read 8:07 a.m. He grabbed his nicest pair of blue jeans from the bedroom closet and hopped down the hallway with one leg in and one out.

"Time to get up!" he hollered.

"Put a sock in it, Tristan!" Cole yelled back.

"Guys, I slept in! Church starts in forty-five minutes and the subway will take at least half an hour! Let's go, let's go!"

Five minutes later, Austin walked into the living room. He tucked the bottom of his bright yellow and purple flowered shirt into his olive green denim pants and pulled up his zipper.

"What in the name of all that's holy are you wearing?" Tristan gasped.

"What?" Austin asked. He turned to look at his reflection in the window.

"You look like you've just been plucked out of some old lady's flower garden."

"You said to dress nice."

"Yeah, nice, not eccentric!" Tristan sighed heavily. He rubbed the familiar spot on his forehead, feeling the pain setting in. "Cole, let's go!"

When Cole entered the room, Tristan was sure he would lose the blueberry muffin he'd just devoured. Cole was sporting a burnt orange and navy blue striped shirt with white corduroy pants that fit a little too tightly.

"Dude," Tristan groaned.

"What's wrong?"

"Those pants look like they belong to your little brother."

"I don't have a brother."

"Exactly!"

"Girls need to see what the good Lord blessed me with," he smirked with self-confidence. He patted his rear end, just to get the point across.

"Not at church!"

"But you said to—"

"Dress nice," Tristan finished. "I know, I know. Let's just go!"

★ ★ ★

The three friends made their train just in the nick of time.

"This has got to be the worst plan you've ever come up with, Tristan," Cole grumbled, scowling. "No morning coffee, no cigarette, and now you're forcing us to go listen to some preacher in a church we know nothing about."

"Oh, I don't know. I think he's done worse," Austin intervened. "Remember the time we stole his father's car and took it on a joyride, only to end up at the police station?"

"Borrowed. I was only borrowing it," Tristan argued.

"Yeah, 'borrowed without asking,' " Austin laughed.

"I stand corrected," Cole said, sighing.

"Have a little faith, will you? This plan is foolproof. Besides, it's only church. It's not like we're breaking the law or something."

"They call it impersonation," Cole said.

"Just act like you know what you're doing, and try not to talk too much."

They got off at Lincoln Center and jogged a block to their destination. Their pace slowed as they watched the others walk into the building. The men were all decked out in suits and ties, and the women wore nice dresses. The first thought Tristan had when he saw the women was how modest they all looked. Although it was warm and sunny, there were no bare shoulders, no dipping necklines, and their dresses hung just below the knee. Not only that, he realized they were walking into the cleanest building Tristan had ever seen in Manhattan.

"Way to go, Tristan! You didn't tell us this was a formal event. We're way underdressed," Austin said.

"Speak for yourself, tulip," Cole said. "I look good."

"Yeah, sure, if it were 1970," Austin said.

"You just—"

"Hey, guys, we're at church, remember?" Tristan interrupted. "I didn't know how they dressed, honest. I wasn't able to finish the whole book. But I don't think they'll kick us out just because of the way we're dressed, so let's go in and find the girls."

The three of them entered the building and stood in the corner of the foyer. They watched several more well-dressed members come in. Some nodded their heads, and others said good morning to them.

"They're going to know we don't belong here. We stand out like a cowboy in the ghetto!" Austin squawked.

"Calm down," Tristan ordered. "Just act casual and follow my lead."

Tristan led his friends over to the chapel doors, where two men were shaking hands with everyone that entered.

"Welcome," the older man said. He held out his hand. "I'm Brother Peterson, the second counselor in the bishopric."

Austin looked at Cole, who shrugged his shoulders. He turned back to the man and shook his hand.

"Whose brother did you say you were?" Austin asked.

"No, I'm Brother Peterson." The man smiled.

"Yeah, but who's Peterson?" Cole asked, still puzzled by this introduction.

"You know what? Just call me Doug," he said with a friendly grin. "Are you new to the ward?"

Tristan quickly scanned the crowd for Rachel. He found her sitting on the second row next to her sisters and smiled to himself. He was the hunter, and she was his unsuspecting prey.

"Yes, we just moved here," Tristan informed the man. "If you'll excuse us, we'll find our seats now."

Tristan eagerly entered the chapel and headed for the front.

"Come on, Tristan, we're sitting in the back," Cole said. He grabbed Tristan by the right arm and directed him to the back of the room. "All we need is to draw more attention to ourselves."

Tristan reluctantly went along. They took their seats on the back row and looked around the chapel. Someone was playing organ music in the front. Those around them whispered to one another. Tristan couldn't help but wonder if they were the topic of discussion.

Tristan kept his sights isolated on Rachel. She pushed a piece of hair out of her face and smiled at something her sister had said. She actually wasn't too bad to look at. She had an innocent beauty to her that was different from all the other women Tristan had dated. *Innocent is good*, Tristan thought. His confidence overflowed. There was no doubt in his mind that she would soon be his.

The meeting opened with a guy who introduced himself as Bishop Anderson conducting. He was an older gentleman with grey hair and bifocals. As he spoke to the members of the congregation, Tristan soon came to realize everyone was referred to as sister or brother, not just who you were related to. Tristan had yet to figure out why, but he thought perhaps it was because everyone felt like family. They were all very friendly and seemed genuinely concerned for one another.

After a few brief announcements, everyone began to sing some hymn that put Austin right to sleep. After the song came the prayer. Everyone around them folded their arms and bowed their heads. Tristan followed the crowd, elbowing Cole, who elbowed Austin to do the same.

Tristan hadn't heard a lot of prayers in his life. About the only time he ever heard God mentioned was when his old man was swearing at him. This prayer was full of thanks and gratitude, as well as an abundance of blessings for their church leaders.

When the prayer ended, Cole raised both hands high in the air and let out an extra loud "amen," a "praise the Lord," and a few "hallelujahs." Tristan couldn't tell if he was sincerely trying to take part in the meeting or just trying to get back at him for dragging him out of bed. Nevertheless, a few people turned around to stare at them. Tristan punched Cole in the side. Cole dropped his arms with a slight whimper.

"What?" he asked.

"I don't think they say those things in this church," Tristan whispered.

"Well, maybe they should."

Tristan continued to watch and listen carefully, taking mental notes to familiarize himself with the routine. The bishop announced the sacrament would be next.

As another song started playing, Tristan was the first one out of his seat to partake in the ceremony. After two steps, Tristan froze in place. He noticed everyone had remained seated. It seemed rather odd, but he quickly sat back down before anyone noticed.

When the song was over, a couple of guys dressed in white shirts and ties prayed over a table covered in a white tablecloth. Another guy dressed in a white shirt and blue tie approached Tristan, holding out a small silver tray that contained tiny pieces of bread. He looked into the tray and realized it must be the sacrament, but he was confused as to what he was supposed to do with it. The one time he'd attended mass with Cole, communion had been done in the front, not in his seat.

He finally opened his mouth and waited to receive the piece of bread on his tongue. The man leaned over and discreetly whispered in Tristan's ear. "If you want to partake of the sacrament, you need to take a piece and eat it," he said.

Tristan shook off his mortification and quickly placed a piece of bread in his mouth. He thanked the man for the bread, but the man continued to stand beside him.

"I don't want any more, thank you," Tristan said.

"You need to pass the tray along," he responded. The man bit his bottom lip and chuckled softly.

Letting out a long sigh, Tristan took the tray from his hand. He'd really blown that one. He elbowed Cole, who was playing around with his cell phone. Cole saw the tray and immediately reached into his pockets.

"I think I have some quarters here somewhere," he said.

"No!" Tristan whispered, a little louder than he intended. But it was too late. The quarters clanged down into the metal tray, echoing through the chapel.

"You idiot! You're supposed to eat the bread," Tristan hissed.

"Well, I don't want any." Cole pushed the tray back toward Tristan.

"Eat one!"

"I'm not hungry!"

"I am," Austin leaned over and whispered. "Pass it down here."

"It's not lunch, it's like Communion. Being that we are Mormons, we're required to eat the bread," Tristan rebuked through clenched teeth.

"Oh," Cole said.

He swiftly picked out the change and put a piece of bread into his mouth. He then passed it along to Austin as more and more spectators turned around in their seats to gawk at them.

Austin took the tray full of bread and swiped up a handful. He stuffed the fistful of bread into his mouth and then passed the half-empty tray down the row.

Tristan slid down in his chair and covered his face with his hands, humiliated by his idiot friends' lack of understanding. If he'd only taken the time to study more about the Mormons, perhaps he could have shined some light on the situation. Now they really did look like incompetent morons instead of knowledgeable Mormons.

When the water came around, Tristan took one of the small white cups and drank the water. Placing the cup into his lap, he passed the tray on to Cole.

"Where's the wine?" Cole questioned.

"They don't drink alcohol, Cole," Tristan said.

"Yeah, but—"

"Just take one and drink it like you know what you're doing."

Cole drank the water and passed the tray to Austin. Austin looked into the tray and gulped down six small cups before passing it down the aisle.

"I like this church," Austin smiled. "You get to eat and drink without ever leaving your chair."

After a sermon on faith and two more speeches about obedience, the meeting closed with a song and a prayer. Tristan looked over at Cole and Austin, who were sound asleep and snoring slightly. He reached over and thumped the back of their chairs, annoyed that they were not taking things seriously.

Finally the meeting and the humiliation came to an end. Tristan, Cole, and Austin followed the three girls to the foyer and then waited patiently while the girls finished their conversation with two other women.

Tristan went right for Rachel. "Hello," he said. "Remember me?"

"Oh yes—Tristan, the Mormon from Chicago." Rachel smirked.

"You remembered my name." Tristan smiled. "These are the friends I was telling you about, Cole and Austin."

"Oh yes, Austin. The shy one," Rachel said.

"What?" Austin began. Tristan bumped Austin out of the way before he could say anything else.

"And these two lovely ladies must be your sisters?"

"Yeah, this is Megan and Marley."

Cole shook hands with Marley but focused on Megan. After speaking with her on the phone at the library, he could sense her intelligence and knew she was the one for him.

"Very nice to meet you," Cole said.

He took her hand in his and gave it a gentle shake. He stood close enough for Megan to smell his alluring scent of Aspen cologne as he focused in on her green eyes. *Tristan's not the only one that can be charming with the ladies,* Cole thought when he saw the excitement that came across her face.

Megan grinned and looked down at the floor. "Nice to meet you too."

Austin could see he was stuck with the one that looked like a bounty hunter. She may as well have had the words, "Don't mess with me" tattooed on her forehead. He took a deep breath and held out his hand.

"Nice to meet you, Marley. I'm Austin," he stuttered.

She looked down at his hand as if he were infected with the plague and rolled her eyes. "How nice for you," she sneered, without taking his hand. "I'm going to class, Rachel. If you want to stand out here and shoot the breeze, be my guest."

Rachel let out a laugh, which sounded a bit more like a snort, and looked back at Tristan. "Come on, Sunday school's this way."

"Actually, we have a prior engagement. Right, Tristan?" Cole spoke up.

"Oh, right. We'll catch the Sunday school next week," Tristan said. "But I heard something about an activity Saturday heading upstate. Are you going?"

"If I said no, would you still go?"

"No, probably not. I thought it'd be nice if we could go together," Tristan said. He could feel his self-esteem dwindling by the second.

"Well, I've got to give you credit. You sure don't give up easily."

"One of my few weaknesses."

"Okay, fine," she said. "The details of the activity are posted on the bulletin board. We'll meet you there." With a flip of her long, shiny hair, she swirled around and walked off, leaving Tristan utterly speechless.

What had he done wrong? He'd used all his best fail-proof lines, his flawless boyish charm, and his unsurpassed flattering facial expressions. She should have fallen right into his arms.

"Wow!" Cole laughed. "I never thought I'd see the day when the almighty Tristan Taylor got the shaft."

"I'm not out of the game yet," Tristan responded with optimism. "I just need to find my angle."

"What angle?" Austin teased. "From the looks of it, she thinks you're a leech. You know, the kind that digs its head into your skin, and you have to light a match to get it out."

"That's a tick, you moron," Tristan said, slapping Austin upside of the head. "She doesn't know me yet. Just wait. After the activity on Saturday, she'll think I'm the Greek God of love."

"Whatever, man," Austin said. "You're not even Jewish!"

Tristan stopped abruptly at the top of the stairs leading down to the subway station and turned to look at Austin in disbelief. Cole bit his bottom lip, holding back the laughter. "Austin, I'm talking about *Greek* mythology," Tristan tried to explain. "You know, like Neptune, Venus, and Jupiter. Does any of this ring a bell?"

"Jeez, I wasn't born yesterday," Austin said.

"Sometimes I wonder," Cole said.

"Wait, so, you're talking about those naked statues, right?" Austin asked.

"Never mind," Cole grunted. "You really think you've still got a chance with her, Tristan?"

"Oh yeah!" Tristan said confidently. "She's just going to be more difficult than I anticipated. But I'll get her."

"I don't know," Cole said. "I have to agree with Austin. She's not very receptive to your Casanova charm. Megan, on the other hand, was entirely captivated by my good looks!"

"Good looks?" Tristan asked. He glanced over at Cole's choice in clothing and chuckled. "Are you sure she wasn't just hypnotized by your colorful stripes?"

"Let's leave my stellar fashion sense out of this. What if Rachel isn't like every other woman and doesn't happen to fall all over you?"

"Leave Rachel to me. You just concentrate on Megan while Austin concentrates on Marley."

"This doesn't seem fair," Austin protested. "I mean, Cole gets the brainy, polite one, and you get the strong-headed but beautiful one. What do I get? The Amazon woman with attitude. She'd just as soon crush me like a cockroach as look at me," Austin grumbled.

"Why don't you try demonstrating some of your outstanding qualities?" Cole suggested. "Like your distinguishing art of clumsiness and your lack of brain activity. Then follow that up with your poor physical condition. You should have no problem impressing her."

"Ha!" Austin croaked nervously. "But seriously, there's no way I can keep up with her."

"Maybe she'll see you as a humanitarian project," Cole said laughing.

"Just do the best you can. No, do better," Tristan encouraged Austin. "We need these girls. I don't know about you, but I don't want to live the rest of my life residing in some old apartment building that should have been condemned years ago and doing grunt work for someone named Bubba."

"You're right, Tristan. The good life sounds very appealing," Cole said. "But what happens when they catch on to us? What then? Do we go to jail for impersonating a Mormon?"

"Don't be ridiculous," Tristan said. "Besides, as long as we play our cards right, they'll never find out."

Five

Tristan pulled his blue jeans out of the dresser drawer and slid them on. His stomach was in knots over seeing Rachel again. Skepticism wasn't an emotion he was used to getting from women. Somehow he'd been thrown off course and washed into unfamiliar waters.

It was true—Rachel was cold and strangely insensitive to his masculine charm. She also seemed completely oblivious to the fact that he was throwing himself at her with every mastered technique he had. Nonetheless, today was a new day, his ego was still intact, and he was headed out to meet her at the singles ward activity.

Paintball had never been something Tristan had been interested in, but he was confident he could pull it off. He thought of himself as a great actor. He could slip into any character with ease. He'd done it many times while growing up.

Wanting to hide the fact that his father was the town drunk and a bum, Tristan would fabricate interesting stories. He would tell people that his father worked for the government and was away on a top-secret mission. The stories were his way of dealing with the disappointment he had for his father. In his boyish mind, he figured if he made his father into a hero, then he might become one.

Cole and Austin knew about his father and were intrigued

with his elaborate stories. Though most of the town knew the truth, they seemed content with letting Tristan live in an imaginary world.

When Tristan was eighteen, he finally realized his father would never be the man that existed in his mind. Graduating from high school was supposed to be a monumental occasion, but when his father showed up drunk, it became the darkest day in Tristan's life.

On that day, Tristan ripped his father from the pedestal he'd placed him on. He took any love he had left for the man, as well as the hurt and disappointments, and locked them away, leaving only anger and hate. He then worked extra hard to be the kid that everyone loved to be around. He wanted everyone to know he was nothing like his old man.

★ ★ ★

Shaking off past memories, Tristan finished dressing and went to find Cole. When he walked into the living room, he noticed Cole sitting on the edge of the couch hunched over the coffee table. He walked around the end of the couch to get a better look.

Cole was frantically tearing through the silver lining of a small package, depositing two green pieces of candy into the palm of his hand. Tristan looked down at the table, reading the label on the package: mint flavored nicotine gum. Cole quickly stuffed the pieces into his mouth and then glared up at Tristan. He chomped on the gum, sounding something like a cow at the feeding trough, as he tried to extract the nicotine.

"You'd better pace yourself, buddy, or you'll never break the habit," Tristan said.

"Don't start with me, Tristan. I wouldn't even need this gum if it wasn't for your lame-brain idea," Cole hissed.

"Okay, okay, I get it." Tristan stepped back and held up both hands in defense. "Anyway, are you ready for some fake, well-supervised, colorful, paint-filled violence?"

"No! As a matter of fact, I'm perfectly content with my butt stuck to this springy, uncomfortable couch watching Rachel Ray cook while I masticate my gum!" Cole yelled.

Cole loved to cook, and it was a good thing he did. Tristan knew how but would rather order out, and Austin's specialty was macaroni and cheese. Cole read food magazines and watched how-to videos, so he was always coming up with some out-of-this-world recipe to try out on Tristan and Austin.

"Jeez, calm down. You're doing this for all of us."

"Tristan, I swear if you tell me one more time it's for the best, I'm dragging you all the way back to Cleveland, even if it means breaking your legs so you fit in my suitcase."

"Oh, come on, I saw the way Megan looked at you. . . . It won't be long before you'll have her eating out of your hand."

"She's not a pigeon, Tristan!"

"It was a figure of speech. But hey, if you want I could give you some pointers."

"Let's just go before I remember why I don't listen to your quirky ideas."

★ ★ ★

Tristan scanned the crowd for Rachel. It was a beautiful spring afternoon without a cloud in the sky. He took a deep breath when he spotted her fully geared up and walking his way.

"All right, boys. Let's go have some fun," Tristan said.

"Well, if it isn't the Chicago trio," Rachel said.

"Hi, Rachel." Tristan smiled. "Nice to see you made it."

"Not a big surprise. I kind of implied I was coming," she said shortly. "I figured I'd see the three of you here."

"You know it!" Cole mocked. "Any Mormon activity that includes guns and girls has to be the bomb!" Cole threw both fists high into the air. Tristan elbowed him in the ribs. "Ouch!" Cole cried, rubbing his side.

Tristan wasn't about to let Cole's bitterness ruin the day. "Yeah, this should be great. Where do we get our gear?" he asked.

"Over by the shed," Rachel responded. She pointed her

finger in the direction of a small blue building.

"I'm not sure where you mean. Do you mind escorting us?"

"What, are you, like, two?" Rachel asked.

"That depends." Cole smirked. "Are you talking actual physical years, or just mental?"

After a threatening look from Tristan, he and Austin headed for the shed while Tristan stood waiting for Rachel to respond.

She cracked a tiny smile that only lasted a brief second, but it was long enough for Tristan to get a glimpse of reassurance.

"Fine, come on," she said.

While they walked, Rachel explained how the game was played and that he would need to choose a partner. That was just what Tristan wanted to hear. It was the opening he'd been waiting for.

"Since you seem to know what you're doing, I can't go wrong with you as my partner," Tristan said with self-assurance. "What do you say?"

Rachel stopped in front of the shed and placed both hands firmly on her hips. "Well, that depends. Are you better with paintball pellets than you are with women?"

"You'll just have to find that out for yourself," he said. He cocked one eyebrow. "I mean with paintball, of course."

"Good looks *and* arrogance. How lucky am I?"

The words "good looks" sent a boost of self-confidence surging through his system. So what if she thought he was arrogant? Handsome was still on her list, and he could live with that for now.

Cole and Austin were already suited up and had somehow talked Megan and Marley into being their partners. As Tristan allowed Rachel to him get fitted with his protective gear, he noticed an unexpected predator coming their way.

He was tall and thin, almost scrawny looking, with bleach-blond hair that was spiked in the front. He walked with confidence, flaunting his designer jeans and black cashmere sweater. High-class was written all over him, which included an I'm-out-of-your-league leer splattered across his pale face.

A deep sigh escaped Rachel's lips as he walked straight up to her with a devious smile and kissed her cheek. Tristan took a quick step back to analyze the new situation unfolding before his eyes.

"Hey, Rae! Are we teaming up?" he said in with a high pitched tone. Tristan could sense he was claiming his territory by his tone of voice.

Watching the expression on Rachel's face turn cold and unfriendly, Tristan was relieved to see she was annoyed by this guy's presence.

"Don't call me that. You know I hate it," Rachel said. "Tristan, this is Stewart. Stewart, Tristan."

"Nice to meet you, Tristan," Stewart said, straining his vocal cords in an attempt to sound friendly. He reached out his hand in a sociable gesture.

Tristan wasn't fooled by his polished manners. He saw the jealous fury flaring from Stewart's green eyes and felt the restraint in his grip.

"Same to you, Stewart," Tristan said.

"Stewart works with me," Rachel explained.

"So, Rachel, we *are* teaming up, right?" As Stewart asked the question, he gave Tristan a patronizing glare out of the corner of his eye.

"Actually Stewart, I already have a partner," she stated.

Tristan perked right up when he realized she was talking about him. He walked around Stewart and took Rachel by the arm.

"That's right, Stewart. I'm her partner today, so if you'll excuse us, we have some paint to splatter."

"Oh. Okay, then. I guess I'll see you later, Rae," Stewart spouted out.

"Thank you for getting me out of there," Rachel said as they walked away. "He just can't seem to understand that there's nothing between us anymore."

"Anymore? Do you want to elaborate on that?"

"Not really," she said.

Though he was curious about her past and how Stewart played into it, he dropped the conversation.

They took their positions on the field, and the horn fired to start the competition.

"Follow me," Rachel whispered. She crouched down and ran behind a stack of straw.

They peeked out just as two others came running out from behind a large barrier. "Fire!" Tristan yelled. They pulled the triggers simultaneously and splattered blue paint across the two men's chests.

Tristan fell back behind the straw. He held his gun tightly in his hands. "Wow, that felt great," he panted. "Is that a bad thing?"

"It's not over yet," Rachel called out as she moved to the next barrier. Tristan followed closely. When no one was in sight, they continued to move from one area to another.

Out of nowhere, the loud pop of a gun filled the air. Tristan took off on a sprint across the field followed by Rachel. It would have been a clean getaway had it not been for the small hole in the ground that caught Tristan's left foot and sent him to the ground.

Following a little too closely and watching over her shoulder instead of in front of her, Rachel tumbled down on top of Tristan. She looked into his face and started laughing. Tristan couldn't help but find the humor in the whole situation and laughed along with her.

He sat up and offered her his hand. At first she seemed hesitant, but then her eyes softened. She placed her hand in his and allowed him to pull her to an upright position.

"Thanks," she said.

When she looked into his eyes again, Tristan could see a slight difference in her expression. Before he had time to react to her sudden change of heart, they were both splattered with red paint.

"Great!" Tristan yelled. He turned to look at Rachel and quickly hid his anger. "Well, I guess that ends that," he said.

"You can't win 'em all," Rachel said. She stood up and reached for her gun.

"Do you do this often?"

"I usually come a few times each summer. I like getting out of the city every now and then. I have to say, though, this particular trip has been the most fun."

"Because of my gracefulness and poise?"

"I think it's because, win or lose, you know how to have a good time," Rachel said. "Thank you."

"For what?"

"Making me laugh. It's been awhile."

Studying her facial expression, Tristan wondered what was going through her mind. "You're welcome," he answered. He kept his eyes locked with hers for a few more seconds. The ice was definitely melting, no matter how slowly. *That's one for me*, Tristan thought. He may have lost the game of paintball, but he'd won with Rachel.

"I guess we should get off the field," Rachel suggested.

Not wanting to rid himself of this crucial bonding moment, Tristan quickly concocted a plan to prolong their time together. "Do you think anyone would miss us if we took off for awhile?"

"And where would we be going?"

"You'll see," he teased.

They returned their gear to the shed and headed for Rachel's car. Her very expensive, luxurious car. Rachel walked beside him, seemingly carefree and comfortable with his suggestion.

"Mind if I drive?" Tristan asked.

"It might be best, since I have no idea where we're going."

Rachel dropped the car keys into his hand, and then Tristan helped her into the passenger seat. He got behind the wheel and started the engine.

"Are you sure your sisters won't miss you?" he asked.

"Do you really care?"

"Right now? No."

Tristan pulled out of the parking lot and headed for his secret destination. He was sure a little one-on-one would help his chances. Without distractions he could pour on the charm. He would send the message loud and clear that he was interested in her, and he was positive he would get the response he wanted.

★ ★ ★

As Cole ran to the next barrier, he caught a glimpse of Tristan and Rachel getting into the car. He abruptly stopped, caught off guard by Tristan's sudden departure.

"Where do they think they're going!" he hollered.

Megan grabbed him by the arm and pulled him behind the barrier. "Get down!" she shouted.

On the other side of the course, Austin struggled to keep up the pace, running breathlessly a few feet behind Marley.

"Hurry up!" she screeched over her shoulder.

When they reached the barrier, Austin collapsed on the ground. He clutched his chest with one hand and wiped the sweat from his forehead with the other. "I can't make it! Go on without me," he wheezed. "Save yourself!"

"I can't, dimwit, you're my partner. Now get up!"

Austin rolled over and pulled himself to his knees. He looked up into her evil, merciless eyes. "You're a heartless slave-driver!" he cried.

"Yeah, maybe, but I don't like to lose. Torture is a small price to pay for victory!" she declared. She reached down, grabbed him by the right arm, and pulled him to his feet.

★ ★ ★

"Do I even get a hint about where we're going?" Rachel asked.

"Not a chance," Tristan smiled. "I'm all about being spontaneous."

"Not me. I have to know every move before it's made."

"Oh, let me guess. You're one of those workaholic types that live life through a Blackberry."

Rachel gave him a smile and pulled a small black device from her purse. "I check it regularly and usually fill my day with too many tasks that I can't possibly accomplish," she said laughing.

"So basically you set yourself up for failure every day?"

"You could say that."

"Wow, you really need to live a little."

As they drove, Tristan continued to quiz Rachel on her likes and dislikes. He discovered that fun hadn't been in her vocabulary for some time. She had been running her father's multi-billion dollar supply company since his death two months ago, which left little time for anything else.

Being careful not to cross the line between curiosity and interrogation, Tristan pried a bit further.

"So, will you eventually take over the entire company?"

"I don't know. I've thought about it, but there's so much responsibility that goes along with it. What if I fail and disappoint my father? I don't know if I could live with myself knowing I'd let him down." Rachel's voice was full of torment over the decision she was facing.

"I think your father would be more disappointed if you didn't even try. You don't want to let him down by placing his company into the hands of some stranger, do you?" Tristan said. If she took over the company that would mean more money in his pocket. "You should do it. You owe him that."

Why was he acting so insensitive to her feelings? Was the money really that important? He shook his head, ridding himself of the accusations. Deep down, he knew the money meant everything to him, and he would go to any lengths to get it.

"You're probably right." She sighed. "I just wish I could make up my mind and get it over with. Instead, I'm torn and confused."

Tristan kept quiet. He knew Rachel was crying out for someone to lift the burden she carried. But he couldn't be that man. His motives were driven by money alone.

"What about your mother?" Tristan asked, trying to change the subject.

"She lives in Saratoga Springs. It's about three hours from Manhattan," Rachel said. Her tone of voice lightened as she talked about her mother. "She hated the city, so my father kept their house there and commuted. She's never really been interested in the company. As long as the money kept rolling in, she didn't care to know anything else about it. My father knew that, so he left her adequate money to live on and left the company to me."

"We're here."

Tristan pulled into a small parking lot and turned off the engine. The tiny cottage was rosy-red with white trim and white shutters. Large trees surrounded the building, while purple and yellow flowers surrounded the front entrance. The wooden sign out front displayed the name "Rosie's."

"Where's here?" Rachel asked.

"You'll see."

Tristan walked around the car and opened the door, taking her hand to help her out. The two glass doors in the front had a rose tint and a small, silver bell at the top to announce their arrival.

When they stepped inside, a sweet, sugary fragrance swirled around them. Rachel tilted her head back and inhaled deeply.

"Mmmmm, it smells delicious," she said.

Tristan seated Rachel on the long wooden bench just inside the doors. He went to the counter and, in a low voice, placed his order. He peeked over his shoulder to make sure she was still seated out of hearing range.

After picking up the order, Tristan walked over to where Rachel was waiting. "Follow me," he said.

Carrying a large brown paper bag in his hands, he led the way with a grin across his face. He had no doubt Rachel would love what she was about to taste.

Rosie's had been, up until now, his secret refuge from the world. It wasn't a place Cole and Austin would appreciate, so he hadn't shared it with anyone.

Rachel walked a step behind him as he directed her out the back door and down a tiny wooden ramp with green artificial turf. The path guided them into a secluded patio completely surrounded by foliage.

In the middle of the brick-laid courtyard was a beautiful rock fountain surrounded by an abundance of more purple, yellow, and orange flowers. The water in the fountain sparkled clearly and cascaded down a mountain of rough rocks. On the far side of the patio was a marble statue of a mother surrounded by her three children.

Tristan sat the paper bag down on one of the six white metal tables that were spread throughout the courtyard. He pulled out a chair for Rachel and then took the seat across from her. When he looked up, he was pleased with the expression that covered her face.

"What do you think?" asked Tristan.

"It's like something right out of a storybook," she said, beaming. "It's absolutely breathtaking."

"Like an escape from reality."

"You surprised me," Rachel confessed.

"How so?"

"I figured you were just another loud-mouth, over-assertive, selfish, egotistical womanizer," Rachel spouted out, all in one breath.

Tristan gulped hard, stunned at how well she knew his type. "Wow, I can't believe you came up with all that in just a week. Have I changed your mind now that you know I have a softer side?"

"Well, I think we can rule out selfish." She grinned. "You chose not to keep this enchanting place all to yourself."

"That's a start."

"How in the world did you find it?"

"I was looking for something that would remind me of Cleveland." He took the bag and pulled out the crispy, sweet surprise. "And I found this."

"I thought you were from Chicago."

"I only ended up there. I was raised in Cleveland."

"Well, it smells delicious. What is it?"

"You've never had a funnel cake?"

"No."

"Oh, you don't know what you've been missing." Tristan pulled a piece off and handed it to Rachel.

She took it from his fingers and popped it into her mouth. Her eyes lit up as the flavor flowed over her tongue and delighted her taste buds.

"Oh wow. It's really good," she said.

"You're preaching to the choir," Tristan assured her, stuffing a huge chunk into his mouth.

"So why does this remind you of Cleveland? Did your mother make this for you?"

"Actually, my mother left when I was seven. I haven't seen or heard from her since."

"Oh, I'm sorry."

"After she left, my father moved me and my older sister from Des Moines, Iowa, to Cleveland. Anyway, when I was—I don't know—ten maybe, my father took me to a carnival in town. He refused to let me ride a single ride, but he did buy me a funnel cake. I've been addicted ever since."

Tristan was careful when he spoke about his past. He kept his tone flat and uncaring to avoid any unnecessary questions.

"Is your father still in Cleveland?"

"As far as I know. About a year after I started college, I moved out. We don't really keep in touch anymore."

"What about your sister?"

"She took off when she was sixteen. We heard she was living in Chicago, but she was long gone by the time I lived there. It's funny, really. My mother ran off with the plumber, my father became a drunk, and my sister became a crack head. We are what you would call the all-American family." Tristan laughed, trying to make light of the situation. *So much for keeping the past buried*, he thought.

"Wow, that's some childhood. So you weren't raised in the

Church?" Rachel asked. She pulled off another piece of funnel cake and stuck it into her mouth, watching him closely.

Tristan hadn't even thought about what he was saying. His childhood sure didn't follow any of the church standards he'd read about so far. He needed to cover it up—fast!

"I'm a convert," he replied.

He strived to keep his face light and unreadable, and he avoided eye contact. If she wanted him to elaborate, he'd surely mess up. He wasn't sure exactly how someone became a member of the Church, and he wasn't eager to try and fake his way through. Extreme panic struck hard and fast as Rachel continued to pry deeper into his imaginary life.

"So, how long have you been a member?" she asked.

Tristan swallowed hard and cleared his throat, unprepared and unrehearsed for the sudden interrogation. He knew his face must have looked as sick as his stomach felt, but she didn't comment.

"Um . . . I . . . ," Tristan stuttered. Rachel's cell phone rang at that very moment, saving him from the boiling pot of water.

"It's Megan," she said, sighing when she saw the caller ID. She answered the call and agreed to return to pick them up. "They're finished, so I guess we should get back."

Tristan walked slowly. He stayed close by her side, touching her arm a few times with his. Rachel seemed relaxed and friendly as she strolled beside him. She talked about the winters in New York and ice skating in Central Park.

Opening the car door for her, Tristan paused. "I had fun today," he remarked.

"I did too," she said.

The transformation he was seeing was astonishing. Within hours she'd gone from cold and unfeeling to warm and inviting. She was opening up to him and responding to his every gesture. It was everything he'd expected plus one thing more—a certain submissive attribute that wasn't present before.

"Would you like to go out with me, you know, on a real date?" Tristan asked.

"I would really like that."

"How about dinner next weekend . . . on Friday night?"

"Oh, I have to work late on Friday."

"Saturday?"

"Saturday's perfect. And I think I have the perfect idea for a date," Rachel said impishly.

"Great! What time should I pick you up?"

Tristan was pleased with her school-girl flirting. Not only was she playing right into his trap, but it was easier than he had anticipated.

"*I'll* pick *you* up at noon."

"Noon? Just what do you have up your sleeve?"

"I guess you'll have to show up to find out."

Tristan watched her face glow with satisfaction. He rather enjoyed letting the woman plan the date for a change, and he was intrigued with this new take-charge mysterious side of her. She was definitely nobody's doormat. She was as strong-headed as he was. But would that be to his disadvantage?

Six

During the next week, Tristan occupied himself by reading up on the Mormons. He was determined to uncover the horrible truth he was sure existed and to find fault with the faith that had millions of followers fooled. He flipped through the pages of *Mormonism for Dummies* and let his mind wander.

Perhaps they danced around a bonfire and sacrificed their firstborn child. No, that wouldn't make sense when they hold families on such a high pedestal. He remembered Cole saying he thought they grew horns on the top of their heads. *Maybe I ought to check that theory out*, Tristan thought.

Mormonism for Dummies was thorough, covering every small detail, including the fact that the official name of the Mormon church was actually "The Church of Jesus Christ of Latter-day Saints." There was no mention of fires, sacrifices, or devil worship.

Tristan continued to read about Joseph Smith and the restoration of the Church. It raised a lot of questions in his mind. After all, Joseph Smith was only fourteen years old when he claimed to see God and his son Jesus Christ.

However, other aspects of the church, things like families being sealed together for eternity, made perfect sense to him.

Although the book captivated him in a way that he'd never

encountered before, he found unsettling information as well. He was dumbfounded to read the Mormon's view on morality.

Complete abstinence before marriage, Tristan thought. He ran his hand through his hair and sighed. If that's what Rachel believed, he'd need to be very careful when he was around her and keep his seductive side hidden. He couldn't afford to slip up now. He had her right where he wanted her.

When Tristan finished the book, he found he was left with an emptiness inside him. His mind seemed to beg for more knowledge and his soul thirsted for answers.

Finding it difficult to deny that the book had sparked his interest, Tristan realized there was only one thing that could help feed the hunger that lurked inside him—he had to read the Book of Mormon for himself.

The yearning to find out what was written inside the book nagged at him terribly. He'd discovered that the book was considered by members of the Church to be another testament of Jesus Christ. That alone intrigued him more than anything else. He stuffed his curiosity aside for the time being and directed his thoughts back to Rachel.

Dialing in the digits to Rachel's cell phone, Tristan nervously paced back and forth with one hand stuffed into the pocket of his jeans.

He counted the rings and breathed deeply. When her silky-smooth voice came across the receiver, Tristan felt his heart unexpectedly leap into his throat and his adrenaline surge through him like wildfire. For some reason he couldn't explain, the sound of her voice had a profound effect on him.

"Hi, Rachel," he spewed out, sounding like an infatuated teenage boy. Tristan cleared his throat and dropped his tone. "It's Tristan. I just called to make sure we're still on for Saturday."

"Definitely. I'm looking forward to it," Rachel said.

"Do I need to bring anything?"

"Yeah, your swimming suit."

"We're going swimming?"

"Not exactly."

"Mud wrestling?"

"Keep dreaming, Romeo," she said with a laugh. "Just wear your suit under your clothes. That way you won't have to change."

"You're loving this suspenseful thing, aren't you?"

"Oh, yeah."

"Fine, I guess I can wait until tomorrow," Tristan sighed. "But it better be good."

"Don't worry. You'll feel like a kid at a carnival."

★ ★ ★

Austin took one grueling step after another, nearly stumbling over his own two feet as he followed in Marley's dust. She was still a good ten feet in front of him, running at a pace that seemed more like warp speed.

His legs burned like hot lava, his lungs felt as though they would explode on impact, and his side squealed out in misery. He knew this was a bad idea. There was no way he could keep up with her. Try as he might to talk his way out of going jogging with Marley, Tristan had insisted it would help break the ice and get things moving.

Austin was skeptical about the whole relationship idea, and for good reason—he and Marley were exact opposites. There was also her pesky habit of glaring at him with witchy eyes that made it evident he was more than just a nuisance to her. He was more like a festering splinter.

Even still, there he was trying his best to keep his lungs from collapsing under the enormous strain of his physical workout, while at the same time trying to appear relaxed and sophisticated.

"Are you going to be all right?" Marley questioned.

For a brief moment, Austin thought he heard the slightest touch of sympathy in her voice. Something that would suggest she was human rather than a cold-hearted mammal.

"Air . . . I need air!" Austin gasped.

"Now you're just being a drama queen."

"Can't . . . breathe!"

"Do you want me to call someone?" Marley snickered. "A dietician perhaps?"

Austin fell to the ground. "No . . . just let me lie here for a minute."

"Well, I have to give you credit. You actually made it around the track one whole time," Marley said. "Tell you what, I'll finish my laps and then come back to make sure you're still breathing." She stood up and ran off, her Nike shoes making a slight squeak.

★ ★ ★

Cole picked up a book and flipped through the pages. The library was packed with men, women, and children, all trying to find that perfect book. Not him. He was there for one purpose only.

Discreetly peeking around the end of the tall bookcase, he watched Megan help a large, round man with a bald head check out his book.

Tristan was right about one thing. Megan was very good looking. Not movie star gorgeous—more like the sweet, innocent, girl-next-door type. She was the kind of girl he could take home to meet his mother. Aside from the fact she was a Mormon, he knew his mother would love him to marry a girl like Megan.

Rubbing his sweaty palms down the side of his blue jeans, he indecisively approached the counter. He placed the book on the counter and gave her a warm smile.

"Have you read this one?" he asked.

"*The Effects of Global Warming*?" Megan asked, somewhat surprised. "Can't say that I have, but it does look interesting."

"What kind of books *do* you like?" Cole asked.

"Wow, about everything on the shelf. But lately I've been into scientific mysteries."

Reaching up to adjust his glasses, Cole leaned one hand

on the counter to get a little closer. He looked into her eyes with intense passion. He didn't care that there was a line of people behind him waiting to check out their books. He kept his sights on Megan and ignored the old lady that was clearing her throat.

"That sounds really interesting. I would love to get together some time and hear about it," he continued. "How about tonight over dinner?"

Megan looked down demurely. "Okay," she giggled.

"Great. If you'll just jot down your address, I'll pick you up around seven."

Megan pulled out a pen and paper. After writing down her information, she meekly handed it over to Cole. He could practically hear her heart fluttering like butterflies, which gave him the self-confidence he desperately needed.

The truth was, most girls wouldn't have given him the time of day let alone their phone number. He found that most of them wanted brawn over brains. Although he felt the tiniest bit guilty about having a hidden agenda, he shot her a strained smile. He knew perfectly well she was way out of his league.

✯ ✯ ✯

Tristan paced back and forth, occupied with one particular aisle of the small secondhand bookstore. He would glance up now and then to make sure the book in question was still in its place. His indecisiveness kept him bound to the row entitled "spiritual reading" as he wore down the thinning blue-green carpet beneath his feet.

"Okay!" he said, sliding the book from its place. Before he could change his mind, Tristan walked briskly to the front of the store and placed the Book of Mormon on the marble countertop and pulled out his wallet. It was time to fulfill his curiosity once and for all. The girl behind the counter stood staring at Tristan with an odd expression on her face.

She was a young, petite girl with long, strawberry-blonde hair that sparkled in the lights of the store. She looked down at the book and then back at Tristan. Her face resembled that of a frightened child and her stance was frigid.

"Is there something wrong?" Tristan asked. He began to wonder if there was some secret code or phrase he needed to disclose in order to purchase the book.

"Are you one of those, you know, Mormons?" she asked, nervously biting her bottom lip.

Tristan couldn't help but be amused by her ghastly reaction. For a moment, he contemplated what his next statement should be. Did he dare push his amusement any further?

"Yes, I am. I'm a Mormon," he announced. He proudly let the phrase roll off his tongue like he'd said it a million times before. To his surprise, it didn't sound odd or unrealistic, but comfortable.

The girl continued to stare without any indication that she would take his money. "Can I ask you a personal question?" she whispered, almost too softly for Tristan to hear.

"Shoot."

She glanced to her left and then to her right, making certain no one was in listening range. "Do you have more than one wife?"

Tristan quickly analyzed the situation, trying his best not to break out in laughter. He had been under the exact same misconception himself. However, he couldn't help but take advantage of this poor, misinformed girl.

"Of course. I only have five wives right now, but I was kind of hoping for an even number."

"*Five?*" she squeaked.

He leaned up a bit closer, almost crossing into her personal space. "You know, you're a very lovely young lady. Are you perhaps single?"

The girl immediately took a step back with a distinct look of disgust plastered across her pale face. "I—I'm not interested," she stuttered. She quickly took his money and then picked the book up by the corner and carefully placed it into a black bag. She kept her distance and held out the bag for Tristan to take.

"That's too bad," he said, frowning. "I think my other wives would have really liked you."

She watched his every move until he was safely out the door. When Tristan was safely absorbed by a swarm of foot traffic, he let out a laugh, causing curious looks around him. So maybe it wasn't the nicest thing to do to someone. But then again, she was the one that so rudely brought it up.

☆ ☆ ☆

When Tristan got home, he found Cole sitting on the edge of the couch chewing nicotine gum like it was his last chance of survival. He closed the door quietly and made his way toward the living room.

Torso rigid and eyes wide, Cole stuffed another piece of gum into his mouth and chomped aggressively.

"Hey man," Tristan mumbled, still keeping a safe distance. "Everything okay?"

Fidgeting with the package, Cole pushed another piece through the silver lining. He glared up at Tristan like an attack dog ready for the kill. Tristan instinctually took a defensive step back, ready to bolt if necessary.

"No, everything is *not* okay!" Cole enunciated clearly in order to eliminate any misunderstanding. "I haven't had a smoke all week, or coffee, or alcohol, and I'm freaking out! To make matters worse, I have a date with Megan tonight, and I'm supposed to portray this in-control-never-sinning-remarkable Mormon!"

"Cole, that's great!" Tristan said.

"How so, Tristan? I don't think I have the strength to convince her that I belong to this ridiculous religion."

"Sure you do. Just try and stay away from the topic of religion and you'll be fine."

Cole shook his head in disagreement and let out a soft, painful groan. "I'll stay away from the subject, but will she? I swear, Tristan, if she starts asking too many questions, I'll probably order a double and drink it right in front of her."

"No you won't."

"Don't be so sure about that."

"Oh, and by the way," Tristan said. He scratched the top of his head nonchalantly and took a deep breath. "The Mormons believe in complete abstinence before marriage, so you might want to watch how you act around her."

"Oh, good, something else to worry about. Gee, thanks."

"You'll be fine," Tristan encouraged. "You've never made it past second base anyway," he chuckled.

"Have too!"

"Oh yeah, that foreign chick. What was her name?"

"Hilda! And she wasn't foreign. She was just very masculine."

Tristan began laughing. "She had more facial hair than you did!"

"I was eighteen!" Cole shouted. "You know, not all of us are born with an automatic chick magnet built in. Some of us actually have to work at it."

Cole finally caught a glimpse of the bag in Tristan's hand and leaned over to get a better look. "What's that?" he questioned.

Tristan nervously took a step back, hiding the bag behind his back. He innocently shrugged his shoulders. "Nothing," he said.

"It's not nothing. What's in the bag?"

"It's just a book."

"What kind of book?"

"Just, you know, an informational book."

"Let me see."

"No."

"Let me see it," Cole snapped. He sprang from the couch and flew at Tristan, reaching for the bag.

Scrambling to avoid the attack, Tristan hurdled the back of the couch and darted for his bedroom. Cole came up from behind and tackled him to the floor before Tristan could make it through the doorway.

"Let me see!" Cole demanded, reaching for the bag.

"No!" Tristan yelled. He tried to stuff the bag under his body, but Cole caught the corner and pulled hard. The corner tore open and sent the book flying across the floor. "Great!" Tristan yelped.

Cole picked up the book and examined it with a displeased expression. "You bought a Book of Mormon? Are you crazy?"

"Yes, I bought a Book of Mormon, and no, I'm not crazy," Tristan stated. He grabbed the book from Cole's hand. "I want to read it. Is that a problem for you?"

"Tristan, it's a cult. They brainwash their victims into thinking it's the truth, but it's all a lie!"

The disgruntled look across Cole's face sent the message loud and clear that he thought Tristan had lost all perspective on reality.

"How do you know that?" Tristan asked. "I mean, we've never actually studied the religion to find out one way or the other."

"And you think by reading their book it's going to make you an expert? Even convert you into one of them?"

"I never said I was going to become one of them. I only said it would be interesting to find out more about them."

"You already read a book about them. You don't have to go reading their so-called Bible too," Cole said, clearly worried for Tristan's well-being, or perhaps his sanity. "What if they have brainwashing material in that book? The next thing we know, you'll be shaving your head and chanting weird satanic phrases."

Tristan took a deep breath and exhaled slowly. The last thing he wanted was to spend the next hour standing in the hallway arguing with Cole. Besides, maybe Cole was right, like usual. He trusted Cole with his life. Cole had never led him astray before.

"Yeah, you're probably right." Tristan sighed. "I'll get rid of it tomorrow."

"First thing?"

"Yup," Tristan replied.

"You'll thank me for this one day," Cole reassured him.

Stashing the book in his night stand, Tristan reluctantly closed the drawer and lay back on the bed. He placed his hands behind his head and stared at the ceiling. Not unexpectedly, his thoughts turned to Rachel. She seemed like an intelligent, strong-willed woman. Why would she get involved with a cult?

Try as he might, Tristan couldn't quite shake Rachel from his mind. She was like a cancerous cell that had seeped into his head, and then, without warning, she had spread through every cell in his brain. The truth was, she was very different from any woman he'd ever been with. Even Jessica.

Being with one woman for six months had been a record for Tristan, so he'd prematurely thought Jessica was the one he was supposed to spend the rest of his life with. However, it was his inability to commit that seemed to hold him back from giving her his whole heart.

Perhaps it was only his desire to have something everyone else wanted that influenced his decision. Jessica was, after all, the top model for Mountain Advertising. Not to mention the most beautiful redhead in all of Chicago.

Putting forth a diligent effort, Tristan had exemplified a supportive and loving boyfriend while keeping his true feelings locked away in his cold heart. Love had never come easily for him. It wasn't that he didn't want to be in love, but rather, it was fear of love itself. Although he seemed to possess a need to have women around him, the anxiety of knowing someone could have that much control over him kept him barricaded inside his own loveless universe.

As night fell, Tristan realized he'd been dwelling on Rachel for close to two hours. The apartment was now quiet, evidence that Cole had finally gotten over his temper tantrum and gone on his date with Megan.

Tristan sat up on the side of his bed, staring silently at the closed drawer that kept his tempting new purchase secluded. He pulled off his jeans and T-shirt, leaving him standing in only his blue and white checkered boxers.

He realized Austin would be closing up Bubba's restaurant and would be considerably late coming up. Since Tristan didn't like being alone, he figured he would hit the sack early rather than mope around the apartment all night dwelling on the complicated life he'd created for himself.

Crawling into bed, he pulled up the covers and reached over to turn out the bedside lamp. He gazed down at the drawer again. Was Cole right? Was this book the Mormons' way to lure innocent people into their cult, innocent people who would never regain any sense of who they once were? But why was he so drawn to it and the secrets it hid inside?

Tristan buried his face in his pillow and groaned, wishing he could find sleep among all of the unanswered questions that burned deep in his mind. Agitated by his mixed emotions, he climbed back out of bed and walked to the window.

The glow of the streetlights shined through the broken mini-blinds and lit his room. He pushed the blinds aside and stared out at the cars and the people rushing to get to their destinations.

There was an older gentleman walking his small dog down the sidewalk. He seemed happy to be out in the night air spending time with his pet. Across the street, a man and woman looked to be having an argument that had the woman very upset. She soon turned and stormed off down the sidewalk, leaving the man standing alone. After a few minutes, the man took off after her. Tristan chuckled to himself, having been in that situation many times before.

As he stood there, watching the world around him, Tristan suddenly realized he wanted to know the purpose behind this crazy, mixed-up life. He wanted to know what it was all leading up to, if anything at all.

He turned and glared back at the night stand again. He wished he could silence the shouting voices in his head. The book tucked away behind the wood seemed to be taunting him, calling his bluff.

Walking back to the bed, Tristan sat down and stared at the drawer. Taking the handle by one finger, he slowly opened the small compartment. What if Cole was wrong? Could he simply close the drawer again and be satisfied with Cole's reasoning, never really finding out for himself?

The uncertainty gnawed at his soul, tearing him into three distinct sections. One side for Cole, one side for Rachel, and the other side his constant desire to know for himself.

Forcing all the agonizing thoughts from his mind, Tristan pulled the book from its hiding place. He flipped it open and began to read.

"I, Nephi, having been born of goodly parents . . ."

Seven

Tristan looked over at Rachel again, searching for clues to their mystery date. A mischievous smile was plastered across her face; obviously, she was pleased with the intrigue.

The cab's window was cracked slightly and the wind swirled her long hair across her face. As she tucked an errant lock of hair behind her ear, Tristan couldn't help but chuckle to himself at Rachel's choice of transportation. With all her money, she could obviously afford a car service—probably the most convenient and luxurious way to get around the city—but he knew she preferred cabs and subways, hiding her wealth so no one would judge her. Not him! With that kind of money, Tristan pictured himself being driven around in a Jaguar by some guy named Randall, just to let everyone know he was better than them.

It was clear Rachel was not going to disclose their destination, so Tristan thought it would be a good time to settle certain . . . suspicions.

He stretched both arms to the ceiling of the car while he tilted his head back in the seat. He glanced over and stared at the top of Rachel's head. He studied it carefully, looking for two distinct bumps but couldn't find anything. He leaned forward in his seat and glanced at the front part of her head. The wind blew her hair across her forehead. Nothing!

Still not satisfied, he leaned over in his seat to take a closer look. "What are you looking at?" Rachel asked with a smile.

"Oh . . . I thought I saw something in your hair. A bug maybe," he stuttered. "Here, let me see."

He scooted over and examined the top of her head more closely, looking through the strands of thick brown hair that smelled of fresh apples.

"Did you get it," she asked anxiously.

"Wait a minute, I think I see it." He pressed his fingers down and rubbed them along the top of her head. It was completely smooth without so much as a pimple. "Oh, there it is!" He closed his finger and thumb together to make it look as though he had something between them. "Got it!" He flicked his fingers to the floor to create the illusion.

"Thanks. I hate bugs!"

Tristan relaxed back in the seat. _Hmm, no horns_, he thought, relieved to put that rumor to rest.

Still watching her, Tristan couldn't help but gawk in amazement at her flawless complexion, glistening in the sunlight.

"You're acting strange today," Rachel said, interrupting his thoughts.

"I'm studying your face for any clue about our destination," he said.

"Any luck?"

"Unfortunately, no."

To his disappointment, Rachel was careful about what she revealed, laughing off his nonchalant interrogation. She was really good at being secretive. _Maybe a little_ too _good_, Tristan thought curiously.

The cab dropped them off near the southeast end of Central Park, and Rachel dragged him along a foot path until they reached a large banner that read, "Children's Research Hospital Annual Carnival." Tristan's mouth dropped open in disbelief. This was their big date? How could she think he would enjoy being around a bunch of sick kids? He diligently tried to tuck his disappointment away and put on a smile.

"Our date is at a carnival? For sick kids?" he questioned.

"What, you can't afford to eat at a real restaurant?"

"I take it you're disappointed?"

"Well, a little, I guess."

"I'll make you a deal," she said, looking him in the eyes. "If at the end of our date you feel like you've been short-changed somehow, I'll let you choose where we have dinner. Anywhere you want, on me."

"You don't need to pay for dinner," he grumbled, feeling insulted.

"But, if you've had the best day of your life, then you can buy me dinner." She smiled, as if she already knew the outcome. "Is it a deal?"

"How do you know I won't lie to you just to get a free meal?"

"Oh, I'll know."

"Then lead the way." Tristan grinned.

Tristan followed Rachel around from booth to booth. He realized he was smiling as he watched the kids playing games. Each game was equipped with an abundance of colorful stuffed animals waiting to be given out as prizes. There was a ring toss, a makeshift fishing pond, a cake walk, face painting, and a beanbag toss.

He observed all the children more closely as he kept up with Rachel. Some of the kids wore scarves over their bald heads and masks over their faces. Others pulled IV stands behind them as they scurried from game to game.

"They're playing," Rachel said. She looked at him with curiosity in her eyes. "Don't worry, they're not contagious."

"I just can't believe they're out playing in the park. Shouldn't they be in bed?"

Rachel stopped walking and turned to face him. "If you act like you're sick, then you'll be sick," she said. "Sunshine and fun are the best medicines in the world. Wouldn't you agree?"

"I guess you're right," Tristan agreed.

They passed by the cotton candy machine, where one happy child was stuffing her mouth full of pink sugar.

"Rachel?" A little voice from behind them squealed with delight. Tristan turned to see a small Hispanic boy wrap his thin arms around her middle. His bald head shimmered in the sunlight, revealing a four-inch scar across crown of his scalp. "I'm so glad you came!"

Rachel dropped to her knees and took the little boy in her arms, holding him tenderly. "Are you kidding? I couldn't miss out on all the fun." She released him and stood up, still holding his hand in hers. "I'd like you to meet a friend of mine," she said, looking down at his wide brown eyes. "Marcus, this is Tristan. Tristan, this is Marcus."

"It's very nice to meet you, Mr. Tristan," Marcus said. He released Rachel's hand and held it out in front of him.

Tristan took his hand and gave it a soft shake. "It's very nice to meet you, Marcus." Tristan chuckled. "How old are you?"

"Four and three quarters," he announced. "How old are you?"

Before Tristan had a chance to answer, a hysterical woman came running over to them. "Marcus Louis Sanchez! Don't you ever run away from me like that again," the woman scolded.

"Uh oh. She used my whole name." Marcus frowned. With wide eyes, he looked up at Tristan. "That's never a good sign."

"Hi, Rachel," the boy's mother said. "I thought I'd lost him this time. I didn't realize you were here."

"Yeah, I'm like a magnet for these kids." Rachel laughed. "Marcus, you always need to tell your mom where you're going, okay?"

"Yeah, yeah," Marcus grumbled. He folded his arms and stomped one foot on the ground. "I'm almost five years old. I can take care of myself."

Tristan leaned over and put his hand against Marcus's ear. "It's a woman thing," he whispered. "It's best to listen to them. They know more than we do."

Marcus put his hand over his mouth and giggled. Rachel introduced Tristan to Marcus's mother, Lucinda.

"Rachel, I can't thank you enough for all this," Lucinda said.

"It's just what the kids needed."

"You don't need to thank me. I love these kids. I'd do anything for them."

Lucinda took Marcus by the hand and led him over to the ring toss. Marcus waved back at them the whole way. Tristan turned to Rachel, amazed by her generosity.

"You did this?" he asked.

"Well, the kids were starting to go stir-crazy just sitting in their hospital beds, so I thought this—"

"Wait, do you see these kids a lot?"

"Once or twice a week. The kids like me to read stories to them or help with crafts."

As they walked, several more kids waved to her or greeted her with hugs and kisses. She was like Santa Claus at Christmas time. The kids idolized her, and she knew each one by name.

"So what's the matter with Marcus?" Tristan finally asked.

"He's been fighting a brain tumor for the last year. He had surgery and chemotherapy, but the tumor keeps coming back. He's going in for more surgery in a few days, and then he'll repeat chemo."

There was a distinct sadness in Rachel's voice as she talked about Marcus and the slim chance he had for survival. Tristan knew she held a special place in her heart for that little boy, but he was baffled as to the reason why she would want to get involved with a bunch of sick kids.

"Why get so attached? I mean, it's just going to be that much harder if things . . . don't end well," Tristan said.

Rachel stopped walking abruptly and stared into Tristan's eyes with a profound look of repugnance. "Tristan, you can't be afraid to care for someone just because you don't know their future. Any of us could be gone tomorrow," she stated conviction. "Life is uncertain. If you dwell on that uncertainty, you'll never let your heart be free to love."

Tristan thought about his past relationships and the fear that had kept him isolated from the rest of the world. Perhaps it was only the insecurities of an seven-year-old boy who had lost his mother that had held him back.

"So you're saying that life's a gamble," he replied. His voice was low and full of frustration, and he sounded a bit grumpier than he intended. "You're just supposed to roll the dice and take whatever you get? That's not very comforting."

"Isn't that why we have the Lord? To make sure our roll is the best it can possibly be?"

As they started walking again, Tristan's heart overflowed with so many emotions, he couldn't tell which one was more powerful—sorrow for Marcus, sorrow for upsetting Rachel, or the self-pity he felt for himself.

"Well, here we are," Rachel announced, throwing her arm out to display a large dunk tank.

"Oh, no!" Tristan gasped. "Is this why you wanted me to wear my swimming suit?"

"Oh, come on, it'll be fun."

"For who? I don't see you wearing your suit."

"Oh yeah," Rachel smiled. She lifted her top up just enough to reveal a red and white striped swimming suit. "I wasn't going to let you have all the fun. Besides, it's for the kids."

"Fine," Tristan growled.

He reluctantly pulled off his jeans and T-shirt, leaving him standing in his blue swimming trunks. When he looked up, he found Rachel staring at his firm, muscle-toned abs. She quickly turned away and looked down at the ground.

"Um . . . yeah," she stuttered. "Okay, I'll run things down here then."

Tristan smiled as he watched Rachel briskly walk away. *So,* he thought, *she's a regular woman after all.* He climbed up the ladder and took his seat. A shiver ran down his spine when he looked down into the clear water beneath him. He really hoped it wasn't as cold as it looked.

"How do I get myself into these things?" he muttered through a clenched smile, as he cheerfully waved one hand at Rachel.

Tristan's first taker was a teenage girl with dark curly hair.

She glared at Tristan and then at the red and white target, holding the ball tightly in one hand.

"You can do it, Cassandra," Rachel said to the girl.

"Don't encourage her!" Tristan bellowed out, a little anxious about the icy plunge awaiting him.

Pulling her arm back, she released the ball, just missing the target. Tristan let out a deep breath and relaxed. Maybe he'd get lucky and nobody would be able to hit the target.

Rachel handed the girl another ball and whispered a few words into her ear. A look of determination came across her face. She looked at the ball and then at the target. When the ball escaped her fingers, it whizzed through the air and nailed the center of the target.

The seat instantly collapsed, sending Tristan plunging into the water. It was cool but, surprisingly, not freezing. Wiping some water from his face, Tristan took hold of the ladder and climbed to the top.

Amazingly, he'd loved it. The drop was exciting and the water exhilarating, not to mention the reaction of the young girl. She danced around with her arms high in the air, giggling as she celebrated her victory.

Tristan was actually thrilled to see he'd made her so happy, and all he had to do was drench himself in a large tank of water. Pulling himself up into the seat, he noticed Rachel standing beside the ladder.

"What are you doing?" she asked. "I thought you didn't want to do this?"

"I don't, but it's for the kids, remember?" A crooked smile came across Rachel's face. "All right, I had fun," he admitted. "And I enjoyed seeing the excitement on the girl's face."

"Well, then you'd better prepare yourself," Rachel said, laughing. She walked back across the yard where a line of children was rapidly forming.

After fourteen more dunks, Tristan relinquished his seat to another volunteer and put on some dry clothes. He looked around and found Rachel helping out at the face painting booth.

LINDA CHADWICK

Face painting wasn't exactly his forte, so he decided to wander around on his own.

On the other side of the carnival, Tristan found a nearly deserted booth with a basketball hoop set up. The only one around was a teenage boy who was confined to a wheelchair. Tristan stood to the side and watched the boy. He rolled in front of the shortened basketball hoop and attempted to hurl the ball through the net but missed.

Without giving up, he collected the ball and continued his quest. Tristan watched with admiration at his extended effort. He didn't get discouraged when the ball would bounce off the rim and roll away. Rather, it seemed to give him more determination the next time around.

After another failed attempt, the ball rolled in front of Tristan, so he bent down and picked it up. He approached the boy and noticed that he had only one leg. He was a good looking kid with short spiky blond hair and blue eyes. Still, his complexion was pale and tense. He wore a basketball jersey with what Tristan could only assume was his last name written across the back.

"How's it going?" Tristan asked.

"Not so good," the younger boy responded. "I can't seem to find my aim."

"Well, I played some basketball in high school. Maybe I could help," Tristan offered.

"I'm not sure anything would help my game right now. If it wasn't for this stupid chair, I would have gone to regionals with my team this season," he grumbled. A sadness came across the boy's face. "I was set up for a scholarship as soon as I graduated."

"Do you mind if I ask what happened?"

"I was walking home one night after a long practice. It was raining, so I took a shortcut down an alley."

Taking a deep breath, the poor kid's face displayed the painful memory that he'd conjured up. Tristan wished now that he'd not brought it up.

"The car was coming so fast I didn't have time to even think about getting out of the way. Not that I would have stood a chance. The cop said the guy's blood alcohol level was three times the legal limit. It's funny if you think about it—he doesn't even remember the accident, but I have to live with the memory every day of my life." Anguish shimmered across the boy's face. Although his life had been changed and his future forever altered, he was determined to make the best of it.

Tristan handed the ball to him and squatted down beside the kid's wheelchair, realizing his own horrible childhood was nothing compared to what this boy had gone through. For the first time in a long time, Tristan didn't think of himself. The only thing that mattered at that moment was helping this boy make a basket.

"How about we try not to live with it for at least one afternoon and concentrate on your game?" Tristan asked.

"I'd like that. My name is Dakota," he said, holding out his hand.

"Nice to meet you, Dakota, I'm Tristan. Now, let's see what we can do about your aim."

Tristan tried to push his heartfelt sympathy aside. It made Tristan angry to think that something so terrible could happen to such a young, talented kid, but Dakota was determined and strong-willed. As the afternoon went on, Dakota got better and better until the basketball finally dropped through the net. Tristan jumped up and down, screaming out so loudly that he was sure everyone would come running. He gave Dakota a satisfying high-five and handed him the basketball.

"I think you're on your way now." Tristan grinned, feeling like a proud coach.

"Thanks to you."

"Don't give up, Dakota," Tristan encouraged. "The chair is only a small obstacle compared to what you've already had to overcome."

Tristan floated off the court, barely noticing his feet touching the ground. His spirits soared to a new high. To help someone in need and actually give something of himself without expecting something in return was incredibly gratifying. It was something he'd never felt before.

When he returned to the yard, he saw Rachel was still at the face painting booth. He stopped and watched her interact with the children. She truly had a pure love for each one of them. Whatever their ailment, she embraced them with understanding and compassion. It was a compassion Tristan was suddenly envious of.

Keeping his distance, Tristan continued to watch Rachel. He was completely captivated by not only her outward appearance, but her inner beauty that was shining through.

Noticing him staring, Rachel waved her hand and shot him a curious grin. She got up and began to walk his way. Tristan never took his eyes off her. He was fascinated with her and yearned to know everything about her. What was in her mind, what was in her heart, and why she sparked his interest.

Her hair blew in the breeze, and her smile never looked so sweet. It was like he was looking at her for the first time.

"Are you okay?" she asked, when she arrived by his side.

"Do you know Dakota?"

"Yes. Let me guess. He was at the basketball booth?"

Tristan nodded his head. "He's a great kid. I guess I can see why you spend so much time here."

"Are you saying you had a good time today?"

"Yeah, you were right." Tristan laughed. "So when am I taking you to dinner?"

Eight

ristan woke to the sound of rain thumping against the window pane. He glanced over at the clock: 2:35 a.m. He kicked off the covers, frustrated that sound sleep would not come easily. He sat up on the edge of the bed and ran both hands through his messy hair, trying to fight the images that haunted his dreams.

Why couldn't he get Rachel off his mind? What was it about her that fascinated him? It wasn't like this was the first time he'd exploited a woman for his own personal gain, even though he'd never actually set out to use any of them specifically before.

Still, there was no way he was going to let some woman demolish his hopes and dreams, even if she was beautiful, intriguing, spunky, and just plain perfect.

"Knock it off, Tristan!" he scolded himself. He let out a loud, disgusted-with-himself grunt and went to the kitchen to get a glass of water.

Sure, being with Rachel was like taking a walk through the park on a brisk fall morning, the kind that sends invigorating jolts of cool air straight through to your soul and revitalizes your spirits.

This was not the way things were supposed to go. It was a simple plan: get the girl, take the money, and run. No commitments, no obligations, no strings attached. So why was his head throbbing with so many doubts? He hoped it was only guilt that weighed heavily on his mind.

Leaning up against the kitchen counter to steady his wobbly knees, Tristan took two aspirin and gulped them down with water. The apartment possessed an eerie silence that sent goose bumps up his arms. The stillness tormented him and enhanced his confused state of mind. It was as though Rachel had unlocked some hidden door inside him—a door he had worked hard to barricade long ago. She released emotions in him that he never expected or even thought existed.

Letting out a deep breath, Tristan took all of his confused thoughts and his weary, aching head back to bed. He pulled the covers up, hoping to finally find serenity behind his heavy eyelids.

★ ★ ★

Two miserably long, drawn-out days went by without a word from Rachel. In an attempt not to come across as obsessive, Tristan had avoided calling her, but it hadn't been easy. She was all he'd thought about. He tried to occupy his days by looking for employment and keeping Cole from breaking his commitment to the plan, though he found it difficult to adhere to his normal everyday activities.

Circumstances had definitely changed since he met Rachel at the restaurant. His mind, his thoughts, even his original objective was now in question.

Finding no other way to put his mind at ease, Tristan decided he had to decide what his real intentions were. Was he driven by money alone, or had Rachel made more of an impact on him than he had the courage to admit? It wasn't something he was eager to find out, considering he'd towed his two best friends into this bizarre charade with him.

Both of his friends seemed to be holding their own. Cole's date with Megan had gone exceptionally well. Austin, however, found it a bit more difficult connecting with Marley. She found him repulsive and annoying, but Austin hadn't given up.

Although Rachel had said she would be working late, Tristan's propensity for overzealous action won over, leaving him no choice but to find a way to see her.

✦ ✦ ✦

Making a quick stop at the deli around the corner, Tristan bought two gourmet spinach salads and added them to his romantic picnic dinner for two, which, among other things, included two crystal glasses and a bottle of pink champagne.

Groceries in hand, Tristan took a cab to McMillan Enterprises. On the way, he thought about the Book of Mormon and the things that seemed to have his mind in a whirlwind. He found the book intriguing and unexpectedly fascinating. Still, he struggled to abide by some of their peculiar rules. Like no smoking, no coffee, and no alcoh—Tristan suddenly swore so loudly, he startled the cab driver. He couldn't believe he had been about to make such a huge mistake.

Alcohol had always been a regular part of his life. Wine or champagne with his meals, especially when those meals involved women, was so natural to him that he'd picked up the champagne without even thinking about the stipulations of the Mormon religion.

Apologizing to the cab driver, Tristan took the bottle from the basket and considered it for a moment. He rested his head back and took a deep breath, slowly blowing it out through his mouth. This new lifestyle was going to take some getting used to. It meant looking at things in an entirely new perspective. It would be difficult at first, but in time it would become second nature to him.

Wait a minute, Tristan thought, shaking his head. He wasn't really supposed to change his lifestyle for good. Just long enough to marry Rachel and take her money. *Get a grip, idiot!* he thought. He clutched the bottle in his hands tighter, feeling the frustration building. He needed to think of this as if he were acting in a play. When the play was finished, he would still be the person he once was.

However tormented he seemed to be, Tristan let one last thought creep into his head before paying the cab driver—and leaving a tip in the form of a bottle of pink champagne: *When it's all over, do I really want to go back to being the person I once was?*

Exiting the elevator on the fourteenth floor, Tristan realized just how difficult it was going to be to hide his self-doubt. With anxiety written plainly across his face and sweat collecting in the palms of his hands, he was sure to make Rachel suspicious.

It was after six in the evening, and most of the lights had been dimmed or turned off completely. The receptionist had left, so Tristan made his own way down the short corridor. A tiny bit of light was coming from a door at the end of the hall. The name plate read "Rachel McMillan." Tristan hesitated in the hallway and watched Rachel through the small crack in the doorway.

Rachel paced back and forth behind her desk. She wore a white button-up shirt and a red and white plaid skirt. Her hair was pulled back into a French braid with strands falling out around her perplexed face. In one hand she held an open folder, and in the other, she twiddled a pen between her fingers.

As she moved back and forth, Tristan could plainly see that she was strained and tired. He noticed her body movements were tense and restrictive, leading him to believe she did not like what she was reading.

Maybe I shouldn't bother her, Tristan thought. *Maybe she doesn't want to see me.*

Maybe I should just knock. He buried his indecision and tapped lightly on the door.

"Come in," Rachel called.

Tristan pushed open the door and took a deep breath before walking in. "Hi, Rachel," he said softly.

"Tristan, what are you doing here?" she asked.

Her eyes were wide, but soft and inviting, so Tristan casually walked to the desk. He sucked in a deep breath of self-confidence.

Rachel's office was roomy and immaculately decorated in blues and musty rose. Behind her, a large window exposed a breathtaking view of the city. In the corner of the room sat a classy damask-patterned love seat and two soft leather chairs.

"I hope I'm not bothering you," he said.

"No . . . not at all. I'm just surprised to see you."

"Well, I lost a bet. Remember?" He smiled, holding up the picnic basket. "I figured I might as well get it over with."

"You brought me dinner?"

"Correction, I brought *us* dinner."

Tristan wasn't about to let her turn him down, so he walked over to the love seat and spread out a small blue blanket on the floor. He sat down and placed the picnic basket in front of him. Rachel still stood, staring at him.

"Are you going to join me?" he finally asked.

Sensing a bit of apprehensiveness, Tristan waited on the floor. Rachel set the folder on her desk and joined him on the blanket. She scooted over next to him, much closer than he thought she might.

"Don't look so shocked," he taunted. "Did you really think I'd forget?"

"I'm just surprised. I mean, I wasn't expecting this."

Tristan smiled with pleasure, reading the delight written across her face. He'd succeeded with making an impression on her, one which he hoped would finally break through any reservation she might be feeling about him.

While they ate their salads, Tristan asked Rachel about her family memories. Tristan kept silent about the majority of his personal life, not wanting to take over the whole conversation. Besides, his childhood was nothing to brag about.

Rachel opened up to him about her father and the unbreakable bond they shared. Tristan saw a small teardrop collect in the corner of her eye. She stayed strong, keeping the tears from falling, but he could see how much she missed her father. With every personal memory she shared, Tristan felt more and more like a traitor.

He listened attentively to her fears of running the company and her lack of self-confidence. Her constant concern of letting her father down was tearing her up inside. Tristan watched helplessly as the anguish grew deeper on her beautiful face. The burden of her distress wrenched at his soul. He wanted nothing more at that moment than to take her in his arms and diminish all of her inner-most doubts.

"Your father loves you, Rachel," Tristan said in a soft, caring tone. "He would never be disappointed in you, no matter what your decision is."

The tension flooded through the air, and Tristan soon realized he needed to change the topic. He couldn't bear to see her emotionally suffering. It was cutting deeply into his tattered heart, though he wasn't sure just why he was letting it get to him like it was.

"So, what do you think my chances are of getting a rematch at paintball?" Tristan asked, replacing the agony with humor.

"You're a glutton for punishment," Rachel said, her eyes suddenly brightening.

"Yeah, maybe, but I had a really good time. Besides, my ribs are finally starting to heal," he said.

"I'll try to watch where I fall from now on. Anyway, our next activity won't be as competitive, but it will be a bit more strenuous."

"That doesn't sound good."

"Oh, come on. A big strong guy like you can surely climb up a mountain?"

"Hiking, huh? Any bets on who can make it to the top first?"

"You like a challenge, don't you?"

"I find that life's more interesting when you can add a little healthy competition," Tristan said.

They stayed on the floor, leaning up against the love seat. Rachel firmly held her position. She seemed relaxed, and a bit more comfortable, by his closeness.

Tristan couldn't seem to keep his eyes off her. He carefully memorized every curve of her face, locking the image away in a secure place in his mind.

Rachel repositioned herself on the floor, coming within inches of him. Being that close to her was torture. He wanted desperately to feel her lips against his and satisfy the desires that burned inside him.

With his strength weakening, Tristan moved in a little closer. The warmth of her breath against his face made his skin tingle with anticipation.

Pushing aside a strand of loose hair from her forehead, he searched her eyes for permission to continue. The scent of her flowery perfume swirled around him. It captured his senses and paralyzed his judgment. He took a deep breath, allowing the smell to flow though his airways. The aroma was intoxicating.

Tristan paused to examine the texture of her smooth, silky lips. Her once-pink lipstick had nearly faded away and her lips were parted just slightly to accommodate her erratic breathing.

He cupped the side of her face with his hand and pressed his anxious lips against hers. Without hesitation, she returned his kiss, sending an electric shock through his entire body—a shock that could have easily jump-started a dead man's heart.

Rachel's lips were soft and sweet, drawing him deeper into their magical force. He wrapped his other arm around her waist and pulled her closer, crushing her body against his. He could feel his wild desires bursting to the surface. At that moment, nothing else mattered. He wanted her more than he'd ever wanted any woman before.

Rachel pressed her hand against Tristan's chest and pushed him away.

"I think we'd better slow it down just a bit," she breathed heavily.

"You're right," Tristan said, struggling to calm his racing heart. "I'm sorry."

Before he had time to catch his breath, an interruption came with the sudden swing of the office door. "Rae?" Stewart said in disbelief.

"Stewart! What do you want?" Rachel barked. The irritation in her voice pleased Tristan immensely, and he couldn't help but smile to himself.

"Oh . . . I didn't realize you had . . . company," Stewart said, unsuccessfully trying hide his contempt. "I'll just leave the budget on your desk." He walked over to the desk with his usual leisurely stride and laid the file on top of a stack of papers.

"Thank you," Rachel said, looking down at her hands.

Stewart glanced over at them one more time before closing the door behind him.

"Sorry about the intrusion," Rachel said with a sigh.

"No problem," Tristan replied. "I should let you get back to work. Can we continue this . . . conversation another time?"

Rachel shot him a smile and cocked one eyebrow. "Are you busy on Saturday?"

"I am now," he said. "What time should I pick you up?"

"Here, let me write down the address where we can meet."

"Is this a trick? I'm not going to show up and be the only one standing in the middle of some deserted field or something, am I?"

Rachel got to her feet and walked to the desk. Tristan picked up the basket and followed her.

"No trick, I promise," Rachel guaranteed him. She wrote something down on a sticky note and handed it to him. "Meet me at this address at 9:00 a.m, sharp. Oh, and you'd better wear some old clothes too."

"Nine? In the morning? Old clothes? Just what kind of a date is this?"

Rachel laughed and shook her head. "Think of it more like a service project. Anyway, thanks for dinner and lending a friendly ear."

"Friendly" wasn't the word he'd been hoping to hear. "Passionate," "loving," or even "devoted" were how he would have described the evening. Besides, all men strive to stay away from one simple phrase, "I just want to be friends." It was the kiss of death.

"Anytime," he said, carefully tucking the paper into his pocket. "Until Saturday then."

Tristan strolled into the elevator, still feeling the touch of her lips against his own. He punched the button for the lobby and leaned his head against the wall. Just before the doors met, an arm stuck through the crack, forcing them open again. It was Stewart.

"Stew!" Tristan chimed, mocking his pet name for Rachel.

"Well, well, well. If it isn't Romeo himself. So you think you've got Rachel right where you want her, don't you?" Stewart asked.

"I would say things are moving in a positive direction, yes," Tristan boasted.

Stewart changed his weight to the other foot and folded his arms. "Rachel and I belong together. Do you understand that? We're cut from the same mold. You, on the other hand, have nothing in common with her, nor can you offer her the kind of life she's accustomed to. I think the honorable thing to do here would be to step back and accept your defeat."

Tristan chuckled under his breath, watching Stewart fidget and fume with jealousy. "Stew, Stew, Stew," he said, shaking his head. "You really need to start paying attention. The mold has been altered. You're yesterday's news, my friend. I think you're the one that needs to step back."

The elevator touched down on the first floor and Tristan rushed out. He was hoping to avoid an unnecessary argument that was sure to ruin his high from kissing Rachel.

Stewart kept pace with Tristan's long strides. "Rachel was mine first, and she will be again. So, if competition is what you want, then let the games begin!" Stewart was yelling so loudly that his voice echoed down the marble hallway.

"I'm not playing games with you, Stewart," Tristan insisted, walking toward the front doors. "I'm with Rachel because she wants me to be."

"She's a woman, for heaven's sake. She doesn't know what she wants. She was in love with me once, so there's one in my favor!"

Tristan stopped at the door and turned to glare at Stewart, annoyed by all of his assumptions. "If you think I'm backing down just because you and her have a 'history,' you're sadly mistaken," Tristan growled, growing tired of Stewart's immaturity. "I care for Rachel, and I'm not about to stand here and be intimidated by you. If you're going to fight for her, then I'll fight even harder. And trust me, I'll win. I always win."

"Well, we'll just have to see about that," Stewart sneered before heading back toward the elevator.

Nine

When Tristan arrived home, the apartment was dark and quiet. He figured Austin was still at work, and Cole was out with Megan. Tossing the keys onto the table, he went to his room and turned on the bedside lamp. He sat on the edge of the bed holding his head in his hands.

Sometime during the ride home, the cloud he'd been floating on burst, and now guilt and shame poured heavily down on his self-esteem. There was something about Rachel that was overwhelmingly enticing. Some magnetic force held his thoughts hostage. He couldn't stay away from her, nor could he bring himself to tell her the truth. The internal conflict raged inside him like a wild beast.

Tristan rubbed his hands across his face and exhaled slowly. He now recognized the truthfulness of his heart, which was something he could no longer deny. He could spend the whole night silently arguing the fact, but in the morning the truth would still be there staring him in the face.

Walking to the dresser, he disgustedly looked at his pale complexion in the small, oval mirror. Grinding his fingertips into the wood, he leaned closer, glaring at the monster he'd become.

Quickly he turned away, repulsed by the image staring back at him. How could he have ever thought of such an unethical, immoral, revolting scheme? It was a plan of destruction and one that would no doubt end in heartache.

What was once a brilliant idea now had become something like a bad dream that he couldn't escape. He walked to the window and slid it open just a crack. The glow of the full moon and the street lights below bathed the room in a soft light. The normal street sounds seemed more muted than normal. He could hear the faint sound of a siren in the distance. He took in a deep, mind-cleansing breath of night air.

Although his mind was a cluttered mess, he knew exactly what was happening. "Am I falling for her?" Tristan whispered. He already knew the answer to his question and was all too aware that there was nothing he could do to stop it.

The funny thing was that deep down, he didn't want to stop it or even slow it down. Rachel made his heart sing and his mind soar. He wanted her with every fiber of his being. He'd only just left her and yet he craved her presence.

Tristan pulled off his clothes and climbed into bed. He closed his eyes and found her lovely face staring back at him. He needed to sidetrack his mind and find a way to ease the emotional distress that had settled in his mind.

Reaching for the night stand, he pulled the Book of Mormon from the drawer. He flipped it open to 2 Nephi and started reading. Aside from Rachel, the Book of Mormon had been the only thing he thought about. He knew there was something more to this book than what Cole had thought. It was almost as if he were being handed answers before he had the chance to ask the questions.

Over the years, Tristan had wondered about life, death, and the meaning behind it all. He'd plunged through life feeling like he was lost in a misty haze, uncertain about his future and blinded by his lack of knowledge. Now, with all he'd read so far, it seemed someone was holding out a brightly lit flashlight, beckoning him to follow. Though he still had small, insignificant doubts about the Mormon faith, following that flashlight was just what he intended to do.

★ ★ ★

On Saturday morning, Tristan was up at first light, getting ready for his so-called service project date. He didn't care if it meant walking through fire as long as he got to spend time with Rachel.

After a quick shower, he threw on some old clothes and checked his appearance in the mirror. He ran his hand through his hair and stepped back to examine his reflection more closely. The look was exactly what he'd been shooting for. *Handsome, mysterious, and . . . trying too hard!* he thought. Giving up, he reached up and shook out his hair.

After almost an hour on the subway, Tristan headed for the address on the pink slip of paper that still smelled of Rachel's peach hand lotion. He held it up to his nose and inhaled deeply, sending memories of the unforgettable kiss raging through his brain. Chuckling to himself, he muttered, "You've got it bad, my friend," almost disappointed in himself for letting his feelings get out of control.

For nine o'clock in the morning, the sun was already warm and soothing. The birds chirped happily in a nearby tree, and the light breeze gave off a refreshing scent of morning air. Tristan inhaled deeply, expanding his lungs with the freshness, and then he put on his sun glasses to hide from the glare of the sun.

Walking up the sidewalk, he paused to inspect his surroundings. Built in the early 1920s, the old walk-up building definitely looked its age, except for the new double-pane windows on the third floor. The white paint was flaking from the weather, and the shingles peeled up.

Instantly Tristan realized what the service project was all about. He followed the six or seven men from church. They were all filing into a large three-bedroom apartment. Tristan grunted and removed his sunglasses. He stuck them on the side on his Levi jeans and glanced around in anticipation, searching for the only person who could brighten his gloomy mood.

The men kept busy sanding and polishing the hardwood floors. Tristan recognized some women from the singles ward on ladders applying a fresh coat of white paint to the walls.

Standing in amazement, Tristan watched everyone hustle around the apartment. He wondered why so many people would want to give up their Saturday morning to be here. No one was obligated. They weren't being paid for their services, and there would be no reward waiting for them at the end of the day. Still, here they were, every person doing their part to help someone in need.

Finally catching a glimpse of Rachel, Tristan moved slowly in her direction. She was standing on the second step of a metal ladder with a paintbrush in one hand. When she spotted him, a huge smile came across her face. With one leap, she was off the ladder and heading his direction. Her long ponytail swooped back and forth as she danced across the room with unrestrained exuberance. The sight of her took his breath away, and he struggled to keep his thoughts under control.

She was dressed in some old, faded blue jeans that had a rip in one knee, and an oversized blue and white striped T-shirt. She had paint splattered across her shirt, in her hair, and down the side of her rosy cheek. She was a mess, but to Tristan she had never looked more attractive.

Taking a deep breath, Tristan sternly reminded himself of the Mormon's view on morality. He should be condemned to purgatory for even thinking what he was, but it wasn't easy for him, especially when she was around. He hadn't been raised that way. Though he respected the Mormons' moral beliefs, his checkered past made it that much harder to resist her.

"You're here," Rachel said, her pleasure written plainly across her face.

Did she have any idea what she was doing to him? Her smile, her body, even her scent was like dangling forbidden fruit in front of him.

Tristan cleared his throat and folded his arms. He took

a small step back to add some much-needed space between them.

"Yeah, so this is our date, huh?" He smiled, breaking up the intensity inside him.

"Oh, come on, don't you find hard work terribly romantic?" she joked.

"I do with you around," Tristan responded. Rachel shyly looked to the ground and blushed. "So what's the story?" he asked.

"Mrs. Brookston lives here with her three children. Her husband was killed six months ago in a car accident and left them with almost nothing to live on. She wants to sell this place so she can move back to California closer to her mother. That's why we're here helping her fix it up."

Out of nowhere, Tristan's perspective on service changed. It really wasn't about the money or the praise after all. It was about helping out this young widow. *Of course!* he thought. He remembered the scripture he'd read just last night. It was in Mosiah, and it said something about when you're in the service of your fellow men, you are in the service of God.

"Well, count me in!" he answered with more enthusiasm in his voice. "Where do I start?"

"The guys are almost ready to wax the floor. You can go check in with one of them." She pointed her finger in the direction of a group of men. "I'll see you a little later." Rachel winked, leaving him with an open invitation to come back later.

Tristan watched her walk away before joining the circle of men. "Hey, I'm Tristan. What can I do to help?"

Two of the men parted, exposing the one person he really hadn't wanted to see. Stewart. He was dressed in his usual designer attire with a gold Rolex watch around his wrist. *Doesn't this guy own any normal clothes?* Tristan thought.

"Well, well, well. If it isn't Tristan "I-can-have-any-woman-I-want" Taylor," Stewart said derisively. "You just can't stay away from her, can you?"

The tension in the air grew stronger, causing the other men

to move back and form their own group.

"On the contrary, Stew. Rachel invited me," Tristan said, loudly enough for the other men to hear and to get his point across to Stewart.

Tristan really had no idea why he felt so possessive of Rachel. It wasn't as though any of the men posed a threat. Other than Stewart, perhaps, but he was more like a pestering fly. So why was he fuming with jealousy?

Stewart's eyes bore down on him like fiery rain falling from the sky. "We really don't need another set of hands. I think we can handle waxing the floor ourselves, so why don't you go make us some lemonade and leave the hard work for the real men?" He reached over and switched on the large machine in his hands.

Tristan recognized the challenge and was powerless to stop the competitive demon that fought to escape. He really would have preferred to deck Stewart and be done with it, but he decided to show him who the real man was—the man that deserved Rachel.

Glaring at Stewart, Tristan walked over to the group of men and snatched up another floor waxer. Though he felt the machine buck painfully at his shoulders, he kept his face tight and carefree.

"Let the games begin," Tristan yelled over the noise with raised eyebrows.

A look of alarm flashed across Stewart's face when he realized the race was on. Nearly tripping over his own feet, Stewart set off in uneven rows toward the dining room, where Rachel was working.

"All for her benefit I'm sure," Tristan huffed. He hurried off to claim his own section of hardwood.

Tristan made swift work of one of the smaller rooms and hallway. He had stepped back to briefly inspect his achievement when he saw Stewart speeding across the apartment with ill-mannered determination.

In a split second, Tristan realized it was a game of speed

not technique. "Oh, no you don't," Tristan grumbled under his breath.

They both took off toward the open living room, Tristan just inches in front of Stewart. Tristan lost control of his machine when his foot got tangled in the power cord, sending him headfirst to the ground. Stewart stopped briefly, standing over Tristan to gloat with satisfaction.

"Stay down and accept defeat!" he roared.

Leaping to his feet, Tristan eyeballed him with unwavering fortitude. "Never!" he shouted.

As they continued to scurry back and forth, bumping elbows at every chance they got, the other men stood back and let the two of them have reign over the expanse of hardwood floor. The group laughed out loud at their clumsiness and mockery as they each tried to out-do the other.

The women were likewise amused by their adolescent behavior. The only one who wasn't laughing was Rachel.

Descending from her ladder, Rachel threw her paintbrush down and headed for Stewart. Her face glowed fiery red as she planted both hands firmly on her hips.

"Stewart, what are you doing?" she demanded.

Stewart was intent on wrestling the waxer in his hands into moving faster. With his mind on the race and his face buried in dirt, he didn't even notice she was standing there.

Shrieking in frustration and throwing both hands up in the air, Rachel stormed off across the apartment to knock some sense into Tristan.

Tristan was down on both knees, the waxer turned on its side, frantically trying to coax his machine into moving again. He was in the process of beating it into submission when Rachel walked up. "Tristan, stop this! You're acting like an idiot!" she scolded. Engrossed in a relentless quest for victory, he went right on working. "Tristan!" she screamed.

Startled by the sudden loud voice, Tristan fell back on the ground. He looked up into a face of fury.

"What?" he panted.

"What are you doing?"

He climbed to his feet and brushed the dirt from his shirt and pants. "Being a complete idiot," he said with a sigh.

"Yes, you are!" Rachel agreed, shaking her head. "Are you trying to prove you're stronger than Stewart? Because I already know you are."

"It's worse than that," he divulged. Dropping his head, Tristan rubbed the back of his neck with one hand. He could feel the humiliation creep to the surface. "I was trying to prove I'm the better man for you."

There were a few seconds of silence that felt like an eternity before she finally spoke.

"Why?" she asked.

Tristan immediately threw both hands up in the air and stared into her perplexed eyes. "If you haven't noticed, Rachel, I don't have the money he has. I don't have the fancy clothes or the important job. I live in a rundown shack in Queens above a grease pit owned by a guy named Bubba," he contested. "What could you possibly want with a guy like me?" Okay, so it was a bit excessive, but for once, Tristan was being honest, though he hated to admit he might be the lesser man.

Rachel stepped in a little closer, clearly not afraid to invade his personal space. Her composed stare was peculiar, leaving Tristan wondering once again what she was thinking. Was it anger or just disappointment in her eyes? Perhaps he'd pointed out the obvious, and now she would go running into Stewart's arms.

Standing incredibly close, she reached out and took his soiled hands, keeping her eyes locked with his. Tristan could feel the coolness of her breath against his hot, sweaty face as she spoke.

"Do you like me?" Rachel asked.

Tristan tilted his head to one side, lost in her majestic eyes, and squeezed her hands tightly. "More than you know." He cocked one eyebrow while concealing his laughter at her innocent, school-girl attributes.

"I feel the same way. Money, clothes—that kind of stuff doesn't matter to me."

"Can you forgive me for acting like a brainless jerk?"

"I already have."

Standing on her toes, she stretched her small frame to meet his taller body. Keeping his hands held hostage, she leaned in and softly pressed her lips against his.

The touch of her lips flooded through him, drenching all of his insecurities and setting his mind free. It was as if the world around them simply disappeared. The kiss was brief, but it had a lingering effect. Rachel had kissed *him*! And more than that, she *wanted* to kiss him!

When she finally released his hands, Tristan no longer gave a squat about Stewart or the competition.

"Now, wasn't that better than battling with Stewart?" she asked.

Tristan vigorously nodded his head, still baffled by her forwardness. "Yes—absolutely—absolutely yes," he answered.

How was it that whenever she was around he acted like a blabbering idiot? This was certainly out of character for him.

"So, no more competing?"

"No, I'm done."

"Good, then I'll see you in a while." She spun around on one foot and trotted off toward her ladder and paintbrush. He could have sworn she was purposely swinging her hips at him.

Taking a deep breath, Tristan rubbed his hand through his hair, his lips still tingling and his head still spinning. He quite enjoyed this new feeling of being wrapped around her finger. Somehow the tides had turned. He was the one who had taken the bait and was now being reeled in by her captivating charm.

By the time he came back out to the living room, the other men had figured the show was over and had taken over the floors. Stewart was pompously leaning in a doorway with an irritated look on his face.

"What is it with you?" Stewart yelled, the open hostility flaring from his eyes.

Realizing Stewart must have seen the kiss, Tristan tried to ignore the other man's threatening posture, although it delighted him to see Stewart squirm.

"Leave it alone, Stew."

Stewart abruptly reached out and grabbed Tristan tightly by the arm to prevent him from walking away. "I told you to back off!" he hissed through clenched teeth.

"Let go of me, Stewart. I don't want any trouble."

"Well, that's too bad, because trouble is exactly what you've got!"

"I mean it, Stewart. I wouldn't want you to hurt yourself," Tristan warned.

Stewart released his grip but kept his icy, hate-filled eyes focused on Tristan. "I'm not afraid of you, with your scroungy hair and your tough-guy attitude. You may have Rachel fooled, but I know different."

Tristan turned around and stared him down angrily. How much did Stewart really know? Regardless, Tristan was getting rather bored with Stewart's constant threats and his overconfident big head.

"You know absolutely nothing about me, Stewart, and it may be in your best interest if you keep it that way," Tristan sneered.

"Don't you want a shot at me, tough guy? Huh?" Stewart asked. He danced around in a small area, like a ballerina turned boxer. He held his fists high in the air with his elbows out. "Come on, let's see what you got!"

"I'm not going to fight you, Stewart. Just back off!"

At that moment, Rachel called out to Tristan, realizing she was witnessing a fight in the works. Tristan turned his head to answer when Stewart's fist came hammering into the right side of his nose. The punch took him off guard and sent him spinning around on one foot.

Stumbling, but not falling, Tristan kept his head down and felt the warm blood start to ooze from his nostril. The ground started spinning, and he heard a ringing in his ears. He wasn't really sure if he was standing or lying on the ground.

Before Tristan had time to regain his balance, another blow came out of nowhere and thumped the other side of his face. This time, the blow sent him to his knees in a stupor.

Someone pulled Stewart away, and soon Rachel was kneeling down beside Tristan. She was blurting out some hideous comment to Stewart, but Tristan couldn't make it out through the constant buzzing in his ears.

"Tristan! Tristan, look at me," Rachel said with urgency in her voice. She gently turned his face to meet hers. "Are you okay?"

He looked into her concerned, sweet, albeit blurry face and grinned. "Perfectly perfect," he muttered.

Holding onto Rachel's arm, Tristan pulled his feet under him. He swayed back and forth, feeling the ground move beneath him.

"I can't believe you, Stewart!" Rachel was practically screaming. "What is your problem!?"

"He deserved it!" Stewart blurted out.

"Go home, Stewart! I can't even look at you right now!"

"Rachel, he's just—"

"Now, Stewart!" she commanded.

Rachel handed Tristan a clean rag to stop the bleeding and then escorted him toward the door. "Come on, Tristan. I'll get us a cab," she instructed, holding out her hand.

"I'm fine. I can just take the subway, really," Tristan insisted. He started off in what he thought was the correct direction.

"Tristan, you're going the wrong way."

"I knew that. I was just making sure you were paying attention."

"Sure you were. Come on, the cab is on its way."

Tristan slid into the back seat of the cab and rested his aching head while holding the rag firmly against his nose. Rachel gave the driver the address, glancing over to see if he was still conscious. Tristan smiled impishly.

"If I'd known it was this easy to get you to come home with

me, I would've let Stewart hit me a long time ago."

"Are you trying to tell me this was a planned attack?" she asked, grinning.

"I'm not admitting to anything that might incriminate me," he replied, chuckling. Chuckling hurt. "Ouch!" He reached up and rubbed his throbbing forehead.

"Just relax. I'll have you home and in bed before you know it," Rachel reassured him.

Even after being knocked silly, his thoughts still wandered into forbidden territory. He knew very well his uncontrolled desires would only get him into trouble, but how could he put down the floodgate and stop the raging waters? What he needed was the perseverance that these Mormons seemed to display with ease.

Curiosity once again set in, and he wondered just where they pulled their strength from. With so many rules and regulations, surely they would crack under the pressures of the world if it were not for some higher power.

As Tristan closed his eyes for the ride home, he recalled the scriptures he'd read on prayer and the powerful effect it has. *That must be it*, he thought. *Prayer must be the key to unlocking the mysteries of restraint.*

If he was going to succeed at suppressing his unwanted desires, he must first test out this theory.

Ten

Tristan was much more focused by the time they reached his apartment. Knowing that money didn't matter to Rachel, he felt better about inviting her into his tiny, rundown dwelling.

The fight with Stewart had actually worked to his advantage. Not only was he with Rachel, but she was now upset with Stewart, which also satisfied Tristan's jealous streak.

It was just a good thing that Stewart had taken that cheap shot. Otherwise, it would have been a one-sided fight, with Stewart being the one driven home by Rachel and Tristan on the chopping block.

Rachel was extremely sympathetic. Although he liked the attention he received, Tristan hated to see her so upset.

For some reason that he couldn't explain, Tristan felt oddly protective of Rachel. He felt the need to shelter her from anything or anyone that might hurt her, including himself. He wanted to be her sole support, her shelter, and her defender, though he knew she really didn't need him.

Over the last few weeks, Tristan grew to understand that Rachel stayed behind an invisible shield that made everyone around her think she was in control and secure. The few times she'd let him cross over, he'd discovered her hidden insecurities.

Rachel came around and helped him out of the cab, sliding one hand under his arm. The irony of the whole situation sent a smile to his face, which she instantly noticed. "What's so funny?"

"You're escorting me to the door like I was an eighty-year-old cripple." He laughed. "Really, I'm not that bad off. Stewart's bark is worse than his bite."

"I'm still going to make sure you make it in. Okay, old man?"

"How will you get home? Did you tell the cab to wait?"

"What, you don't want me to sleep over?" she teased. "I'm hurt."

A half-smile came across his face as he continued to shake dangerous thoughts from his mind. He took her by the right hand and slowly pressed it to his lips, kissing her velvety-soft knuckles.

"You're too much of a temptation for me to have around all night."

Rachel blushed timidly, leaving Tristan to wonder if it might be a temptation for her as well.

When Tristan opened the front door, a distinct odor swirled around them—one he recognized a moment too late. Rachel walked through the open doorway into a cloud of second-hand smoke. Tristan glared at Cole, who was sitting on the couch smoking a cigarette.

Tristan's slaughtering glare shot straight across the room with a loud message attached. Cole's flabbergasted face paled, and he instantly doused the butt into the ashtray.

"You're home early," he gasped, waving his hand in the air while he placed the glass ashtray on the floor.

"Cole, I thought you said you'd quit!" Tristan squawked. He walked over to Cole and glared at him.

"Wow! What happened to your face?" Cole asked.

"Never mind that. What about your *promise*?" Tristan asked. He emphasized the last word, trying to direct Cole in the conversation.

Cole broke out in tears of remorse, playing along with whatever Tristan had up his sleeve.

"I'm . . . so . . . sorry," he whimpered. "I'm really trying, I swear. But I'm weak. I am a disappointment to all the people I care about . . . and my religion."

Tristan discreetly made a motion with his hand to take it down a notch. He wanted it believable without the day-time-talk-show emotions.

Rachel stood silently in the corner of the room, her face full of curiosity, or perhaps suspicion. Tristan wasn't quite sure which.

"Hand them over," he demanded.

"No," Cole whispered. He quickly buried them behind his back.

"Give them to me."

"No!"

Hurling himself at Cole, Tristan pinned him to the couch, fighting to take the pack from the death-grip Cole had around them.

"I'm going to help you quit!"

"I don't need your help!"

"Cole, there is a lady in the room. We don't want to make a scene," Tristan reminded him.

"Fine," Cole growled. He reluctantly placed the pack into Tristan's hand. "I hate you," he whispered.

"Now, don't you feel better already?"

Cole stared up at Tristan with a fire raging from both eyes. Tristan knew he'd pay for it later, but all that mattered right now was making their story believable.

"Why, yes I do." Cole scowled. "Thanks to you, my *friend*. What would I do without you? Because, you know, *friends* like you are so rare. Yep, my *friend* Tristan, always looking out for me—"

"Okay, okay. You don't need to thank me," Tristan interrupted nervously.

Walking back over to Rachel, Tristan smiled and let out a

sigh. He hoped she wouldn't notice the sweat that had collected on his forehead.

"Sorry about that. Austin and I have been trying our best to help him stay clean, but sometimes . . ." he said. He was more disappointed in himself for lying to Rachel than he was in Cole for smoking.

There was a vague look on Rachel's face that Tristan couldn't quite place as she walked past him and went to sit next to Cole on the couch. Tristan watched apprehensively, holding his breath. The room suddenly became very humid, and he found it difficult to breath. Had Cole blown it for them?

"Cole, did you start up again because of Megan?" Rachel asked. Full of compassion, she placed her hand on top of his and looked into his eyes. Cole dropped his eyes and nodded his head. "It's going to be okay. She'll only be gone for a year, and you can call her every day. Shoot, I'll even fly you over there," Rachel offered in a soft-spoken tone of voice.

"What's going on?" Tristan asked. He was trying his best to follow the conversation, but he was irritated at her sudden interest in Cole.

Ignoring Tristan, Rachel continued to focus on Cole. "I can call Megan and see if she's home. You should go see her."

"That would be great," Cole said, whipping up a few more tears to create the illusion of sadness.

He leaned over and took Rachel in his arms, squeezing her tightly as he glanced up and gave Tristan a sleazy smile. Their closeness ignited the jealous fuse inside, and Tristan blew. He folded his arms and walked to the couch, furious that they held some secret they weren't telling him.

"Okay, somebody better tell me what's going on right now," he demanded.

Rachel pulled back and held up one finger, indicating to him that she would fill him in later. She pulled out her silver cell phone and called Megan, informing her that Cole was on his way over. She placed the phone on the coffee table and smiled at Cole.

"She's waiting for you," Rachel said.

"Thank you," Cole said.

Cole rose from the couch and walked past Tristan, mocking him with a half-smile and raised eyebrows. He grabbed the keys off the table and headed out the door. Cole really was disappointed Megan was leaving, but he was playing it up a bit. Seeing the look on Tristan's face as he hugged Rachel was priceless.

After the door was shut, Tristan turned to Rachel for an explanation. "Megan was offered the chance to study archaeology in Europe," she explained. "She leaves tomorrow and will be gone for a year. I'm pretty sure that's why Cole started smoking again."

"Oh, well, that explains a lot. The hug was a little much, though, don't you think?"

"Don't get upset. I was only trying to comfort him."

"You're right, I'm being stupid again." Tristan sighed. "Okay . . . so, would you like a tour of the apartment?"

"Absolutely."

Walking to the small area that connected the kitchen and the living room, Tristan stood and motioned for Rachel to join him.

"Okay, from this particular location you can actually see the entire apartment without ever moving," he said, still amused at how tiny the apartment actually was. "You have the kitchen and conjoined living room here, which Austin finds extremely convenient during football season. Down the hall, we have Cole's room, Austin's room, one pathetically small bathroom, which you should probably stay away from if you value your sense of smell, and, of course, my room to your left."

Tristan pointed to each room, acting a little like a pushy real estate agent, just to add some fun in the midst of humiliation. "The good thing is you can walk to any room in two seconds flat."

"It's really not that bad," Rachel reassured him. "Now, let's see how long it takes to walk to your room." She darted past him and headed for his bedroom.

She walked in and made a complete circle while Tristan stood silently at the door and watched her expression closely. An old wood desk holding a computer sat in the corner. Beside the small, single-pane window was a tall bookshelf made out of cheap compressed wood. Two of the four shelves were filled with books while the other two held several trophies and ribbons he'd received in high school. Three were for wrestling and the other five were for basketball. Rachel stopped in front of the shelf to examine the awards.

Tristan kept his eyes on her, wondering if she'd think he was just boasting about his accomplishments, which he usually liked to do. In Rachel's case, he'd rather have placed them in the drawer.

"Wrestling and basketball, huh?" She grinned and walked back over to where he was still standing. "Very impressive. And I think this room is perfectly cozy."

"Well, you know, the penthouse was already taken, so . . ." He sat down on the edge of the bed. "You can sit down with me. I don't bite."

"I don't know about that."

"I'll be right back. Don't move," Tristan said, and then left the room.

He hurried to the kitchen and retrieved a roll of gray duct tape from the drawer. He returned to the bedroom to find Rachel standing exactly where he'd left her.

Sitting on the edge of the bed, Tristan unrolled a long piece of tape and ripped it off the roll. He stuck one end of the tape to his wrist and the other end into his mouth, gripping it tightly between his front teeth. Using his mouth as the leverage, he proceeded to wrap the tape around both wrists several times, binding his hands securely together.

When he was finished, he looked up into Rachel's questioning eyes. "There, you're completely safe now," he teased, holding up his bound hands for her to inspect. "Well, are you going to sit down?"

Scooting to the top of the mattress, he leaned up against

the headboard and stretched out his legs. He crossed his ankles and laid his hands in his lap. He gave her an innocent, angel-boy smile—the one he used back in school to get himself out of trouble.

Rachel returned his smile and moved to the bed. She sat down on the very end of the firm single mattress. Her posture was stiff, and her face was full of anxiety. Tristan wished she wouldn't be frightened of him. The last thing he wanted was to scare her off.

"You never cease to amaze me, Tristan Taylor," she said, shaking her head.

"I'm perfectly harmless, really."

"Yeah, I know your type. You portray the innocent kitten but you're actually a lion," she taunted.

Laughing off her accusation, Tristan could sense she was beginning to relax and really felt no threat from him. Nonetheless, she kept her distance at the end of the bed.

"I'll make sure I keep the beast locked up, at least for the night," Tristan joked. "So tell me, you've got one sister that wants to study in Europe and one that obviously wants to be the next women's body-building champion. I don't think you've ever told me what you want."

A heavy sigh passed through her lips, making a hissing sound as it crept out. She repositioned herself on the bed in order to face Tristan. "I don't know," she finally confessed. "I know what everyone expects me to want. They all look at me and think I have it all—the company, the title, the money—everything that could possibly make me happy. The truth is, I don't know if it will make me happy, if it's what I need. Some days it seems to be enough, but other days it feels all wrong."

"Why do you care what everybody else thinks? Do what makes you happy. Don't try so hard to please everyone."

"I guess. I just don't want to let my family down."

As they talked, Tristan could feel his fingertips start to tingle. He twisted his hands a little, but he could get no relief from the pressure of the tightly wrapped tape.

"Is there something wrong?" Rachel asked.

"I think I've cut the circulation off to my hands."

"Take it off, Tristan, quick!"

"I'm trying, but I seem to have bound myself more tightly than I intended."

"Here, let me help you." Rachel tried to rip the tape with her fingers, but to no avail. She then placed the tape between her front teeth, gently tearing it apart until his wrists were free. "There, does that feel better?"

He wiggled his fingers, sending the blood back where it belonged. "Aren't you afraid you've let the lion out of its cage?" he asked, smiling.

"I'm not afraid of you," she said firmly. "In fact, I'll prove it." She walked around the bed and slid right up next to him. She picked up his hand and intertwined her fingers with his. "There. Satisfied?"

Although her closeness was getting easier to handle, he still fought to hold back the inappropriate feeling that stirred inside him. "I think I may be the one that's in danger here."

"I'll try to control myself."

Tristan let out a long, frustrated sigh. Feeling the touch of her soft skin and the warmth of her body next to his ignited the fuel.

"Could you excuse me for a few minutes?" he asked.

Leaping from the bed, he headed straight for the door. He could feel his heart beat rapidly with excitement. His forbidden desires were once again creeping to the surface. The truth was, he didn't know if he could be trusted. He was more of a lion than she realized. But he cared enough for her to know he had to do something to stop the inferno.

"Is there something wrong?" Rachel asked.

"No . . . nothing's wrong," he lied. "I'm just filthy from chasing Stewart around all day. I thought I'd take a quick shower. Will you wait for me?"

"Of course."

"Just give me ten minutes."

Tristan escaped to the refuge of the bathroom and turned on the water. Staring at himself in the mirror, he breathed in deeply and exhaled loudly.

"Get a hold of yourself, Tristan," he ordered. He wanted her to stay, wanted to hold her in his arms without fear of crossing the line. He needed strength to overcome his weakness. "You can do this," he told himself. "Just stay in control."

After a cold shower, his confidence and his self-control returned. Tristan entered the room and found Rachel sitting on the edge of the bed looking through his high school yearbook.

"This was laying on your desk. I hope you don't mind," she said.

"Be my guest," he answered, a little leery.

"You must have been quite the ladies' man," she observed, holding up the book. "All of the signatures in here are from girls. In fact, five of them left you their phone numbers."

"Um . . . well, you know how the girls like the jocks," he said, dismissing the accusations.

"I can't blame them."

"You can't?"

"Well, you're the whole package—you've got supreme characteristics that outshine even your most handsome attributes."

Wow, she thinks I'm handsome and . . . and . . . what? "What characteristics?" he questioned.

"You're compassionate, caring, thoughtful, and a pure gentleman."

More like a liar, a sinner, and a pure disgrace to all mankind. He wondered how she could possibly see all those redeeming qualities in him.

Rachel set the book down and took her place back on the bed. Tristan immediately joined her. They talked about everything. He even opened up about his catastrophic advertising campaign. Tristan shared his most personal thoughts: the loss of his mother, his damaged career, and his fear of letting his two best friends down. He told her things he never thought he'd ever share with a woman—things dearest to his heart.

He only stopped when he heard Rachel's stomach growling. It was after 8:00 p.m., and his stomach was protesting as well.

He led the way to the kitchen and pulled out one of the three old chairs at the table. He then prepared a bachelor's dinner of ham and cheese sandwiches and potato chips.

As they ate, Rachel brought up something he'd been trying to avoid—his future.

"So, what will you do if you can't find a job here in New York?" Rachel asked, sounding deeply concerned for him. "Will you move back to Cleveland?"

"I'm not sure. Cole and Austin quit their jobs just to come with me. I feel horrible about that, and I don't wish to go back home as a failure."

"You're not a failure, Tristan. So you had one bad advertisement." Rachel knew all about the ad, so he shot her an incredulous look. "Okay, a really disgustingly horrendous advertisement," she said, smiling. "But you'll find something soon, I'm sure of it."

When they were finished, they returned to the bedroom and continued their conversation. Tristan was afraid she would grow tired of his company and want to leave, but she seemed to be enjoying herself, so he continued. He found it was easy to talk to her, though he still kept quiet about most of his childhood and was content to let her do most of the talking.

As the hours of the night slipped away, Rachel yawned more frequently. She slid down in the bed and rested her head on the pillow. Before long Tristan noticed the silence and glanced over to find her sound asleep. He sat very still so he wouldn't disturb her peaceful slumber.

He gently ran one finger down the side of her cheek. Her skin was warm and soft, and she stirred just a little at his touch. Placing both hands behind his head, Tristan sat quietly and listened to her breathing. He knew he should wake her and send her home, but his selfish side took over. He didn't want to let her go.

Tristan studied her exquisite features. Everything about her was undeniably wholesome. She was the real thing. The kind of woman men like him only dream about, and there she was, lying next to him. He only wished their relationship hadn't come with such a high price—one which he would be forced to pay if she ever found out the truth about him. He couldn't let that happen. Not just because of the money, but because she meant too much to him now to risk losing her.

☆　☆　☆

"Rachel . . . Rachel, wake up," Austin whispered into her ear.

Rachel was sleeping peacefully with her head resting comfortably on Tristan's chest. Her left arm was draped across his stomach, and she snuggled close beside him. Tristan had likewise fallen asleep and was gently holding her with one arm around her shoulders and the other around her waist.

Austin grunted irritably, wishing he had saved just one of the firecrackers from last year's Fourth of July parade. A loud noise was just what they needed. They looked a little too cozy. Austin leaned in closer.

"Rachel!" he shouted.

Rachel sprang up in shock, nailing Tristan in the jaw with her head. "Ouch!" he yelped, blinking his eyes and holding his chin in pain.

"I'm so sorry," she exclaimed. "Oh my gosh, what time is it?" She jumped from the bed and checked her pockets. "Where's my phone?"

Austin watched from the background, happy to have succeeded at getting them out of bed. "You left it on the coffee table. It rang, but I didn't answer it. I figured it was none of my business," Austin said. He handed it to Rachel and left the room, closing the door behind him. It cut off the little bit of light that had been shining into the dark room.

"Um . . . Tristan, the light please."

"Oh, right." Tristan sat up and flipped on the bedside lamp.

"What's the matter?" he asked, observing her bizarre behavior.

"Tristan, it's two o'clock in the morning."

"So?"

"I fell asleep."

"So did I."

Tristan rose from the bed and went to stand next to her. He perceived that there was something very wrong, but he couldn't understand what it might be. He hadn't tried anything. In fact, he was praising himself for enduring it so well.

"When I woke up, I—I was in your arms, lying on your chest," Rachel stuttered, grasping at each word.

"Trust me, you were no bother," he said, smiling at her worry.

Taking Rachel by the hand, Tristan gazed into her troubled eyes, hoping to calm her anxiety. He thought for sure his statement would bring a smile to her face, but instead her eyes were wide with apprehension. She stood nervously biting her bottom lip.

"It was wrong. I shouldn't have led you on like that. You know, making you think . . ." Her voice trailed off as her eyes fell to the floor.

Well, he'd never claimed to be intelligent, just handsome. It took Tristan a few more seconds to understand what was going through her head. He took his finger and gently placed it under her chin, raising her head to meet his eyes.

"I wasn't tempted," he whispered.

"Oh," she frowned. Her look of frustration immediately changed to disappointment.

Smiling at her innocence, Tristan raised both her hands to his mouth and softly kissed her knuckles, keeping his eyes locked with hers.

"Rachel, I would never do anything to hurt you or make you feel uncomfortable," he clarified. "But I'd be lying if I said I didn't enjoy holding you, and I wish the night didn't have to end."

As her face lightened and the distress vanished, Tristan could see she shared his feelings. She would only be a temptation if he let her, and he was determined to stay in control. Nevertheless, he would make sure their conversations were in a more appropriate place next time.

leven

Tristan tapped softly on the door and waited for an answer. When the door opened, he found the face that he yearned to see every day.

The glow from her face radiated through the room as he walked in. He loved to see her face light up every time he was around. It reassured him to know that they shared the same feelings.

"Tristan," Rachel said, her smile growing by the instant. His heart leaped at the sound of her enthusiasm. "What are you doing here?"

Walking over to her, Tristan immediately wrapped both arms tightly around her waist and pressed his lips softly to hers. It was the sweet taste he longed for. Something to temporarily fill the emptiness inside him when he was without her. Although he could have stayed lost in her kiss, he knew his inner demons would soon surface and threaten his ability to stay in control.

Pulling away from her, Tristan looked into her perfect face. "I missed you," he confessed.

"I just saw you two days ago," said Rachel.

Dropping his eyes to the floor in embarrassment, Tristan let out a quiet sigh and cleared his throat. "Yeah, I know."

"But it seems more like weeks," she said, laughing.

Tristan shook his head and let out a small huff. "You had me worried there for a minute. I thought I was going to have to kidnap you just so I could be with you," he joked.

"I don't know. Being your prisoner doesn't sound that bad."

"You better be careful what you say. I can feel the lion rattling his cage," he teased. He kissed her on the nose and then wrapped his arms around her. "How about dinner tonight?"

"I can't. I have some stupid meeting."

He let go of her and looked into her eyes. "Okay, how about tomorrow night? I'm a patient man. I can wait until tomorrow."

"Oh, I thought you might be going to the fireside tomorrow night."

"A fireside? Do I need to bring the marshmallows?"

"Very funny," Rachel chuckled. "Why don't we meet at the stake house at seven."

A bland stare came over Tristan's face as confusion occupied his brain. *What's a fireside? Was that in the book? What is she talking about?*

"Yeah, a place called the Stake House. Um, why are they having a fireside at a restaurant?" he asked.

"Tristan, are you feeling all right?"

"No, not really." Shaking his head, he rubbed the back of his neck, feeling a bit disoriented.

"The church building is also our stake's meeting house," she clarified, watching him closely.

"Oh, yeah, I knew that. I was just kidding around."

"I figured as much," she said, shaking her head. "Oh by the way—"

Just then the door flew open. "Hey Rae, I've got those invoices you wanted," Stewart said.

Tristan let out a despondent sigh. *Doesn't that guy know how to knock?* he thought, aggravated by the intrusion.

"Oh, excuse me. I didn't realize you were doing charity work today," Stewart snapped.

"Be nice, Stewart!" Rachel scolded. "By the way, wasn't

there something you wanted to say to Tristan?" She placed both hands on her hips, her lips pressed tightly together as she glared at Stewart.

"Oh right, something I wanted to say to him. No, I don't think it would be appropriate to say any of those things in the presence of a respectable girl like you," Stewart said smirking.

"Stewart!"

Tristan reached out and softly touched her arm. "It's okay. I'm not here to fight. I'll see you at the fireside." He leaned over and gave her a quick kiss.

Tristan walked past Stewart and whispered, "Don't you dare upset her!"

Tristan waited anxiously around the corner, listening to their conversation. He realized how childish it was to eavesdrop, but he couldn't help his male instincts.

Stewart was talking quietly, and Tristan had to strain to hear each word. Stewart was saying something about being suspicious of him or that he knew something. "Speak up," Tristan mumbled under his breath, frustrated that he was only getting bits and pieces of the conversation.

Placing his ear to the door, he listened closer. He'd missed something important. Stewart was waiting on important information from someone. Was it someone that knew Tristan? Was it information that could ruin everything for good? Stewart said he was expecting a fax later that evening.

Hearing footsteps, Tristan retreated out of view just as Stewart opened the door.

"I don't care, Stewart," Rachel hissed.

"You will when you see what Mark has to say," Stewart continued. "You'll see that I'm right about this."

Stewart returned to his office and shut the door, as did Rachel, giving Tristan the opportunity to escape undetected.

Tristan could only imagine what horrible information Stewart might have discovered. Tristan was sure of one thing: he needed to get his hands on that information before Stewart could give it to Rachel. But how?

There was no other choice. If he wanted to keep Rachel from finding out the truth, he'd have to break into Stewart's house and steal the information.

Twelve

Austin walked into the recreation center with his blue duffel bag in hand. Feeling it was his duty to at least attempt to make a play for Marley, he'd decided to try his hand at racquetball, her favorite sport.

Dressed in blue and white shorts and a blue sports shirt, he bent over to tighten his shoelaces and then went to meet up with Marley. He twirled the racquet around and around in one hand while he pranced down the hallway with confidence.

While he waited for her to come out of the locker room, Austin practiced his swings. He stood with his feet slightly apart, his knees partially bent, as he swooped the racquet—first to his left and then to his right, feeling a bit over-confident.

When Marley stepped out and started down the hall toward the racquetball courts, she was dressed in a sinfully short white tennis skirt and a tight red tank top. Austin's mouth hit the floor. He'd been right in the middle of swinging his racquet when he saw her, and he lost his grip on the rubber handle. The racquet flew a good five feet into the air before nailing an unexpected bystander in the back of the head.

The muscular man was large—very large. He spun around and glared into the crowd of people, rubbing the back of his head. Austin felt his heart pound rapidly against his chest. *He's going to kill me*, Austin thought. He walked quickly down the hall, whistling an unfamiliar tune as though nothing had happened.

Once out of danger, he found Marley. She was in front of the courts retying her shoelaces. Taking a deep breath for added support, he casually strolled up to her and cleared his swollen throat.

"Hey, Marley," he choked out. "Need a racquetball partner today?"

She stood straight up, her shoulders held stiffly back and her hands planted firmly on her hips. She stared at him with a look of disbelief.

"Why?" Marley asked.

"Um . . . well . . . because I want to get into shape, and I think you're just the person that can help me."

The phrase spewed out of his mouth like the taste of bad food, and terror seized his body so that he couldn't move. His breathing became shallow, and his knees felt weak. It was at that moment that he realized the words he'd spoken would most likely condemn him to a long, painful death by physical exertion.

It wasn't a complete lie. He really *did* need to get into shape. He'd always just assumed he had a low metabolism and there really wasn't anything he could do about it. Both of his parents were heavier, so he just figured there was no use trying to fight with genetics. Since meeting Marley, however, he realized just how out of shape he really was.

"Let me get this straight," she said. "You want me to help you get into shape?"

"Um . . . well . . . yeah," Austin muttered. He dropped his eyes to the floor, afraid he may be struck down by bolts of fire shooting from her eyes.

Austin stood silent, chalking up her silence as evidence of her obvious annoyance with him. After spending only a short time with Marley, Austin had come to the conclusion that she was tough and vindictive. She was also extremely domineering and seemed to possess the need to control everything and everyone around her. If there was one compassionate bone in her body, Austin had yet to discover it. Aside from that, he figured she was relatively normal.

"Fine," Marley finally spoke in a low, flat tone. "Follow me."

Austin reluctantly went along, ignoring the small voice inside his head that was screaming at him to run the other way.

Marley led him into the court and gave him some instructions on how to play the game. She pulled another racquet from her bag and handed it to him.

"I'll start," she said, with a bit of sarcasm in her voice.

Marley threw the ball up and gave it a forceful smack, plunging it into the wall on the other side of the court. Austin saw it coming and fervently darted across to hit it.

When the ball bounced off his racquet, he could hardly believe it. He took a moment to silently boast about his achievement, but he took a moment too long. The small green ball bounced off the wall and flew back, nailing him directly in the side of the head.

Stumbling just a bit, he shook off the ringing in his ears and continued with the game. He sprinted back and forth across the court as he tried to focus on the yellow blur that seemed to be moving faster than the speed of light. The ball instantaneously bounced from the wall to Marley's racquet and then back again.

Once in a while, the ball would get past her and Austin would leap for it with unwavering determination, only to end up splattered across the floor or into the wall.

The sweat flowed down his face and his breathing became strained. His pulse raced and his arms dangled at his sides. It felt like heavy bricks were tied to his fingertips.

Ignoring the growing ache in his lower back, Austin raced back and forth, trying his best to keep up with Marley. His feet seemed like suction cups against the glossy gym floor. Nevertheless, he was determined to win the battle against the hideous rubber ball.

"Do you need to stop?" Marley asked, sounding a bit concerned, but mostly annoyed.

She held the ball in one hand and her racquet in the other while she watched him gasping for air. Austin bent over and clutched one arm around his waist while he wiped the sweat from his forehead with the other.

"No . . . no I'm good," he panted. He slowly pulled himself into an upright position, feeling the ache turn to jolts of excruciating pain that shot down both legs.

"I think you've had enough punishment for one day," she grunted. She headed for the door without looking back to see if he would follow.

"Great, I'll call you tomorrow. We'll go running," Austin wheezed. His tortured body hit the floor with a loud thump.

"Sure," she said, actually laughing, and she waved her racquet high in the air.

✭ ✭ ✭

"Come on, Cole, I need you," Tristan pleaded after explaining his planned criminal excursion at Stewart's.

"You've totally lost your mind, Tristan," he sneered. "You've taken this way too far."

"I can't lose her, Cole. If that means breaking into Stewart's house to get that fax, so be it."

"We could be arrested!"

"So? It's not like we haven't spent the night in jail before."

"Why do you care so much? Is the money so important that you would break the law?"

Hiding his true motive, Tristan struggled to come up with some reasonable explanation for his actions. He thought about telling Cole how he really felt about Rachel—that he would do anything humanly possible to keep her from finding out his secret and losing her forever. But how could he do that after pulling Cole into this horrible nightmare with him? Maybe after he and Rachel were married, he'd break the news to Cole. As for now, he knew it was best to avoid the subject.

He sat down in the chair across from Cole at the kitchen table and watched him stuff his sandwich into his mouth while he waited for Tristan to answer.

"We're talking about a lot of money, Cole. Do you realize how different our lives could be with that kind of money? Think about it. You would never need to rely on your parents again." Tristan leaned over the table and looked into Cole's eyes. Using Cole's parents as leverage was probably hitting below the belt. He knew it was a touchy subject with Cole.

"I don't rely on my parents . . . much," said Cole.

"Still, are you willing to sit by and watch Stewart weasel the money out from underneath us?"

Cole drank the rest of his milk and placed his elbows on the table, mimicking Tristan's behavior.

"Tristan, I'm going to say this because I'm your friend and I care about you," Cole stated in a very serious tone. "You need professional help."

Tristan grinned. "So, you're in?"

Thirteen

As Stewart hailed a cab in front the entrance to McMillan Enterprises, Cole motioned for their own cab driver to pulled out behind him, keeping a safe two-car distance behind Stewart. A mixture of luck and the promise of a huge chunk of their savings convinced the driver to go along with their plan.

"I can't believe we're doing this!" Austin gasped from the backseat. He nervously bounced one leg up and down as he chewed on one fingernail after another. "We're going to get caught! You know that, right? We'll be arrested! Oh, man, they'll call my dad for sure!"

"Austin, will you calm down? You're twenty-four years old. They're not going to call your parents," Tristan said.

"I'd just like to know who's going to bail us out of jail when all three of us are locked up together," Cole pointed out.

"Look, he's getting out!" Tristan interrupted. Stewart walked up to an older three-story townhouse, not far from where the service project was earlier that week.

"This is where he lives?" Cole asked, noticing the exquisite flower boxes in the windows.

"Let's go," Tristan said when Stewart was inside.

According to their agreement, Tristan paid the cab the "half now" part of the deal and walked across the street before he noticed he was alone. Letting out a loud grunt, he walked back over to cab and leaned in the window.

"Will you come on already?" Tristan growled.

Grudgingly, Cole and Austin retreated from the car and followed Tristan across the street. They stopped at the mailbox and read the name: Allen B. Tingle.

"Dude! This isn't even his house," Austin whispered in panic.

"Relax. It must be his parents' house," Tristan said.

"He still lives with his mom and dad?" Austin snickered. "And I thought Cole was bad."

"Hey, I was only staying around to help them out."

"Help them what, clean out their savings account?"

"You know what, smart guy? I think—"

"Guys, come on, we're in the middle of breaking and entering," Tristan intervened.

"Oh right, how thoughtless of us," Cole said, rolling his eyes.

Tristan motioned for them to follow him as he ran up to the front of the house. They squatted down in some bushes by the large bay window and peeked through the sheer curtains.

Only one light shone from a rear window—no one besides Stewart seemed to be home. It was after ten o'clock, so the neighborhood was mostly dark and quiet.

"Stay here while I look around," Tristan whispered.

Keeping his eyes on the house, Tristan crept around to the side of the house, spying in each window as he passed by. He probably should have felt guilty sneaking around in the dark, peeking into someone's windows, and planning to break in, but all he felt was a little uneasiness about the whole situation.

On the other side of the house, Tristan found a small window that was cracked just slightly and dimly lit by the glow from the other room. Tristan squatted down, keeping himself from view while he peered over the window sill.

Inside was a small office. It had a couch, a coffee table, and a desk in the corner of the room. Tristan could see the computer and fax machine sitting in plain sight.

Suddenly Stewart walked into the room and flipped on the light. Tristan ducked down even more and stayed very still, holding his position. Stewart went straight over to the fax machine and picked up a sheet of paper that had just come in. As he read through the page, a pleased expression splattered across his devious face.

Tristan's heart raced and sweat broke out over his forehead. Was he too late? Stewart casually placed the paper on the desk. He shut off the light and walked out. Tristan hurried to follow him from the outside, trying his best to watch his every move.

A large rose bush around the corner seemed to come out of nowhere. Tristan clumsily stumbled into it, receiving a few painful thorns to his bare arms. "Ouch," he mumbled.

Stopping at the back of the house, Tristan peeked through the small space between the flowered curtains that hung in the window of the back door. Stewart walked into another room and closed the door behind him.

Instantly, Tristan realized this was the opportunity he'd been waiting for. He quickly made his way back to the front of the house to round up Cole and Austin.

When Tristan reached the front of the house, he noticed Austin crunched down on the ground in attack mode. Austin had smudged mud under both eyes, down his cheeks, and across his forehead.

"What are you doing?" Tristan asked, surprised at Austin's combat appearance.

"I tried to tell him how ridiculous he looks." Cole laughed. "He looks like some freaky version of G. I. Joe!"

"It's called *camouflage*," Austin insisted. "All good burglars do it."

"Well, that leaves us out, because we don't have a clue what we're doing," Cole stated.

Tristan shook his head, sighed heavily, and wished he'd came alone.

"Follow me," he instructed.

Tristan led them around to the office window. He tugged

on the window to open it a little more.

"Wow. I love Upper West Siders. They're so trusting," Cole said.

"Austin, you stand guard over there in case his parents show up," Tristan ordered.

"Good idea. If I see anyone coming I'll give you the secret signal," Austin said. He darted off and took refuge behind the trunk of a large maple tree.

Cole looked at Tristan, trying not to laugh. Tristan let out an aggravated grunt before turning to Austin.

"Austin," Tristan called in a low tone, motioning for him to come back.

Austin looked around before getting to the ground and crawling back over to the house. He stood up to meet Tristan's annoyed glare.

"What?" Austin asked.

"It might be nice if you let us know what the secret signal is," Tristan said.

"Oh, of course. What was I thinking?" Austin laughed, slapping himself on the forehead with the palm of his hand.

Leaning in, Austin grabbed Tristan and Cole around their necks and pulled them in to form a huddle. He looked to his left and then to his right. "Run," he whispered.

"Run?" Cole asked. "That's your big secret signal?"

"What would you use? Something like, 'Excuse me guys, but I think someone might be coming'?"

"We'll use 'run,'" Tristan said. He shoved Austin back toward his maple tree.

With Austin in position, Tristan opened the window even more and paused to listen for an alarm. To his relief, he heard only silence coming from the house. Tristan slid through the opening and motioned for Cole to follow.

"What now?" Cole whispered, once they were inside.

"You watch the door while I find the fax," Tristan instructed.

Tristan walked over to the desk and picked up a pile of

papers. He noticed several framed pictures sitting on top of the desk. All of them were of Stewart and Rachel. Together.

In one picture, they were lying arm and arm on a sandy beach. Another was of the two of them kissing in front of the Eiffel Tower.

Tristan put down the papers and picked up the small silver frame that held the photo of them kissing. He stared at the snapshot, feeling the painful blow of her past wrench at his stomach. The glow on Rachel's face was irrefutable; their closeness was right in front of him.

The stronger of two emotions won over and he felt the stabbing pain surge from his stomach straight to his heart. She had been really happy with Stewart, finding comfort in his wealthy arms. Worse than that, it looked like she was truly in love with him. That thought alone sent Tristan's mind plunging into a cyclone of questions about how she felt about him and his destitute state and how she really felt about Stewart.

Was Stewart right? Could he offer her the kind of life she was accustomed to? She had obviously traveled the world. He'd never even held a passport. *Huh. Right now I couldn't even afford to take her out of the state, let alone the country!* Tristan thought.

"Tristan, do you have the fax or not?" Cole croaked, interrupting Tristan's distressful thoughts.

With a long sigh, Tristan replaced the photo back in its position. As he did, he noticed a small blue ring box sitting next to the frame. Curiously, he picked it up, already knowing what he would find inside. When he opened it, he saw three diamonds sparkling from a beautiful platinum band.

Feeling weak in the knees, Tristan fell back into the soft leather chair, staring down at the ring. He let out a long sigh and rubbed his forehead. It was at that precise moment that Tristan realized what he was up against. Stewart was more than a lovesick ex-boyfriend. He was a real threat. It was clear that Stewart had big plans to get Rachel back, and his intentions had not been altered by Tristan's presence.

"What's wrong with you?" Cole asked.

Replacing the box, Tristan shook off the shock and disappointment and continued on his quest to find the fax.

"I got it," Tristan confirmed.

He folded it up and stuck it into the front pocket of his pants. He took one last look at the display of photos before returning to Cole's side.

They walked to the window but stopped when they heard a strange sound coming from outside. It sounded somewhat like a terribly sick owl.

They both looked out the window, and their eyes immediately fell on Austin, who was hiding behind the tree trunk. He held both hands to his mouth and gave a long, shrill *hoot* sounding like an owl with a horrible case of laryngitis. Just then Cole and Tristan noticed the well-dressed couple coming up the walk.

"Great! Now what?" Cole hissed as he ran a hand through his hair.

"We wait until they come inside. Then we'll make a break for it," Tristan said.

As soon as Stewart's parents entered the house, Austin darted across the yard, running with full force.

"So much for backup," Cole quipped.

Cole slipped through the window just as Stewart came out of the bathroom patting his wet hair with a towel.

With no time to escape, Tristan scanned the room for a hiding place. He closed the window and promptly took refuge under the desk. He pulled his knees up tightly against his chest and could feel his heart beating so loudly it echoed in his ears. Hearing footsteps enter the room, he slowed his breathing and froze in place.

"Stewart, honey, are you home?" a woman's voice called out.

"Yeah, Mom, I'm in the den," Stewart answered.

The overpowering aroma of sweet flowered perfume soon filled the room. Tristan had to cover his nose to keep from sneezing.

"How was your day, sweetie?" an elderly woman asked.

"Fine."

"Did you find your dinner in the refrigerator?"

"Yes, thanks, Mom. Did you deposit the money into my account today?"

"Of course, and don't tell your father, but there is a little extra just in case you want to take Rachel out for a nice dinner."

Tristan swallowed hard, agitated by hearing Rachel's name spoken. How dare they even talk about her! Stewart had no claim on her anymore!

"Thanks, Mom, but it's going to take more than money if I want to get her away from that big-talking hillbilly," Stewart said.

Feeling his temper rising, Tristan fought to keep his composure. He stayed quiet while he listened to them converse about Rachel and the relationship she and Stewart once shared.

Gripping his hands tightly together, Tristan bit his bottom lip in annoyance, fighting the instinct to attack.

"Well, sweetheart, you'll get her back. I know she still loves you."

"She'll soon realize that. Especially once that low-life womanizer is out of the way. Then she'll be all mine," Stewart boasted.

"Do you have a plan?"

"Oh, yeah."

"Come have some ice cream and tell me all about it," his mother replied.

Tristan heard footsteps again and peeked out from beneath the desk to find the room empty. He made his escape out the window and headed for the waiting cab as fast as his legs would go. He kept his sights on the vehicle, not looking back to see if anyone was watching.

"Man, I didn't think you were going to make it out of there," Austin said. "What happened?"

"I hid under the desk until they left the room."

"I tried to warn you guys," Austin pointed out.

"Yeah, what happened to 'run'?" Tristan questioned.

"I couldn't very well yell 'run' with them walking up to the house. That's why I used my back-up signal."

"Sure, because sounding like a terminally ill owl was less conspicuous." Cole smirked.

"I did the best I could."

"We're in the city, Austin. There aren't too many owls around here!"

Tristan had been reading through the fax, not really listening to their argument. His eyes narrowed as he read the important information. When he finished, he let out a long sigh and rubbed the back of his neck.

"Well, what does it say?" Cole finally asked, ignoring Austin's dispute.

Folding up the paper, Tristan stuffed it into the front pocket of his pants and shrugged his shoulders. "I guess I was wrong," he said. He cleared his throat and turned to meet their confused stares. "It wasn't about me at all. It was from Mark Miller Enterprises. They want to merge with Rachel's company."

"What?" Cole and Austin both blurted out at the same time.

"Yeah," Tristan said sheepishly. "My bad."

"You mean we broke into someone's house for nothing?" Cole yelled.

"It wasn't for nothing. I found out some very important information."

"What? That you can fall back on a career as a felon?" Cole asked.

"I found out that Stewart has a plan to remove me from Rachel's life for good. That piece of information alone was well worth the risk. Wouldn't you agree?" asked Tristan.

"That hardly justifies breaking the law!"

"Well, we got away with it, so what are you worried about?"

"Tristan, I swear if you weren't my friend, I would have suffocated you in your sleep years ago," Cole grumbled.

"Yeah, but just think how boring your life would be without me in it."

"Come to think of it, you'd better sleep with one eye open."

★ ★ ★

Throwing himself on his bed, Tristan groaned loudly and covered his face with both hands. "What am I doing?" he mumbled. "How did things get this complicated?" He waited for someone to give him an answer but heard nothing in the tormenting silence surrounding him. The stillness of the room added to his frustration and made it difficult for him to think straight.

Sitting up on the edge of the bed, Tristan rubbed the back of his neck, feeling the pressures of his dishonesty weighing heavily on his shoulders. Images of the photos on Stewart's desk still haunted him. They burned deep into his mind, leaving a permanent mark.

The sight of Rachel's happy face and the knowledge that she'd once found comfort in Stewart's arms shattered his confidence and drenched his hopes.

Unanswered questions gnawed at his mind. Was he really the best man for her? How could he give her all of the things that Stewart had provided? A relationship that started off with a lie could only end in disaster. With Stewart in the picture, just waiting for him to mess up, the odds were quickly stacking up against him.

As Tristan sat in the dark, thinking about Rachel, Stewart, and the Book of Mormon, he realized what a horrendous triangle he'd created. "One thing at a time," he whispered.

Tristan turned out the bedside lamp and crawled beneath his covers. He realized if he wanted an honest relationship with Rachel, one in which his intentions had nothing to do with money, he needed to change some things, and the first thing on his list was to talk to the bishop of the singles ward. It was time he confessed he was not a Mormon.

Fourteen

The next morning, as Tristan struggled to find his apartment key while juggling two full bags of groceries, he felt his cell phone vibrate in his pocket. There was a text message from one of the ward members who informed him that the fireside that night was going to be a toga party. Wow, it was a good thing someone had clarified what a fireside was before he showed up looking like a complete idiot.

After conjuring up an outfit from an old white bed sheet, he made a laurel leaf headband out of a metal hanger and plastic leaves. He completed the ensemble with a brown pair of leather sandals that he stole from Cole's personal collection of geek-wear.

After attracting more than a few strange looks on the subway, Tristan hurried into the church building running a little late but feeling very satisfied with his costume. He would definitely win the best dressed award. With his bed sheet draped across him and a pair of white shorts underneath, he pulled open the door to the gymnasium and took one giant step inside.

Sitting there in perfectly aligned iron chairs was a group of people dressed in their Sunday best. When they heard the door, they curiously gawked at him. To make matters worse, he'd entered through the front doors instead of the rear, making his arrival that much more prominent.

Semi-quiet chuckles broke out around the room. Some people just watched in amusement or utter shock—Tristan wasn't quite sure which.

His eyes fell directly on Rachel, who was sitting in the middle, two rows back, with a stunned look across her face. Next to her was none other than Stewart, who was sitting a little too close to Rachel, in Tristan's opinion. He covered his mouth with one hand to hide his laughter.

In an instant, Tristan realized he'd been set up horribly by the person he despised the most. He snapped his gaping mouth shut and collected his dignity. He shoved a leaf out of his eyes and took another step in, letting the door close behind him.

Determined to prove himself victorious, Tristan cleared his throat and nodded to the speaker. "Sorry I'm late," he said with a confident grin. "I couldn't find a thing to wear."

He casually strolled over to the row of chairs with a smile on his face. He gave a few amused people a friendly wink and then excused himself several times as he scooted his way past the endless array of legs until he came to the empty chair Rachel had been saving for him.

"Why are you wearing that?" she whispered.

Glancing around the room, he found that everyone's attention had been directed back to the speaker. All but Stewart, who was smirking at him around Rachel, seemingly pleased with his crude prank.

"I was misinformed about the proper attire," Tristan replied, sending Stewart an icy-cold glare.

He slid down in the chair and rested his right leg across his left knee and placed one arm securely around Rachel's shoulders. He snuggled up against her and looked behind her head at Stewart. Tristan smiled and gave him a not-so-friendly wink to let him know he'd won this round.

Although nothing more was said about Tristan's choice in clothing, Rachel eyed Stewart with a disappointed look, as if she knew who the culprit was.

Throughout the fireside, Tristan silently plotted his revenge.

If Stewart wanted a battle, then Tristan would give him a war!

✶ ✶ ✶

Try as he might, Tristan could not fight the inferno that was brewing deep inside him. Stewart had gone too far. Tristan was now bound and determined to seek vengeance.

After filling Cole and Austin in on the fireside fiasco, Tristan was gratified to know his friends were more than willing to help even the score. They discussed all their options—the legal ones and the not-so-legal ones.

Cole wanted to pour sugar into his gas tank. Tristan thought hiring some thugs to fake a holdup and scare the pants off him sounded like a good idea. But, surprisingly, it was Austin who came up with the ideal plan.

The next morning, a personal ad ran in the *New York Times* that read:

"Single white male, big and bad, looking for a companion who enjoys riding Harleys, intimidating strangers, and getting tattoos."

They included Stewart's cell phone number. At the very least, Stewart would be kept busy answering the numerous solicitations. Not to mention that he really deserved what he got.

✶ ✶ ✶

During the next week, Rachel was, once again, all Tristan thought about. He had a hunger that only she could satisfy. He called her daily just to hear the sound of her voice, which temporarily filled the void. They'd talk for hours on the phone, but it was never quite the same as seeing her. She'd been caught up in meetings nearly every day. When Sunday finally came, it was not a minute too soon.

Walking into the chapel, Tristan scanned the crowd and found her sitting near the front dressed in a modest blue flowered skirt and white top. She glanced over her shoulder, looking for him as well. He briskly walked to the front, his heart pounding harder with each step he took. Cole and Austin followed him up the aisle, dressed a little more appropriately this time.

Rachel scooted over so Tristan could sit next to her. Feeling the touch of her bare skin against his arm was like finally getting oxygen to his brain.

"I thought maybe you weren't coming," she whispered.

"I had to pull a few individuals out of bed this morning." Tristan grinned.

"Oh, there's the bishop. I need to give him my tithing," she said, standing from the bench.

"Come again?"

"Yeah, you know, it pays to pay the Lord first." She smiled and made her way to the end of the row.

Tristan recalled what he'd read about tithing and remembered that Mormons were supposed to give ten percent of their income to the Church. Why hadn't he thought about that before?

"Cole, give me twenty bucks," Tristan demanded.

"What for?"

"We're supposed to pay the preacher for his sermon."

"No."

"Come on. I'll pay you back later."

"No, you won't."

"I'll let you use my Metro pass for a week."

"Two weeks."

"Fine."

Cole pulled a twenty-dollar bill from his wallet and reluctantly handed it over to Tristan. Tristan quickly shot up from his seat, eager to show his loyalty to the Church and impress Rachel.

"Well, Brother Taylor, good morning," said the bishop.

"Good morning, Bishop," Tristan said. As they shook hands, he discreetly deposited the bill into the Bishop's hand.

"What's this?" Bishop Anderson questioned.

"For your services," Tristan replied. "I always pay the Lord first." He gave him a slap on the back and winked at Rachel.

"Brother Taylor, I was wondering if you could come by my office later today, say around seven?"

"Am I in trouble for something?" Tristan asked, a little leery.

"No, no trouble. I'd just like to discuss something with you."

"All right," Tristan replied

When Tristan took his seat next to Rachel, she leaned over to whisper in his ear, "Remind me later to show you where the tithing slips are," she said.

This week was an unfamiliar meeting for Tristan. People from the congregation got up to talk about their conviction of the gospel. Others seemed to be content with talking about their lives and the ways the gospel had affected them.

Tristan was actually enjoying this new meeting until Austin decided to follow the group. It was just like him to do what everyone else was doing, no matter how crazy or bizarre. He was the guy who would jump off the proverbial cliff just because his friends did.

When Austin rose from his seat and started for the front, Tristan's heart jumped into his throat, making a terrible gagging sound. He knew Austin usually only ran on one cylinder, but that didn't excuse his erratic behavior.

Swallowing his shock, Tristan leaned over to Cole, who was watching wide-eyed with an empty expression.

"What does he think he's doing?" Tristan whispered.

"Being Austin," Cole said, chuckling. "This should add some spark to an otherwise dull meeting." Although Cole seemed to be entertained with Austin's brainless adventure, Tristan was mortified.

When Austin reached the front, he glanced out into the congregation, grinning sheepishly. "I would like to tell all of you how grateful I am that you have accepted me into your . . . um . . . group." His voice cracked and the tears began to collect in his eyes.

Tristan covered his face with his hand and sank down in his seat, humiliated by the scene going on in front of him. *Is he really going to start crying?* Tristan thought. He glanced over at Rachel, who seemed to be intrigued by Austin's pathetic performance.

"I want to tell my two best friends how much they mean to me," he continued. "Cole, Tristan: I love you, guys!" His bottom lip began to quiver and for a moment Tristan wondered just how much was fabricated.

Austin reached over and pulled out a tissue from the box near the podium and continued to weep softly. He paused briefly to regain his poise. Tristan thought it was finally over . . . until Austin unexpectedly confessed he was a sinner and needed to repent.

He finished his performance by raising both hands high in the air and praised God for his generous compassion. He said an extra loud "amen," just before Tristan could climb under the bench and die of embarrassment.

Casually sitting back down, Austin glanced over at Cole, who was hiding his laughter beneath his hand, and Tristan, who was close to wringing his neck right there in front of everyone. Austin wore a satisfied smirk across his face, as if he'd just done Cole and Tristan a huge favor.

When the meeting was over, Tristan found Rachel standing in the foyer, where she was cornered by Stewart. Her face was tense and unreadable. She held her arms crossed tightly in front of her.

When Stewart walked away, Tristan approached Rachel with caution. He was worried Stewart had said something to upset her. He couldn't bear to see the anxiety in her beautiful face. It tortured him.

"Everything okay?" he asked.

"Yes." She sighed. "Stewart is just being Stewart."

"Uh-oh, I don't like the sound of that. What did he say?"

"Well, he thinks you're only trying to get my money." She looked to the floor as if searching for the answers in the rust colored carpet.

Tristan remained quiet, closely watching for any indication that she might doubt his intentions. After a few awkward moments of silence, Rachel finally raised her head. Her eyes were sad and her forehead crinkled.

"I'm sorry. I'm humiliated for even thinking he could be right. It's just . . . well . . . it's hard to believe someone like you would want to be with someone like me," she admitted.

With his eyes still focused on her face and the insecurity written across it, Tristan took her by the hand. He gently unraveled her stiff arms and held her hands in his.

"Rachel, you are, by far, the most beautiful, most compassionate, most captivating woman I've ever met," he declared earnestly. "I am the one honored that you would want to be with me."

Pulling her hands to his mouth, he gently kissed her soft skin. He wished she wouldn't think of herself like that. She was far from ordinary. In fact, if she knew the truth about him and his not-so-favorable past, she would run away screaming.

"How do you do that?" she asked. She kept her eyes fixed on his as if searching for answers.

"Do what?"

"Make me go weak in the knees."

"Do I?"

"Yeah," she whispered.

There could have been a million people around them, but at that moment, Tristan felt like they were the only two people on the planet. If she only knew how she affected him. Every muscle in his body weakened by her slightest touch.

"He also has the idea that you placed this crazy ad in the personal column about him. Do you want to confess anything while we're at church?" Rachel asked, trying not to smile.

"Wow, he really thinks it's me?"

"Wasn't it?"

"Absolutely!"

"You know, he's had everyone from devil worshipers to biker men calling him for a date."

"Did he find anyone he liked?"

Rachel broke out in laughter, and Tristan finally felt like he'd gotten his revenge.

"I guess he deserved it after the fireside and all," Rachel said.

Just then, Marley showed up to drag Rachel away. After promising to call, Tristan rushed out to the street, worried he'd been left behind. He was eager to let Cole and Austin know that their idea had been a success.

Outside the building, Tristan found Stewart waiting by the glass doors. He paused briefly, sending Stewart a hostile look warning him to back off. It didn't take long for Stewart to return the same signal.

The look itself was nothing new coming from Stewart. Tristan had seen that same hateful glare several times before. However, there was something very different about him today. Maybe it was the way he strategically positioned himself with one hand placed firmly against the building, the other stuck in the pocket of his neatly-pressed black suit pants. His posture was stiff and motionless, like he was made of stone. Stewart's head was slightly down with his accusing eyes fiercely throwing caution to the wind.

If looks could kill, Tristan thought. He sarcastically waved his hand in Stewart's direction and then calmly walked away, making a mental note to stay on his guard. Any little slip-up would give Stewart the chance to shatter his future with Rachel.

Tristan realized he may have won the last battle, but the war was far from over.

Fifteen

Tristan entered the church building feeling unexpectedly overwhelmed. Although he realized his road to conversion needed to start with the bishop, he felt uneasy about the whole thing. Did he have the strength to reveal his sins, both past and present? What if he wasn't ready for this? Or worse, what if the bishop threw him out and told him never to come back?

Wiping his sweating palms down the side of his pants, Tristan took a deep breath and reached out to knock on the heavy wood door. His mind told him he was crazy, and Cole's words rang loudly through his head, "It's a cult!"

He dropped his hand and breathed heavily. Deep down, his soul was pushing him forward, making the conflict inside him almost unbearable.

No! he thought. *I've come too far to quit now.*

He smacked his knuckles against the door and waited for an answer. The door opened and Bishop Anderson extended his hand in a friendly handshake.

"Come in, Brother Taylor."

Grabbing the first chair he came to, which happened to be next to the door, convenient in case he needed to bolt from the room, Tristan rested his shaking knees. Bishop Anderson sat down in his high-back leather chair and leaned his elbows on the desk.

This was unlike any confessional Tristan had ever heard of. It was much more personal sitting face-to-face with the bishop, who was watching his every reaction. There would be no beating around the bush, no leaving out any of the smaller details, no trying to make the big mistakes seem small. The bishop could read every expression on his face, not to mention his body language.

"Brother Taylor, I was wondering about your membership records? Have you had them transferred yet?" Bishop Anderson asked.

"You need to have a membership to be in this church?" Tristan asked.

"Your membership records include your baptismal date, blessing date, and endowment date. Have you had these ordinances performed?"

Blessing? Endowment? Ordinances? Tristan couldn't remember if he'd read about them or not.

"Bishop, I think now would be a good time to confess something." Tristan sighed heavily.

"Go ahead, Brother Taylor. Everything you say will be kept confidential."

"Well . . . you see . . . I wasn't . . . I mean . . . I'm not, you know . . . of your faith," he stuttered.

"You mean, you haven't been baptized?"

"No . . . I mean . . . yes, that's correct, but there's more. Before a few months ago, I'd never stepped foot inside a Mormon church."

"I see," the bishop said, leaning back in his chair. He kept his eyes on Tristan, causing Tristan to squirm in his seat. "And everyone here assumed you and your friends were already members. How did that happen?"

"I guess I kind of led them to believe that. Before I tell you the whole story, I want you to know that everything I used to believe in has changed. I've changed." With a deep breath, Tristan told the bishop everything, starting from the first day he arrived in New York City. He didn't hold anything back.

When he was finished, Tristan sat back in his chair and watched for Bishop Anderson's reaction. Tristan folded his arms in front of him and nervously bounced one knee. All of his lies, his deceit, and his true feelings were laid out in front of him. For the first time, Tristan was ready to confront them all.

"Wow, that's some story. Have you told Rachel the truth?" he asked. His voice was not of judgment, but of compassion.

"Not yet. I was hoping if I joined the Church before I told her, she might see I've really changed."

"If you're joining the Church for Rachel, you're joining for the wrong reasons."

"I know. And at first, I thought it was just about Rachel and wanting to be a part of what she believed in. But now . . . now I'm not so sure it *is* just for her. I'm almost finished with the Book of Mormon, and I want to know more. Not for Rachel, not to prove Cole wrong—though, let's be honest, that would be a plus—but I want to do it for me. There is something to this book. I can feel it."

Tristan released a breath and looked down at the floor. It sounded strange saying these things out loud. Strange because he never thought the Mormons and their church would ever affect him this way.

"Well, you've come a lot further than I ever thought you might." The bishop smiled.

"Wait, what? You *knew* we weren't Mormons?"

"Let's just say I had my suspicions. I wanted to wait and see how it was all going to play out. Are Cole and Austin as interested in the gospel as you are?"

"Unfortunately, no. In fact, if they knew I was here right now, I'd probably have to find a new place to live."

"And yet you're here nonetheless. That tells me a lot about you."

"What, that I sneak around, never telling anyone the truth about anything? Yeah, I'm a wonderful person, let me tell you," Tristan answered.

"It tells me that your heart is in the right place. It tells me that you've made up your mind to find the truth and to take the next step. Where would you like to go from here, Brother Taylor? Would you like to take part in the missionary lessons?"

"Yes, but, if it's all right, I'd like to do that discreetly. I know I need to tell Rachel the truth, and I will, but for now, I would like to keep this between us."

"I understand your predicament. You can come to my home to meet with the missionaries, if you'd like."

"Thank you, Bishop. I'd really appreciate that."

"But Tristan, the lie still needs to be addressed. Dishonesty has a funny way of growing until its out of control. Not to mention the fact that the Lord doesn't approve."

"You don't need to tell me that. I already know. First hand," Tristan said.

Tristan talked with the bishop for an hour about life, death, and repentance. In that hour, he learned more about the gospel, the Church, and himself. He felt optimistic about being forgiven for his mistakes and overjoyed to learn he was no longer alone in his quest.

Sixteen

Tristan found himself breathing heavily regardless of how fit he thought he was. Hiking up a mountain was certainly more physical than he had anticipated, but he was with Rachel, which made the pain bearable. The best part of the whole day came when Tristan was informed that Stewart had a prior engagement and would not be joining them.

The singles ward had been planning this trip upstate for months. Even though New Yorkers did plenty of walking, actual mountains for actual hiking were somewhat hard to come by in New York City.

Without much effort, Marley was a good thirty feet ahead of the pack. She vigorously tackled each hill with ease, seeming almost possessive of the trail.

Hanging in the back, fighting for each and every breath, Austin tried not to draw attention to himself. He stayed close enough to keep the group in sight, but far enough away that they couldn't hear him wheezing.

As the sweat poured from his forehead, back, and underarms, Austin dragged one foot in front of the other up the unreasonably steep slope.

Tristan and Rachel stayed somewhere in between, laughing at Marley's egotism and Austin's infinite determination to make it to the top. Actually, Tristan was rather impressed by

Austin's efforts. He only wished Marley could understand the sacrifice Austin was making by trying to get into shape—he'd all but given up Bubba's free leftovers from the restaurant.

With the peak of the hill in sight, Tristan dug his black hiking boots into the dusty trail for leverage and sprinted past Rachel to gain his victory. Rachel let out a loud huff and darted up the hill after him.

"Oh, no you don't," she shouted.

When she was close enough, she reached out and latched onto the back of his shirt. Tugging hard, she sent him off balance and planted him face first into the ground. With determination, she climbed over the top of him to win the race.

She hadn't gotten more than two steps when Tristan clasped his hand around her ankle. He pulled on her leg, causing her to fall flat into the dirt. She accepted her defeat and looked back to meet his laughter.

Slowly, Tristan crawled up and flopped down on his back next to her. The others didn't seem to care that they were blocking the trail. They walked around them with knowing smiles on their faces.

Rachel propped herself up on one elbow. "Do you think anyone would notice if we just didn't get up?" she asked.

"By the way they all looked at us just now, I'd say they might even appreciate it," Tristan answered. "Ugh, I had no idea hiking was this strenuous."

Just then Austin came staggering up the trail. Once in front of them, he fell to his knees.

"What . . . are . . . you . . . .two . . . doing," he wheezed, fighting to get each word out.

"You look like you're in need of some serious oxygen, my friend," Tristan joked. He stood up and brushed the dirt off his pants.

Rachel expressed a little more concern for Austin's condition. "Are you okay?" she asked. Austin didn't answer. He was too busy concentrating on getting more air into his depleted lungs.

Austin rested both hands on the ground, letting the sweat

run from his head. It formed a small puddle of mud beneath him. He grabbed the bottle of water from his pouch, popped open the lid, and took a long swig, letting the cool water drench his scratchy throat. He then dumped the rest of the water over his head, cooling the explosive fire.

"He's fine," Tristan confirmed. He reached down and snatched Austin under one arm. He pulled him to his feet and gave him a hard slap on the back. "See, he's good to go."

Austin shot Tristan an intimidating glare as he tried to smile for Rachel's sake. "Yep. I'm just getting my second wind."

Rachel stayed close to Austin, apprehensive about his worsening condition. Tristan likewise was starting to wonder if Austin was going to make it to the top. He stood on the other side of him, whispering words of encouragement.

When they'd made it to the top of the mountain, the group stopped to catch their breath and appreciate the incredible view of the valley below.

Taking a seat on a large rock, Austin leaned his elbows on his knees. He rubbed a sore spot on the back of his neck and breathed deeply. The small breeze helped to calm the burning inferno in his face and made it easier to breath.

When he felt his heartbeat slow back to normal, he looked around for Marley. He wanted to gloat about his accomplishment.

In the distance, he noticed Marley walking away from the group. She veered off from the designated trail and vanished in the cluster of large trees.

Letting his curiosity take over, Austin followed Marley into the forest, keeping his distance so he wouldn't be detected. She walked a fairly long way before she stopped beside a tall aspen tree. Austin continued to watch her but kept his distance.

Marley seemed to be frozen in place, vigilantly watching something in the distance. Her short brown hair blew in the breeze while she braced herself with one hand against the tree trunk. She was certainly being very careful not to be discovered. But what held her interest?

Austin couldn't stand it any longer. He had to know what she was so interested in. He tiptoed over to the tree to get a glimpse. He'd never seen her so engrossed in anything—other than exercise—but something held her attention, and he was determined to find out what. As careful as he was, though, the snap of a tree branch under his foot abruptly announced his arrival.

Marley turned her head, saw Austin, and scowled. *"Quiet"* she hissed, placing a finger to her lips. She returned her focus on the area in front of her without so much as a wisecrack about his carelessness, which simply wasn't like her.

Taking even smaller steps, Austin made his way over to the tree. He stood just slightly behind Marley and glanced out into the open meadow. Several feet away, grazing on a patch of fresh green grass, was a small golden-brown fawn. It tore off a long stem and look around as it chomped.

"It's beautiful," Austin whispered.

Marley nodded her head in agreement. "There doesn't seem to be a mother around anywhere," she said. "I wonder if it wandered off."

Smiling to himself, Austin could see she was genuinely concerned about this tiny animal. This definitely was not the usual hard-core attitude he'd grown accustomed to.

Just then something startled the fawn, and it darted off into a patch of trees on the other side of the meadow. Austin turned to leave when Marley caught him by the arm.

"Let's see where it's going," she insisted, towing him along behind her.

"Shouldn't we catch up with the others?"

"I know the way down. Come on."

Reluctantly, Austin followed her into the heavily wooded area, a little leery about being separated from the group. His sense of direction had always been slightly off, which was a fact he had realized at the early age of nine when he'd gotten lost in a carnival fun house. After two hours, his father finally came in and rescued him. It was a nightmare he never forgot, nor could he ever look at clowns the same way again. On the other hand, Marley seemed to be confident in her sense of direction.

They trudged deeper and deeper into the secluded foliage. The wind was picking up, blowing leaves around in the air. Though it was a warm wind, it made the hairs on the back of Austin's neck stand on end.

Marley was like a courteous tour guide, moving branches out of his way and pointing out obstacles in his path.

Finally, the line of trees ended, and there was again a magnificent meadow with purple and yellow wildflowers growing throughout the long stems of green grass. Across the field of blossoms, gathered close together, a massive herd of deer, including their tiny friend, stood feeding on the greenery.

A smile came over Marley's face as they stood covered by several large trees. "I guess he does have a family after all," she said.

But Austin wasn't looking at the deer. He was staring up at the sky, no longer amused by their adventures. Thick grey clouds had collected overhead, bringing with them a lingering scent of rain.

"Uh . . . Marley, don't you think we'd better be getting back?" he asked.

Glancing up, Marley's face mirrored Austin's distress. "That might be a good idea," she agreed.

They started back through the forest of tall pine and aspen trees, searching for the clearing they'd first seen the fawn in. They walked for what seemed like an hour. Every tree and every rock looked exactly the same as the last. Austin tried to stay quiet. The last thing he wanted to do was to challenge her leadership skills, but he was sure they were going in circles. It was like the jungle had gulped them up, forbidding their escape.

"Hey, Marley? Are you sure you know where you're going?" Austin finally spoke up.

Flashbacks of the fun house raced through his head as he strived to stay calm. A loud crack of thunder shook the ground and sent a crushing blow of terror through Austin's trembling body. Marley stopped dead in her tracks and spun around to face him. Her eyes were wide and full of anxiety.

"We need to find shelter. Now!" she said with a strained voice.

Marley took off in the other direction, doing a little more than a fast jog while Austin hustled to keep up with her.

"Why? What's the matter?" he yelled, not really sure his words were reaching her.

Sprinting back through the now-deserted meadow, the stillness of the mountainside sent an eerie feeling to the pit of his sick stomach. Even the deer must have sensed the coming storm. Marley began the climb up a steep hill in front of them.

Great, Austin thought. *Another mountain.*

"Come on!" Marley shouted. "I saw a cave just a little ways up."

Lightning flashed around them, the mountainside grew darker by the minute, and the thunder roared loudly. The climb went a little easier than the first time. Austin was surprised he was able to keep pace with her. His fear pumped adrenaline through his system, creating enough strength for him to carry himself up the steep slope.

They soon came to a deep, secluded cave in the side of the mountain. Marley ran inside, but Austin stopped at the entrance, staring in with apprehension.

"Well, come on," Marley insisted.

"What if there's a bear in there?"

"There aren't any bears in this area."

"Are you sure?"

Marley grunted irritably and latched onto his shirt, yanking him inside just as the clouds burst open.

✦ ✦ ✦

Staring through the set of binoculars Rachel gave him, Tristan marveled at the spectacular view. He'd missed out on so much taking care of his lazy, drunken, no-good father. He never took the time to just be a kid.

Extracurricular activities had been few and far between. Nothing had come close to the overpowering feeling that surged through him as he stood and looked out over the cliff. It was simply breathtaking.

He inhaled the fresh, cleansing, pine scent. It was like therapy for his soul. It rejuvenated every inch of his aching body. For a moment, he wished that Cole had come with them. He would have loved the view. Instead, he was at home wallowing in self-sacrificing defeat stemming from Megan's recent departure.

Taking in every inch of the scenery, Tristan couldn't help but wonder how many times he'd unknowingly passed by nature's true beauty without ever giving it a second glance. Now, every rock formation, every crevice, and even the tiny stream far below distinctively stood out. It was more beautiful than he could have ever imagined.

After that point, he really wasn't sure what happened—perhaps it was the overwhelming beauty of the atmosphere, or maybe it was just the high altitude—but something instantly sent his mind into a whirlwind of self-discovery.

The phrase "take time to stop and smell the roses" popped into his head. He'd heard that line a hundred times, but at that moment he understood it completely.

Never wanting to play by the rules, Tristan spent most of his life trying to find that one single loophole that would put him over the top. He yearned for fame and glory, always searching for the treasures of the world. What he didn't realize was that on his quest for wealth, he'd missed out on something even more valuable—life itself.

Glancing around the group, he spotted Rachel standing alone, looking out over the mountainside. In an instant so short that he may have missed it if he weren't paying attention, it dawned on him that he was looking at things backwards. The true treasures of life didn't come with a price tag.

Tristan stood frozen to the soft ground beneath his feet, unable to move and barely able to breathe. How could he have not seen this coming? Was it because it was too terrifying to admit? But he knew it now, just as sure as he was standing there.

Letting the binoculars slip from his fingers and then fall to the ground, he started walking. Slowly at first, but he soon picked up speed. It was more like he was floating off the ground as he moved in her direction.

It was her! Rachel was the pot of gold he'd been searching for his whole life, and it wasn't because of her sizeable bank account. He'd known it for a long time—it was that unfamiliar feeling that pumped through his veins when her skin touched his. Tristan was undeniably and thoroughly in love with Rachel, and he could no longer dispute his true feelings.

Pacing himself so he wouldn't stumble over his own clumsy feet, Tristan rehearsed in his head what he would say. He would first sweep her up in his arms and divulge his undying love for her, making her blush with delight. Then he would kiss her soft, sweet lips, making her knees tremble with pleasure. After she was putty in his hands, he would confess his deep, dark secret, and, if she didn't immediately throw him off the cliff, they would live happily ever after.

"Piece of cake," Tristan hissed with skepticism.

Coming up behind her, he wrapped both arms around her waist and rested his chin on her shoulder, ready to reveal his hidden secret. *At least there are plenty of people around*, he thought with a sigh. *Maybe homicide will seem less appealing if there are witnesses.*

"A penny for your thoughts?" Tristan whispered softly in her ear. He closed his eyes and deluded himself into thinking this blissful moment would last even after he told her the truth.

Rachel sighed. "The clouds have moved in, and Marley and Austin have disappeared."

Before he could respond, the group leader announced they would be taking off earlier than planned in order to avoid the definite threat of rain. As everyone filed down the path, Rachel spun around with horror on her pale face.

"What should we do?" she asked.

Tristan instantly took command, feeling a bit apprehensive himself. "Wait!" he shouted to the group. "Marley and Austin aren't with us. Did anyone see them leave?"

The group chatted amongst themselves, but no one had a response. The group leader immediately approached Tristan. "When was the last time you saw them?"

"Maybe thirty minutes ago," Tristan replied.

"Well, it's already four o'clock. If we don't get moving, not only will we be caught in a rain storm, but it'll also be dark. Believe me, you don't want to be on top of this mountain during a thunderstorm. It can get really bad," he complained like a stubborn child. "I think we should all go back and call search and rescue."

"By the time we do that, they could be royally lost."

"Hey, you can do whatever you want, but the rest of us are leaving before the storm hits." He turned and swiftly walked away.

It was perfectly clear to Tristan that solving this problem was completely up to him. Austin was like his brother, and Marley was Rachel's little sister. He couldn't just leave them up on the mountain alone. He turned to Rachel, who had been silent through the whole conversation.

"Maybe you should go back with the others," he suggested.

"You're crazy if you think I'm going to let you go wandering around the mountains by yourself. I'm coming with you!" she stated. She threw her backpack over her shoulder and headed for the heavy patch of trees where she had last seen Marley. She turned briefly. "Coming?"

Tristan let out a loud huff and followed Rachel into the trees. She had to be the most stubborn woman he'd ever met. Most of the women he'd known would have been the first ones down the mountain, worried that the rain might ruin their hair.

"He's right, you know," Rachel said. "The rain can get very heavy up here. Not to mention the lightning."

"My only concern is finding Marley and Austin—and

protecting you, of course," he said. "If I see a lightning bolt coming your way I'll jump in front of it. Heaven knows I probably deserve to die by electrocution anyway."

Rachel stopped and placed both hands on her hips as she gave him "the look"—the one a woman gives a man when he's said something really stupid.

"Why would you say something like that?" she snapped.

Tristan produced a big smile and gently touched her face. "Never mind." He laughed, but he really found no humor in it whatsoever. "Come on, I think I felt a raindrop."

They walked through the forest calling out for Austin and Marley, but the only sound they heard was the treetops rattling in the wind. A loud clap of thunder echoed through the mountainside, and the raindrops slowly began to fall.

"I don't suppose you have an umbrella in that backpack of yours?" Tristan asked.

"No, but if you're worried about getting a sunburn, I have something for that," Rachel joked.

"I think it's safe to say we won't be needing that anytime soon." He looked up into the gray sky as the clouds above them threatened to burst. "I think we better find cover and wait out the storm," he suggested. Taking her by the hand, he hurried back the way they'd come.

"Where are we going?" asked Rachel.

"I saw something back here I think we can use for shelter."

When they came to the edge of the mountain, there was a small indentation in the rocks. Tristan began to clear some of the foliage from the opening.

"That's your idea of shelter?"

"Well, it's better than getting drenched."

"We'll never fit."

"Sure we will. I'll get in first and you can squish in too."

Tristan crawled in and scooted to the back. He opened his arms and shifted his legs, making room for her to come in. Rachel stood silent, blinking her eyes against the now more constant rain.

"I don't know, Tristan," she said, obviously wary of how little room was left and how close she would need to squeeze next to Tristan.

"Rachel, you can't stay out there in the pouring rain."

Just then the sky lit up brightly and another thunderous boom rang out through the trees. Swallowing her principles, she ducked her head and crawled into the small opening. She had to slide up very close to him in order to get her entire body out of the rain.

Her wet ponytail flipped Tristan in the face, causing him to snort. "Sorry," she said. She glanced around their miniature refuge. A feeling of claustrophobia became apparent. Her eyes met his, just inches away. "Well, this is cozy," she said.

"Cozy's my middle name." Tristan smiled, hoping to calm her anxiety. He could see the worry in her eyes, and her face expressed fatigue. "You look so exhausted, Rachel. Here, lean your head back and try and get some rest until the rain lets up." He inched down a little to make it easier for her to rest her head on his shoulder.

"How can anyone sleep like this?" she grunted, repositioning her knees.

"Why don't you try? I promise I'll be on my best behavior. Trust me."

Rachel stared into his eyes. Her face lightened and her tense posture relaxed into his cold, wet arms.

"I do," she whispered.

She snuggled her head between his neck and shoulder, shivering just a bit.

"Don't worry," Tristan said. "We'll find them."

Seventeen

Austin stuffed his hands into the pockets of his Levi jeans and anxiously paced back and forth in front of the entrance of the cave. He would periodically check behind him to make sure some bear wasn't lurking in the darkness waiting to make its move.

"Will you please stop that annoying pacing?" Marley hissed. "You're making me nervous." She sat on a large boulder, leaning her elbows on her knees, seemingly quite relaxed for the circumstances they were in.

"Well, good!" Austin yelled. "Because I'm already a nervous wreck!"

"There's nothing to be worried about. When the rain lets up, we'll find the trail and head back down."

"And what if we can't find the trail again, huh? What then? Do we set up residence in this hideously dark dungeon?"

"Will you calm down? We'll find the trail. I just got a little lost before."

"A little?"

"Okay, then, smart guy. Why don't you leave right now and see if you can find the trail!" Marley hollered.

"Maybe I will!" he shouted back.

"Fine!"

"Fine!"

Austin bolted from the cave and started down the steep slope. The mud was horrendous and overpowered his tired legs. His foot slipped, and when he started sliding down the steep ravine, he reached out to catch hold of a small branch of a nearby tree, but the flimsy bark was not adequate support, and the branch slid effortlessly through his wet hands. His attempts to gain leverage were useless, and he went head first down the muddy rift.

The rain was streaming down much harder than before, and the lightning flashed in every direction. Austin could see this was not the brightest idea he'd ever had.

Raising his face into the rain, he washed off some of the mud splatters and started the tedious climb back to the top. "There will be no living with her now," he grumbled.

When Austin finally reached the cave, there wasn't an inch of him that wasn't covered in mud. He stretched out his arms and shook the mud off his hands. He didn't have to wait long to receive his verbal lashing. Marley was standing at the entrance with her arms folded, laughing hysterically.

"Go ahead," Austin spat. "Laugh it up, jungle girl. But if it wasn't for the rain . . . and the lightning . . . and, of course, the mud, I totally would have made it back!" He looked down at himself and realized he looked like something right out of *Swamp Thing*. He caught Marley's eye and broke out laughing.

"That was really stupid, wasn't it?" He chuckled.

He took a seat on the large rock and wiped more mud from his face. Marley walked over and sat down on the rock next to him. Her closeness made him uneasy, but her face was light and carefree. She really was quite gorgeous, for an ice queen.

"I'm sorry," she said. "I should have warned you about the mud."

"Oh, you knew about that, huh?"

"You know, you're kind of cute . . . when your face is all covered in mud," she said, smiling. She reached up and wiped a small amount away from the corner of his eye. The sudden movement made him flinch just a bit, but he hoped she hadn't noticed.

"Thanks," he muttered in a low voice. "And you're actually

quite beautiful when you're not trying to push people away."

Leaning in a bit closer, their faces almost touching, Austin could feel the warmth of her breath on his cold, wet face. He couldn't help but wonder if this was the part where she slapped him across the face. But there was nothing, not even the tiniest protest.

Watching her closely, he saw something that he hadn't noticed before. A distinct look of passion. He figured it had always been there; it had just been hidden under the hard-core shell she'd put up for the rest of the world.

Placing one hand behind her head, he gently brought her lips in to meet his. It was, without doubt, all that he thought it would be. To his relief, there was no hesitation in her lips, no protest, and no sympathy. She eagerly pressed her mouth to his. Her lips were soft and warm against his cool mouth, causing every muscle in his body to weaken.

Austin let out a faint groan as she broke contact and pulled away. "Well . . . that was . . . unexpected," she whispered.

"Very," he agreed with a pleased smile. "Can we do it again?"

*　*　*

"Rachel," Tristan whispered.

He was reluctant to wake her. He not only was enjoying holding her in his arms, but he also loved watching her sleep. However, the rain had finally stopped, and it would be getting dark soon. He was eager to find Austin and Marley before it was impossible to see anything at all.

Stirring a little, Rachel opened one eye and looked up. "Do we have to leave already?" she said, nudging herself into his chest even more.

Tristan grinned. He liked the fact that she found comfort in his arms. "If it were up to me, we'd stay like this all night."

"Did the rain stop?"

"Yeah, about five minutes ago. How do you feel?"

"Mmm, like I'm in heaven," she said. "I'm more worried

about you. How do your legs feel?" She pulled away, scooting towards the opening.

"Never better."

"I didn't cut off the circulation?"

"Are you kidding? This was nothing. You should have been there the time Cole, Austin, and I had to travel two hundred miles in the back of a Volkswagen." He crawled out after Rachel, stretching his legs and inspecting his clothes. They were mostly dry except for a few spots.

After taking a few minutes to stretch, Tristan and Rachel continued on their search. The ground was wet and squished under their feet, and they tried their best to avoid the really muddy spots. The collected rainwater dripped from the leaves overhead, occasionally catching them off guard by sending a wet surprise down on their heads. The scent of wet woodland was invigorating. It helped to settle their apprehension and rejuvenate their tired bodies.

"So, tell me about your uncomfortable two-hour journey," Rachel asked.

"What, in the Volkswagen?"

"Please?" she begged. "You don't share very much of your past with me. I, on the other hand, am like a broken record that just won't stop playing."

"I like listening to you. You're . . . intriguing," he said. He took her by the hand and continued to lead her through the wet forest.

"Thanks, I think. But really, I would still like to hear about it."

"Well, let's see, I was probably about seventeen at the time. There was this concert in Columbus, Ohio, about two and a half hours away. Of course, my father forbade me to go, as did Cole's and Austin's parents. Being the mischievous teenagers that we were, we told them we were going camping and took off on the road."

"We made it as far as the next town when Austin's old Ford pickup truck broke down. Unfortunately, being young and invincible, we were not easily deterred." Tristan chuckled at the memory. He looked over to see if she was bored to tears, but her face was bright with enthusiasm.

"What did you do?"

"We hitchhiked."

"Three seventeen-year-olds hitchhiking down the freeway? Kind of reckless. Who gave you a ride?"

"These two blondes. Older ones," he said, wagging his eyebrows. "We thought we'd died and gone to heaven. Of course, they shoved all three of us in the back seat and then proceeded to talk on their cell phones, ignoring us completely. I don't think we were able to straighten out our legs for a week, but that wasn't the worst of it."

"There's more?"

"Just ten minutes before we were to arrive at the concert, we got pulled over."

"Oh no!"

"I wasn't worried at first, but then we found out one of the girls had stolen the car from her mother, who had, of course, reported it. The cops took us back to the station and called our parents. Cole and Austin were grounded for a month."

"And you?"

Tristan cringed and cleared his throat. His pace slowed, and he dropped his head as he remembered the beating. It was another memory he wished he could leave behind. He'd spent his entire adulthood trying to forget his childhood, but there was always something that sent his mind racing to the past.

"Let's just say my crime didn't go unpunished," he said in almost a whisper.

"Oh," Rachel breathed.

Sorrow stretched across her face, and Tristan could see she understood what he meant. It was difficult to hide the hurt and anger of his past from her. Although the surface wounds had vanished, the permanent scars ran much deeper than the skin.

Rachel reached over and gently touched his arm. "I'm sorry," she said.

"The funny thing was, I knew what the consequences would be. I knew exactly what would happen if I disobeyed him, but I chose to do it anyway. I don't know—maybe I thought I had old scores to settle." Tristan sighed heavily. He thought about the abandonment of his mother and his loser father.

"Tristan, you were just being a kid. Kids make mistakes all the time."

"Not in my father's eyes," Tristan said.

He stopped walking and dropped her hand. Gazing off into the trees, Tristan thought about his childhood. The bitterness he felt for his father was overpowering. Although he knew it would be best to keep the information about his upbringing locked away, his anger clouded his judgment.

It wasn't something he normally talked about. In fact the only people who knew how he really felt about his father were Cole and Austin. But with Rachel, everything seemed to just roll off his tongue with ease. So without hesitation, Tristan divulged his secret qualms.

"You don't understand. I had to be the grown-up. I had no other choice. By the age of fourteen, I was dragging him out of the local bars so drunk he couldn't stand up. I would drive him home in his truck, praying that we didn't get pulled over so he wouldn't go to jail again."

"Then, at fifteen, I went to work part-time as a tire buster for a local garage just to put food on the table. But it still wasn't good enough. Nothing was ever good enough for him, because nothing would change the fact that he blamed me for my mother leaving. Every slap, every punch, every degrading remark was his way of getting back at my mom."

Tristan hung his head in shame, wishing he hadn't just dumped his whole pathetic life into her lap. Then again, it felt liberating to share his burdens with her. Revealing his dark, disturbing childhood hadn't seemed too difficult. Perhaps now would be a good time to continue with his confessions.

Opening his mouth to disclose his secret, Tristan was stopped by the soft and gentle touch of Rachel's hand on his cheek.

After feeling her sympathetic touch, Tristan hadn't the heart, nor the courage, to tell her any more of the truth.

As they walked out into the clearing, they caught sight of Marley and Austin coming through the trees on the other side. "Marley!" Rachel shouted with joy. She ran across the wet grass to meet her sister.

Tristan walked swiftly behind her, watching as she ran into Marley's arms and hugged her tightly.

"It's good to see you, bro!" Tristan exclaimed. He gave Austin a brotherly embrace, but he jumped back rather quickly as he eyed Austin up and down. "Austin, have you been playing in the mud again?" he teased with a motherly gesture.

"Don't even start," Austin growled.

Eighteen

Tristan stood in the shower, letting the hot water flow down over his cool skin. He lingered longer than usual. The water was just too refreshing to leave.

He thought about Rachel and his new understanding of his true feelings. *Why can't I just tell her the truth?* he thought. He'd shared so many personal truths about himself without seeming to deter her feelings, so why couldn't he tell her the one thing that mattered the most?

Tristan climbed out of the shower and quickly dried himself. With the towel in hand, he wiped a small circle in the middle of the steamed mirror. He glared at his reflection and grumbled, "You're a coward, Tristan Taylor!"

He pulled on his sweat pants and T-shirt before heading to the living room. He was finally starting to feel normal again. Apparently, Austin had been much too tired to worry about cleanliness, as he had flopped out on his bed as soon as they got home.

The rain-soaked trail had devoured them with mud up to their knees, and nightfall had come before they were off the mountain. Through it all, they were able to find their way back, no thanks to the so-called tour guide.

When Tristan walked into the living room, he found Cole slumped down on the couch, holding the phone.

"Is something wrong?" Tristan asked.

"Well, it's all up to you now. I just hope you share your good fortune with your two best friends that went along with your scheme," he croaked.

"What are you talking about?"

"Megan! She's already found someone new. She just called me to let me know I shouldn't hold out hope for us."

"She found someone that soon? She's only been gone for a week."

"Yeah, I know. Supposedly she dated him off and on before he went away on a mission. Now he's there with her, and I'm here getting the rejection call."

Standing in front of Cole, Tristan wondered if he'd gotten closer to Megan than he intended, too. "I'm sorry man. You two were getting pretty close."

"Close nothing! The money was in the bag!" Cole threw his hands up in the air.

At that point, Tristan realized Cole didn't share the same feelings for Megan as he did for Rachel. It was still all about the money to him, and now he'd missed his opportunity.

"Right . . . the money," Tristan grumbled. "Well . . . you know . . . money isn't everything. I mean, if you really like someone, that stuff doesn't matter, right?"

Cole scooted to the edge of the couch and rested his elbows on his knees. He looked up at Tristan with questioning eyes.

"Has something changed, Tristan?" Cole asked.

"Um . . . no, nothing. I was just saying that sometimes money isn't as important as being with that person."

"I know you, Tristan. What's going on?" His voice was sympathetic, though Tristan could tell there was a slight irritation to his tone.

Plopping himself down on the couch, Tristan kept his eyes on the floor to avoid Cole's interrogating stare. He could never hide anything from his best friend—Cole could read him like an open book. At first it drove Tristan crazy, but then, Cole and Austin had always been more like brothers to him than friends. He trusted them with his life, and he knew they felt the same way. They had a bond that was set in stone at the age of ten—the year they became blood brothers.

They had been sitting in Austin's backyard tree house when Cole decided they should secure their friendship through the ancient ritual of blood. He took out his pocket knife and made a tiny slice in the palm of his hand. Then he did the same to Tristan and Austin. Just before Austin fainted, they placed their hands, swearing loyalty for the rest of their lives. If Tristan was going to share his innermost feelings with anyone, it would be with them.

"She's wonderful, Cole," Tristan confessed. "She's thoughtful, sensitive, witty, and passionate. Not to mention she's the most beautiful—"

"Wait, wait, wait," Cole interrupted, holding up his hand in protest. "This isn't about the money anymore, is it?"

Tristan looked up into his eyes and let out a heavy sigh, shaking his head. "No, it's not," he said.

"Are you going to tell her the truth?" Cole asked.

The word "truth" stabbed at Tristan like the cold, dull blade of a knife cutting straight into his heart. He felt a twinge of pain run through his chest and shuddered at the thought of Rachel ever finding out the truth.

"I want to. I almost did, but I don't want to lose her; I can't lose her," Tristan said in a low voice.

"She deserves to know."

Tristan kept his eyes focused on the carpet and squeezed his hands tightly together.

"I can't," he whispered. "I love her."

Cole scooted up to get a little closer. He gently placed his arm around Tristan's shoulder. Tristan could feel his compassion through his touch and knew that as much as Cole may be frustrated with his change of heart, he also understood.

"If you love her, you need to be honest with her," Cole said. "I'll leave it up to you. You know Austin and I won't say anything."

Tristan looked into Cole's gaze, somewhat comforted by his genuine concern. "I appreciate that."

Cole stood, followed by Tristan. They clutched hands and leaned into a masculine embrace. As Cole patted Tristan on the back, he said, "I know you better than you know yourself, Tristan. You'll tell her the truth."

Tristan pulled away, eager to escape the torturous thoughts that burned into his mind. "It's harder than you know, man."

"Well, I'm here for you," Cole said, starting to crack a smile. "Because, you know, you're my hero." He smirked, as he laid his head on Tristan's shoulder and batted his eyes up at him.

Tristan laughed. "And you, my friend, are the wind beneath my wings."

"Um . . . excuse me," Austin gulped, suddenly appearing in the living room. "I . . . I didn't mean to interrupt your male bonding moment."

There was an awkward tone to his voice, as if he wasn't sure what he'd just witnessed. He slowly moved toward the door, keeping his eyes locked on them.

Tristan and Cole shared a devious glance. They both leaped for Austin at the same time and wrapped their arms tightly around him.

"Oh, Austin, you know you're our inspiration!" Tristan sparked off in a high-pitched squeal.

"Yeah, you're the reason we live," Cole cried.

"Okay, guys, I get it. Now get off!"

✯ ✯ ✯

The darkness closed in around him. Tristan struggled to focus on the tiny, dim light that wasn't more than ten feet in front of him. There was a peaceful, comforting feeling that seemed to radiate from the glow, making him want to reach it all that much more.

Slowly, he moved forward, feeling the tranquility beckoning to him. Getting closer, he could see a beautiful face within the glimmer, encouraging him to continue. It was a face that he trusted and even loved.

Although the light grew brighter with every step he took, the shadows around him quickly closed in, drawing him back into a massive cloud of blackness. The shadows seemed angry, even outraged that he wanted to embrace the light.

Tristan fought with mind, body, and soul to elude the darkness that held him hostage. He was distinctively aware of the hopelessness that was contained within the powerful shadows.

Out of the murky mist around him came thousands of hands. They reached out from the dark crevices, clutching him around his arms and legs. They screeched out loudly in protest, mocking his futile efforts to reach the light. Terrified, Tristan tried to run, but he found his legs were like heavy bricks that had sunk into cold, black tar. When he cried out for help, he found his voice was silent. As despair crept in and overtook his very essence, he closed his eyes to the bitter darkness, feeling nothing but coldness around him. Despair sunk in as his hope to reach the light slowly faded away.

Just as he was ready to surrender himself to the unearthly gloom, he heard a voice—faint at first but growing louder. Tristan tried to concentrate on the sound coming from the distance. It was the face in the light. The voice was calling out his name, encouraging him to fight the evil that surrounded him.

Finding his inner strength, Tristan fought even harder than before, resisting the dark's pleas for him to stay and its constant ridicule. He had to reach the light. He didn't know why, but he knew it was safe there, and it had a serenity he'd longed for.

Letting the voice be his guide, Tristan pulled himself through his surroundings, fighting against the dark's powerful grip until he reached the edge of the light. Soon the blackness faded away, leaving only vivid brightness around him.

Standing motionless, Tristan soaked up the peaceful atmosphere that now surrounded him both physically and spiritually. This was where he was supposed to be, what he'd been searching for his entire life.

Looking to his left, he could see an enormous castle that

stood taller than any other structure in the vicinity. The castle was lit up brighter than the noonday sun. He walked a little closer, wanting to inspect its exquisite beauty.

The thought came into his mind that this lovely structure was the Mormon temple. Around the temple blossomed flowers of every kind and color, growing tall and in abundance, as if placed there by a magical force. The rich green grass stretched out around the flowers, and the trees grew plentiful.

A large crowd surrounded the breathtaking building. Tristan was instantly hypnotized by its beauty and found himself drawn to it.

As he moved even closer, he could see two distinct people standing at the entrance of the temple. They were dressed completely in white.

Curious about the couple, Tristan pushed his way through the crowd of unfamiliar faces. When he got closer, he could see the woman more clearly. It was Rachel! She was wearing a long, silk wedding gown. Her hair was pulled back under her white full-length veil. Her whole being seemed to glisten like diamonds in the sunlight.

The man beside her was more difficult to see; his face was a blur. Tristan had to find out who the mystery man was. He continued to push and shove his way to the front. He needed to know who held Rachel's heart. Who was the one that had been worthy enough to be married to her for eternity?

Finally, breaking through the crowd, Tristan looked closely at the man standing directly in front of him.

He saw his own blue eyes staring back.

★ ★ ★

Tristan jerked up in alarm and gasped for air. His body trembled uncontrollably, frightened by the disturbing images.

Pulling his knees to his chest and resting his elbows on them, he held his head in his hands. He could feel the thumping of his heart beating rapidly against his chest. Cold sweat trickled down the side of his face and bare back. He struggled to slow his breathing and heart rate.

Running his hands through his damp hair, he breathed deeply, trying to gain control over his unsettling emotions. The horrifying images of the dark danced freely around his mind, sending a cold chill down his spine. But then there was the beam of light, so loving and comforting, sending out feelings of peace and happiness.

Quickly searching his thoughts, Tristan recalled what had happened in his vivid dream—seeing himself with Rachel at the entrance of the temple. He felt happier than he ever thought possible, but it was more than just being there with Rachel. There was a feeling of fulfillment, like the void inside him had instantly been filled. It was a feeling he'd been longing to find.

What did it all mean? Was he going to marry Rachel? What did the shadows represent? Were his lies and deceit holding him back from gaining the one thing he wanted the most? But if he told Rachel the truth, he could lose her forever.

These tormenting questions bounced around his mind, with no indication of relief. Throwing back the covers, Tristan sat on the edge of the bed, staring at the red numbers on the alarm clock. It was only five in the morning, but there was no time to try and get any more sleep. Rachel would be picking him up in two hours.

She was taking him home to meet her mother. Tristan had known for some time that this point in their relationship would arrive, but knowing didn't make it any easier.

From what he'd observed from Cole and Austin's mothers, they were extremely protective of their children. The genuine love they felt for their children turned them into defensive guard dogs.

Because of that fact, he was afraid Rachel's mother would see right through him. Although he was still toying with the idea of soon coming clean, he didn't want anything to ruin their visit. So for now, he would continue with the charade and put up with the likely interrogation.

Pulling on his blue jeans, Tristan walked to the kitchen without turning on any lights. He poured himself a glass of milk and sat down at the table, soaking up the welcoming silence of the apartment.

Cole was right—Tristan needed to tell Rachel the truth. So why was he retracting from his original intention? On the top of the mountain, everything seemed so clear, but now it was the most difficult task he'd ever tried to conquer.

His reasons for not telling her didn't just stem from his own selfish motives. It was more than that. The thought of telling Rachel the truth and causing her pain tortured him worse than the idea of spending a decade in hell.

Resting his elbows on the table, he groaned miserably, wishing he could be the one Rachel wanted, not this prefabricated man he saw in his dream. Was it really so bad that he wasn't a Mormon? Or that he could only marry her until "death do they part"? After all, he'd been truthful about everything else, divulging all of his insecurities about the future and his hatred for his father.

Tristan let out another long, dispirited sigh. Deep down he knew Rachel was not just any woman, and he was only rationalizing his betrayal. So what if two-thirds was truth and the rest a lie? A lie was still a lie, no matter how small a portion it was.

Feeling miserable and utterly despicable, Tristan returned to his room. He flopped himself down on the bed and glanced over to the nightstand where his copy of the Book of Mormon lay.

He'd been reading nearly every night. The missionary lessons were going well. He'd had the first three and already knew he wanted to be baptized, which was another secret he was keeping to himself.

The stories of the ancient people in the Book of Mormon sparked his interest and seemed to give him direction. There was one concept that was so important every prophet preached it continuously. "Repent and be baptized." The Lord had also made a promise: if Tristan would endure to the end, he would inherit the kingdom of heaven.

Tristan recalled the last discussion with the missionaries at Bishop Anderson's house about the Atonement. Although he didn't understand it completely, he knew that repentance was necessary to progress. More than anything, Tristan wanted to find peace within himself and endure to the end.

Pondering on the word "endure," Tristan remembered Lehi's dream. He recalled the rod of iron that led to the tree of eternal life. Many souls never made it to the tree. They were enticed away by others, or they merely fell into the murky waters only to be lost forever.

Lehi's dream had made a huge impact on Tristan. The message was perfectly clear: if he could hold tightly to the rod, he wouldn't perish. *I could really use an iron rod right about now,* Tristan thought. *Something to hold firmly to, leading me in the right direction.*

Tristan did, however, hold to the belief that strength and abstinence could only be achieved through the power of prayer. Why he was so sure about this, he couldn't really explain, but he knew it was what he needed to make it through two whole days with Rachel.

He loved and respected her. The last thing he wanted was to let his unruly thoughts cloud his judgment.

Tristan knew what he needed to do and slowly crawled out of bed. He got down onto his knees and leaned on the mattress. As he knelt there, he couldn't help but wonder if he was going about this whole prayer thing in the right way. Should he fold his arms, like they do in church? Should he speak out loud, or just in his mind? Why hadn't the missionaries or Bishop Anderson told him the right way to pray?

He felt awkward and full of embarrassment, not to mention that his flawed past, as well as his present deceptions, seemed to be screaming out at him, telling him he wasn't worthy to speak to God and that he was a fool. The voices grew louder by the second. Tristan tightly shut his eyes and replayed the words to the last song they had sung in sacrament meeting. "Did You Think to Pray" affected Tristan in a way that no song had. The words of the song stuck in his mind and gave him hope.

Finally, the voices faded away and Tristan continued. He clutched his hands together, interlocking his fingers, and took a deep breath for reinforcement. He cleared his mind and thought of the scriptures he'd read on prayer and forgiveness. The guilt and shame quickly vanished. He was left with a feeling of tranquility that seemed to encourage him to continue.

Feeling as though his knees were cemented to the floor, he realized he couldn't have moved even if he'd wanted to. He cleared his throat for the second time and forced the stubborn words past his lips.

Tristan prayed for the strength to overcome his faults as well as for control over his unwanted thoughts and desires. He asked for forgiveness, for compassion, and for the courage to tell Rachel the truth.

Resting his elbows on the edge of the bed, his pulse raced and his breathing became heavy. He realized there was one last question he needed to ask—the question that had invaded his mind for the last several weeks.

Tristan inhaled deeply, holding his breath for a moment before releasing any and all reservations. He proceeded to ask for confirmation of the truthfulness of the Book of Mormon. He asked with a clear mind and an open heart, having complete faith that he would receive an answer

Holding his position after closing his prayer, Tristan stayed very quiet. The silence of the room surrounded him, leaving a lonesome feeling in the pit of his stomach. His anxiety grew with passing second. He wasn't quite sure what to expect, really. Perhaps the earth would begin to shake, or a loud voice from the heavens would speak to him.

Suddenly, it was as if he'd walked from a dark room into the bright sunlight. A new sense of understanding surged through his mind, and a complete comprehension of morality settled in. At that moment, Tristan understood the significance of following the principles of the gospel.

After the knowledge came the feeling like someone had ignited a flame inside his chest. It started out slowly, like the warmth coming from a lit candle. It didn't take long before the small flame became a full-blown blaze. It burned so deeply and so intensely that Tristan found himself gasping for air.

When the warmth subsided, an overpowering feeling of peace surrounded him, wrapping around him like a heavy blanket. It was so comforting that Tristan didn't dare move. The feeling engulfed his body and seeped deep down into his soul.

Tears welled up in Tristan's eyes when he realized what had just happened. He had been touched by the Spirit, just like the missionaries had described. Above all, he'd been given the confirmation he'd asked for. God had answered his prayer.

* * *

Tristan took an extra long shower, soaking up the warm water. He had been reluctant to leave the spot on his bedroom floor, afraid he'd lose the new comforting feeling he'd gained. It made his spirit soar with optimism. For the first time in years, he felt content with his surroundings and had a new understanding of the meaning of life.

Tristan carried his duffel bag out to the front room. He wished he could share his excitement with Rachel. She was the one person that could relate to his experience. He couldn't share this with Cole. It would only cause more contention between them. So for now he had to contain his enthusiasm, which would be like a small child holding onto a secret. He would keep silent on the outside but would be screaming out loud on the inside.

Tristan went to the window and watched the sun as it rose and sent its radiant beams shooting across the city. Tristan realized he had to find a way to tell Rachel the truth. He could no longer go on with the lies and deception. He was undeniably in love with her, and it was time to tell her, regardless of the outcome.

Nineteen

Rachel arrived not a moment too soon to rescue Tristan from his torturous anxiety. All he had to do was gaze into her captivating eyes and all his worries faded away.

The train ride was a little more than five hours, which seemed more like minutes in her presence. Their conversation was light, and they avoided such topics as his childhood, her family's expectations, and of course, the lie. It seemed they were both determined to keep the mood light and cheerful.

A car was waiting at the train station, and by the time they pulled into the long driveway that led up to the house, Tristan was already impressed. He always figured her mother lived in a mansion, but it still took his breath away. The lengthy driveway twisted up through a forest of leafy green trees that were perfectly aligned with the pavement. The long, sturdy branches hung out over the road, providing a nice, shady drive.

When they emerged from the wooded area, the driveway encircled a life-size marble statue of a woman dumping a pitcher of water into the round base of a fountain. The clear water flowed freely down, making a soft splashing sound as it hit and swirled around.

The enormous home sat on a beautifully landscaped plot, surrounded by exquisite flower beds. The entrance was magnificent. Four large marble pillars surrounded the porch covered by thick green vines.

The exterior of the home consisted mostly of dark maroon brick, with two chimneys sticking out of the roof. The attached garage was also very roomy with four white doors.

Gawking in bewilderment, Tristan stood glued to the driveway. He'd always known these kind of dwellings existed, but he'd never actually seen one, let alone had the opportunity to stay in one.

"Everything okay?" Rachel asked, briefly stopping in front of him.

"It's just . . . wow," he gasped.

Rachel took him by the hand and noticed the flabbergasted look on his face. "It's just a house, Tristan," she reminded him. "It doesn't make me any different than you."

Putting on a serious face, he returned her gaze. "Are you kidding? This changes everything."

"What?" Rachel questioned. Her eyes narrowed, and a perplexed look came across her face.

"Yeah! From now on, *you're* buying dinner."

"Jerk!" Rachel laughed, punching him in the shoulder.

Tristan pulled her close and gave her a quick kiss to reassure her of his loyalty. He placed one hand tenderly against the side of her cheek.

"I don't care what kind of house you live in," he said truthfully. "As long as it doesn't bother you that I live in something a little less extravagant."

"You should know me better than that," she said, smiling. "One thing I know for sure, money doesn't equal happiness. And you, Tristan Taylor, make me very happy—rich or poor."

Dropping his hand from her face, he met her smile.

"Now you've gone and made me blush," he croaked, mimicking the tone of a red neck Southerner. "Come on. Let's go meet your mother."

Tristan relieved their driver of the luggage and followed Rachel to the door. Money obviously didn't matter to Rachel, but how would her mother react when she learned he was jobless and broke?

Rachel walked beside him, playfully elbowing him in the side to lighten the mood. "Mom, we're here!" Rachel called out.

A tall, thin brunette, who looked as though she was in her early forties instead of her mid-fifties, came strolling down the spiral staircase that stood just a few feet inside the front door.

Her face was flawless, thanks to noticeable coats of foundation that were spread across her skin. Her long, curly hair was much like Rachel's, and it was flowing down over thin shoulders. She wore a bright pink blouse, designer trousers, and brown leather sandals.

Tristan couldn't help but wonder how many surgeries she'd had in order to make her look more like Rachel's older sister rather than her mother. Her fingernails were perfectly manicured, as were her matching toes, displaying a bright red polish to match her lipstick.

"Rachel!" she squealed with delight. She wrapped her arms around Rachel's neck, her gold bracelets shimmering in the sunlight.

"Hi, Mom," Rachel said.

"It's so good to have you home. I've missed you terribly!"

"Mom, I just saw you four weeks ago."

"I know, but that's *still* too long." She sighed, releasing her grip. At that point she eyed Tristan up and down with a pleasing smile. Rachel made the introduction.

"Mom, this is Tristan Taylor. Tristan, this is my mother, Eleanor."

Tristan held out his hand. "It's nice to finally—"

Eleanor reached out and grabbed him around the neck, pulling him into a firm hold before he could say any more. "It's very nice to meet you," she rejoiced, hugging him a little more tightly than Tristan felt was actually appropriate.

Maintaining her close contact, Eleanor released him from her embrace. "You sure are a handsome one," she squeaked, cocking one eyebrow in approval.

Speechless and a bit overwhelmed, Tristan couldn't help but wonder if she was this forward with all of Rachel's dates.

"*Mom!*" Rachel roared from behind.

"Well, he is," she stated, dropping her hands. She turned to confront her humiliated daughter. "Not at all like that other boy you dated. What was his name? Wart something?"

A chuckle escaped Tristan's lips. Rachel shot him a look to let him know she didn't find her mother's insulting remark at all amusing.

"It was Stewart, Mother, and I'm not dating him anymore," Rachel clarified.

"Well, of course you're not!" she said. Reaching over she snatched Tristan's chin between her thumb and fingers, shaking it gently. "Not when you've got this face staring back at you."

"Why, thank you, Eleanor! And you are even more lovely than Rachel described," Tristan answered, using his soft, velvety voice.

She puckered her lips, and for a moment Tristan thought she might kiss him. "*Mother!*" Rachel hissed. "Come on, Tristan. I'll show you to your room." She eyed her mother with a warning. Rachel reached over and took Tristan by the hand and pulled him toward the stairs.

"I'll have Marcia make us some lunch," Eleanor called out while they made their way up the flight of stairs.

"Thank you, Mother," Rachel said. When they reached the top of the stairs, Rachel turned to Tristan. "Sorry about that. I should have warned you about my mother. She can be a bit . . . fanatical at times."

"Really? I hadn't noticed," he teased. "Don't worry about it. It's kind of nice to have a mother dote over me. Even if it isn't my own."

A sad look came over Rachel's face. "Oh, I'm so sorry. Here I am complaining about my mother when you lost yours at such a young age. Nice one, Rachel."

Tristan took her by the hand and stood close, looking into

her troubled eyes. "You are far from thoughtless, Rachel. You don't ever need to apologize for something that happened in my past."

Rachel gave him a small smile, but something in her face made Tristan wonder if she felt sorry for him. He didn't want sympathy. Not from her.

"Well, here's your room," Rachel said, opening the door for him.

The guest room was decorated in a outdoors motif with ducks and geese, light blue walls, and a blue and gray checkered bedspread on the king-sized mattress.

After Rachel left to unpack, Tristan went to the window to inspect the view.

He glanced around the yard, but his thoughts returned to Rachel. He wondered if she would ever be able to see beyond his flawed past. They were raised so differently. Rachel was born into money, he had none. She had a loving, supportive family. He had a missing mother and an abusive father. She was raised with wholesome morals and religion. Tristan was taught to take whatever he wanted, even if he didn't deserve it.

How could they ever build a strong, lasting relationship when they came from such different worlds? Tristan's thoughts once again tortured him, crucifying him for what he'd done and who he'd become.

"I'm no better than my old man," Tristan whispered. Now, instead of being the strong one in the relationship, he had become a sympathy case.

"Ready for lunch?" Rachel asked, interrupting Tristan's thoughts. He turned around to find her smiling face in the doorway.

He followed Rachel downstairs, where they enjoyed a light lunch provided by the kitchen staff. The home was all over-whelming: the expensive decor, the paid wait staff—the whole atmosphere screamed money.

It was a lifestyle he could get used to and one he'd always wanted. This was the reason he'd come up with the plan in the first place—to live high on the hog, surrounded by nice things and plenty of money. It was all so enticing; at least, it used to be. Now the only thing that really appealed to him was Rachel.

When they were finished eating, Rachel took Tristan on a tour of the grounds. There was an oval swimming pool directly out the French doors of the kitchen. It was complete with diving board and space for a wet bar, which amused Tristan because he knew Rachel's mother didn't drink. Several padded lounge chairs lined the tiled area around the pool. Plush kitchen chairs were set up around a portable roasting fire off to the left.

There was also a white gazebo decorated with tiny white lights and leafy vines. The patio was equipped with an outdoor kitchen that even a professional chef would be envious of.

After the pool came the flower garden. Perfectly manicured shrubbery lined the sculptured rock walkways that led them through the garden area. An assortment of colorful flowers covered just about all other available space. It was clear there had been careful planning and special consideration, as well as hours upon hours of labor.

Three unique granite statues of children playing were strategically placed at all three entrances into the garden.

Tristan took Rachel by the hand, slightly swinging it back and forth as they walked. "It must have been a blast growing up here," Tristan said.

Rachel let a loud sigh pass her lips. "We weren't allowed to play in the garden, or in the yards. They were for appearances only," she said. "With my mother, it's always been about keeping up with the Joneses. Unfortunately for us kids, it meant no lemonade stand, no sidewalk chalk, and no tree house. Basically we could be kids, but we just couldn't show it to the rest of the neighborhood."

"You mean to tell me you had all this open space, all these great places to play hide-and-seek, but you weren't allowed to?" Tristan was both shocked and angry. He'd hoped that at least one of them had enjoyed a normal upbringing.

Rachel let out a grunt and bit her bottom lip. "My father

worked a lot, so my mother was home with us. Or at least, she had the staff watch us. She was usually getting her hair or nails done, or having some little place on her body nipped or tucked."

Sitting down on one of the wrought-iron benches, Rachel took a deep breath. "My father, on the other hand, was wonderful. He was so down to earth and just all-around easygoing. Not at all like my mother." She looked down at the ground with a frown. "That's why nothing has made much sense since he died."

"What do you mean?" Tristan asked. He sat down next to her, hoping she would open up to him about her feelings.

"Well, when I told you he left me his company, it wasn't exactly the whole story. He put things in his will that just don't make any sense. Why he would put those things in there, when he was never the kind to . . ."

Her voice trailed off as she kept her eyes to the ground and rubbed her hands together. Tristan realized what she was talking about but kept quiet.

"You can talk to me, Rachel," Tristan said.

"Well, it's just . . . he added this stupid stipulation in his will. I mean, I knew how he felt about us girls getting married. He thought if a girl wasn't married by the time she was twenty-five she was destined to be an old maid. I figured he'd change his mind when he saw that times had changed. I guess I was wrong."

"So, the stipulation was to be married?" Tristan asked. He wanted her to reaffirm what he already knew.

Rachel nodded her head, without looking up. Tristan wondered if she was embarrassed or heartbroken by her father's unrealistic request.

"It doesn't really matter anymore. It's too late for me. Megan and Marley still have a chance, but my inheritance will be dissolved into the company." Rachel sighed again and looked into Tristan's eyes. "I could have done so much with that money— helped out so many people. I'm sorry," she said. "I shouldn't have dumped all that on you. It's not your problem."

Although Tristan held his tongue, he realized the money meant more to Rachel than he'd thought, though not because she would have spent it on fancy clothes or a lavish home. She was definitely the kind of person that would share what she had with others.

"We make quite a pair, don't we? I always had to be the grown-up, and you had to hide your childhood. Doesn't seem fair, does it?" Tristan said.

"Nothing like getting ripped off," Rachel agreed.

Watching the disappointment in her face was just too much for him. He thought about it for a moment and then shot her a mischievous smile. He reached up and tapped her on the shoulder.

"Tag, you're it!" he hollered, before darting off through the rows of bushes.

Rachel sat for a moment, and then, just before losing sight of him, she took off on a dead run.

Catching a glimpse of Tristan as he darted in and out of the trees, Rachel rounded another corner, knowing there was a shortcut to his destination. Tristan ran out into the green fresh-cut yard, glancing over his shoulder to see if she was anywhere close.

What he hadn't expected was for her to come shooting out from behind the bushes. When he turned back around, she rammed into him and knocked him to the ground. Concerned she might have hurt herself, he got up to inspect her condition.

"Are you okay?" Tristan asked.

"Caught you!" she said. She reached up and snatched him by the shirt to pull him to the ground.

After the laughter died down, Rachel propped herself up on one elbow while Tristan lay flat. He wished she could see into his heart, to really know how much he truly loved her. If she understood that, then nothing else would matter. Not even a lie.

"What are you thinking about?" she finally asked. Scooting

over a little more, she gazed down at him with her pure, care-free eyes, earnestly searching his face for answers.

He could feel the soft, bare skin of her arm touch his own and the warmth of her breath on his face. It was like a flash of hot flames that instantly awakened all of his senses—even the ones he'd wished would stay asleep.

Although he let his mind wander for a brief moment, he quickly brought it back into focus. It was amazing how much more strength he had since praying earlier that morning. It was as though someone had handed him the remote and given him back control of his life and feelings.

"Are you going to tell me, or do I have to beat it out of you?" Rachel asked.

Tristan hadn't realized he'd been silently staring, perhaps searching for his future in her eyes. *Tell her now! Tell her the truth right now!* his mind shouted, encouraging him to do the right thing.

Opening his mouth, Tristan breathed heavily, almost hoping the words would just roll out without any effort on his part. But they didn't.

"I was just thinking how very beautiful you are," he murmured. He reached up and wrapped his hand around the back of her neck and pulled her face down to meet his lips.

Rachel's response surprised him. Pressing her body close to his, she reached up with both hands and weaved her fingers into his thick hair, crushing her lips harder to his.

The kiss was unlike any they had shared before. It was powerfully intense, full of affection, and somehow more meaningful. It was unlike anything he'd ever experienced, and it was unexpected coming from her.

Imprisoned by her smoldering mouth, he draped his arms tightly around her, feeling the force behind her passion. As the kiss lingered, Tristan could feel his urges bubbling up inside him. He would not let that demon out again. He'd come too far.

Gently, he gripped her face in his hands and pushed her

away. "Wow," he whispered, breathing heavily. "Now who's let the animal out of its cage?" he teased.

Rachel immediately moved away with a look of embarrassment across her face. "Sorry," she panted.

"You have nothing to be sorry about. It was my fault."

"I hate to burst your bubble, Tristan Taylor, but *I* attacked *you*," she said, pouting. "You're not the only one that feels the burdens of temptation."

Taking her hand inside of his, he kissed it softly and smiled. "Just when I think I have you all figured out, you surprise me."

"Oh, you think you have me figured out? Okay, look at me now, and tell me what you see. I'll let you know when you're getting close." She smirked.

"This should be interesting," Tristan grunted. "Well, I see an absolutely gorgeous, intelligent, mature woman that knows exactly what she wants in life but is afraid to go after it."

Rachel tilted her head to one side, and her eyes narrowed. "I'll give you that one on account of you think I'm gorgeous," she said. "What else?"

"Hmm . . . I see someone that's had her heart broken by someone she trusted, and now she is afraid to give it out to someone new." Tristan watched her expression change from playful to serious.

For a few seconds, she was silent, obviously contemplating his accusation. Did she trust him enough to give him her whole heart?

"Maybe . . . I'm waiting for an exchange," she whispered, staying focused on his eyes.

Giving her a soft, reassuring smile, Tristan prayed that she would see the sincerity behind his answer. "Rachel, you already hold the key to my heart."

Twenty

Out of the blackness of the bedroom, a hand reached out and touched Tristan on the arm, sending him to an upright position with his mind racing. *Not another nightmare*, he thought, panic-stricken by the memory of his previous night's sleep.

"Tristan, it's Rachel." Her silky-sweet voice rang out through the darkness, easing his fears. Through the dim lighting that emerged from the hallway, he could see her silhouette bending over his bed.

"Jeez, are you trying to give me a heart attack?" he said, panting heavily and clutching his hand to his chest. He scooted up in the bed, wiping the sweat from his forehead.

"Sorry, I didn't think you'd be asleep yet," she responded with a sound of disappointment in her voice.

"No, it's fine. I just dozed off. Is something wrong?"

Taking his hand, she gave him a slight tug to let him know she wanted him to follow her. "No, nothing's wrong. I'm kidnapping you."

"As much as I like the sound of that," he said, "would you mind if I put some pants on first?"

Abruptly releasing his hand, Rachel shyly turned around and looked down at the floor. Tristan climbed out of bed and pulled on his jeans and T-shirt.

"Ready?" Rachel asked over her shoulder.

"Did you want to tie me up?" he teased. "You know, I might try to escape."

Rachel reached out and again grabbed him by the hand, leading him to the door. "Oh, I don't think I'm in any danger of that," she said. "Curiosity is more powerful than bondage."

Following her out the back door, Tristan couldn't help but admit he was more than a little intrigued by her secrecy. Keeping the suspense going, Rachel stayed quiet.

As they approached the stables, Tristan let a loud sigh pass his lips. Rachel only smiled at him and opened the door.

"You've got to be kidding me," Tristan snorted. He looked over at the two horses tied up to a post already saddled and ready to ride.

"If you're scared, I can always walk beside you," she snickered.

"Not on your life!"

"Okay then, climb on." Rachel handed Tristan the reins of a silky, honey-colored horse. "His name is Duncan," she said.

Tristan stood for a moment, staring down the horse in an attempt to bully the animal into doing what he wanted.

"Don't worry. He doesn't bite," said Rachel.

"I know that."

"I was talking to Duncan." She laughed, patting Duncan on the nose. She leaned in and gave Duncan a kiss.

"Oh, I see how it is," Tristan said.

Swallowing the lump in his throat, Tristan stood to the left of the horse and grabbed hold of the reins. Slipping his right foot into the stirrup, he soon determined it was the wrong foot and pulled it out again.

Rachel remained quiet while Tristan analyzed the situation. He tried again by placing his left foot into the stirrup. Grabbing tightly to the saddle, he hurled his right leg in an upward motion. What he didn't anticipate was the height of the horse. His leg smacked Duncan's rear end. The force set him off balance and knocked him to the ground.

Rachel giggled. She put out her hand to help him up. "Here, watch how I do it," Rachel instructed. With ease, she placed her left leg into the stirrup and pulled herself up into the saddle. "See? Nothing to it."

Tristan grunted, not liking the fact that she'd already shown him up, and he wasn't even on the horse yet. He followed her example, finally securing a seat safely in the saddle. Once there, he thought for sure he was home free. How hard could it be to ride a horse?

They rode along side by side, Rachel looking competent and comfortable in the saddle, but clearly going slower than she would have liked. She made conversation by telling Tristan all about her horse. His name was Chestnut because of the different shades of brown in his coat. Chestnut was her sixteenth birthday present, so he was definitely getting up there in horse years. Tristan could see there was a noticeable connection between the two of them. Chestnut was much more than just a horse to her.

"So, do you think you can pick up the pace a little? I mean, if you're not too nervous," she asked.

Feeling a bit overconfident, Tristan decided he would demonstrate his natural horseback-riding ability by giving the reins a hard smack against Duncan's neck and slapping his legs against Duncan's torso.

The last thing Tristan heard was the sound of Rachel's voice. She yelled something he didn't have time to make out before a thunderous jolt ignited beneath him. Tristan let out a high-pitched squeal and hung on for his life.

Duncan sprinted across the pasture like a racehorse heading for the finish line. Tristan's stomach was left somewhere in the dust, but his arms held tightly to the reins.

When they reached the fence at the far end of the pasture, Duncan didn't stop like Tristan had anticipated. Instead, he effortlessly leaped over it. Tristan's body violently bounced high off the saddle, knocking him forward. He came back down in the saddle with a hard blow to his backside.

Duncan got going even faster with Tristan bouncing up and

down in the saddle like a rag doll, having no control over his body movement. He clung desperately to the two leather straps that seemed to be his only support, and his adrenaline escalated.

The night wind whipped across his face like millions of cold, stiff hands slapping him all at once. It was almost unbearable to keep his eyes open against the wicked night air. He realized he needed to gain control over this unruly beast before he ended up on the ground.

With every bit of strength he had left in his arms, Tristan pulled hard against the reins and let out an extra loud "Whoa!" He'd seen it done in the old cowboy movies, so maybe it would work for him.

Regrettably, he realized he was not in Hollywood, and the horrible creature seemed to have a mind of his own. It became agonizingly clear that he was in this bumpy ride for the long haul. All he could do now was hold on and hope Duncan would decide to stop before they reached Connecticut.

Out of the misty haze that whizzed past him, Rachel's voice rang out like an angel of mercy. She was suddenly there beside him, her old horse having no trouble keeping up with the young stud.

"Hold on," she yelled.

"Like I'm not?" Tristan yelled back. If he hadn't been so scared, he may have laughed out loud at her demand.

Rachel brought Chestnut closer to Duncan while Tristan's terrified face pleaded for help. She reached out with one hand and took hold of the reins on Duncan's nose. She gave them a hard tug. "Whoa, Duncan."

At her command, the horse began to slow to a semi-fast pace and then retreated to a slow gallop. Rachel continued to hold onto the reins until Duncan finally stopped.

"Are you all right?" she asked.

Watching her in amazement, Tristan took in a deep breath and exhaled while running his hand through his hair. He could feel his heart finally slowing down.

"Are you talking to me or the horse?" he mocked.

"You, of course."

"Well, you know before, when you asked if I wanted you to walk beside me?"

"Yeah."

"I'm retracting my original statement," he panted. "I really think he was trying to kill me."

Rachel chuckled and turned the horses around to head back to the pasture. She let go of the reins and let Tristan take control.

"You spooked him, that's all. He's really not a bad horse."

"*I* spooked him? Somehow I doubt that."

"I'm sorry. It's really my fault. I forgot Duncan gets spooked so easily. I should have let you ride Chestnut."

"You forgot? Oh, you owe me big time for this one!"

"Hey, I just saved your life, tough guy."

"Not even close," he said.

The night was warmer now that the wind wasn't blasting him in the face. It was actually quite a nice night. Tristan hadn't noticed how far Duncan had run. They were a long way from the stables, out in the middle of nowhere.

Even through the dim moonlight, Tristan could see they were riding through some kind of meadow with tall blades of lush green grass. Purple wildflowers covered most of the meadow, with a few large trees here and there. The meadow was breathtaking in the moonlight. With the starlit sky above them, it was almost mystical.

Tristan looked over at Rachel, realizing she had been very quiet for the last several minutes. Her skin glistened bronze in the heavy moonlight and her hair shimmered. She was exceptionally beautiful by moonlight.

It was peaceful there, riding through the deserted meadow. The silence was hypnotic. The only sound was the soft footfall of their horses and the faint sound of crickets chirping in the distance.

"Is this part of your land?" Tristan finally asked, breaking the awkward silence.

"I think so, but I never knew how beautiful it was out here."

"Would it sound cheesy if I said it suffers in comparison next to you?"

Rachel shook her head and smiled, looking away momentarily. Tristan could swear he saw her blush, even through the darkness.

Stopping the horses, Rachel repositioned herself in the saddle. "Tristan, if I ask you a question, will you give me a completely honest answer?"

Tristan shuddered to think what she might have on her mind. He could see the seriousness of the question written plainly across her face. From the beginning of their ride, he could sense there was something different about her tonight. She was keeping something from him.

"Of course," he replied.

"Well, with your looks and your line of work, you could have any woman you want. So, why are you here with me?" Her voice was genuinely full of distress.

It was obvious that she still doubted his intentions. Tristan stared deeply into her inquiring eyes, wondering how he could tell her the truth without losing her forever. It was like having your cake and eating it too—a concept that has always baffled him.

"Rachel, I . . . I don't know where to begin," he stuttered, feeling his heart thumping rapidly against his chest. The words once again rang out inside his head. *Do it now! Tell her the truth!*

"Just tell me why you want to be with me."

Since she didn't actually ask a direct question, he didn't need to give her a direct answer. *Wimp!* his mind cruelly mocked.

"You already know the answer to that," he said in relief.

"Humor me again, please."

"Rachel, I can't imagine not having you in my life. You're like warm sunshine and cool rain. You take my breath away, and at the same time, you make it possible for me to breathe. You inspire me to be a better man, even when I don't believe in myself. You're the first person I think about when I wake up and the last before I go to bed. I never knew life could be this good. Do you want me to go on?"

"I . . . um . . . no. I think that will do," she breathed.

"Don't ever doubt how beautiful you are. You are more real than any model I have ever met. You're beautiful on the inside *and* on the outside. True beauty like that is rare."

Tristan leaned over and placed one hand on the side of her face, focusing on her unsettling eyes. He pulled her over, swiftly finding her moist, warm lips through the moonlight. Both horses stood perfectly still, respecting their closeness.

When Rachel kissed him, it was soft like feathers sweeping across his lips. Still, it was different than before, more reserved. There was jagged emotion behind the kiss, as if she were trying to decide whether to let go or lock up.

When Tristan released her from his kiss, he saw something in her eyes that worried him. It was almost like she was ashamed of the kiss. What had changed? Had he come on too strong again?

The ride back was painfully quiet; the silence tortured his confidence. Tristan wanted to ask what she was thinking. He needed to know if she had decided he wasn't good enough for her after all. But the words would not come.

There was something she wasn't telling him. Something that wasn't there before. A resistance to her feelings. But why?

Persecuting doubt rushed into his mind, but Tristan tried his best to stay optimistic. After tying up the horses, they walked slowly back to the house. He reached out and took Rachel by the hand, but he could feel the resistance even in her touch. She was harboring something—something he probably didn't want to hear.

When they reached the swimming pool, Rachel stopped abruptly. She turned to face him with a distressed look on her face.

"I need to talk to you about something," she said, sounding a bit indecisive.

"Anything," Tristan replied. He gulped down the lump in his throat and braced himself for the worst.

"Well, I don't really know how to begin." She let out a heavy sigh. "I'm not very good at this kind of thing."

Her rapidly beating heart and erratic breathing was anguish to him. Whatever she was going to say had to be bad. Was she breaking it off? Was this the end for him and the beginning for Stewart? Tristan stood his ground, ready for anything, but then again, how does anyone prepare to have their heart crushed?

The few moments she stood silent were awful. *Please don't say it*, thought Tristan. *Don't say it's over!*

"Rachel, please, you're killing me over here," he grunted.

The pool was lit up by several underwater bulbs, and the gazebo's lights shimmered brightly. It made the stress on her face that much clearer. Tristan wished the night was dark enough to hide his agony.

"Okay, here it goes," she whispered, more to herself. Taking a deep breath, she looked up into his eyes. "Tristan, I think— no—I know I'm in love with you."

Tristan's mouth dropped open. His heart skipped a beat, maybe two. Was his heart beating at all? His head was spinning, and his knees felt like jelly. Did he hear her right? Did she really just tell him what he'd hoped to hear?

Standing motionless in shock, Tristan stared into her pale face. He tried to speak, but his lips were frozen. Rachel's eyes pleaded for a response, but he was paralyzed. Questions flashed through his mind as he struggled to react.

He wondered what he'd done to deserve someone this wonderful. He also thought about the lie and what that would mean now that he knew how she felt.

Her strained smile faded, and her eyes dropped to the ground. Unintentionally, his lingering silence had sent the wrong message. Rachel quickly stepped around Tristan's stiff, unresponsive body.

"I'm sorry," she said. "I shouldn't have said that. Just forget that last part."

Hearing the sorrow in her voice snapped Tristan out of his stupor. "Wait," he said softly.

Tristan quickly spun around on one foot to stop her from leaving. Not seeing the small table that was sitting directly behind him, his leg caught the white metal, sending him staggering to catch his footing. He stumbled to his left, and then to his right, trying to regain his balance. Just when he thought he had it under control, his foot slipped from the edge of the pool. With a large splash of water, Tristan was immersed in a chlorine bath.

When he surfaced, Tristan flipped his wet hair out of his eyes and wiped the water from his face. Other than being fully dressed, the warm water felt refreshing and seemed to calm his embarrassment.

"Tristan, are you okay?" Rachel asked, bending over the edge of the pool.

"That was graceful," he joked, swimming over to the edge. Rachel was on her knees, laughing hysterically. "Oh, you think this is funny?"

"Well, yeah," she choked out.

"Just help me out, please," he complained, holding out his hand. Rachel reached out and took it, only to be yanked headfirst into the water next to him.

Rachel surfaced and wiped the water from her face. Tristan immediately pulled her over to him. "You're right—it is funny," he said, laughing. He removed a strand of wet hair from her face and gazed into her eyes.

"I guess I deserved that," she said. "After all, I just dropped a bombshell on you. But, it's okay if you don't feel the—"

Tristan grabbed her around the waist and wedged his lips around hers to stop her from saying any more. He released her from his kiss but kept her close. He affectionately ran his fingers down the side of her wet face.

"Rachel, I'm in love with you too," he whispered.

"But I thought—"

Tristan placed a finger on her lips. "Shhh. I'm sorry about my earlier reaction," he said. "You shocked me. I was under the impression you were trying to tell me good-bye."

"You thought I wanted to break it off?"

Tristan shook his head, humiliated he'd even thought about it. "I'm glad I was wrong." He ran his fingers through her long, wet hair and then pulled her into another passionate kiss.

He could sense the difference right away. There was no hesitation like before. Just unrestrained passion. She clutched her arms tightly around his neck, pulling herself deeper into his lips.

For a few more minutes, he was lost in what he thought could only be heaven, surrounded by her arms, her lips, and her love for him. The feeling was overpowering and may have brought him to his knees if he weren't submerged in water.

When he returned to his room, Tristan changed out of his wet clothes and flopped down on the bed. He should have known heaven couldn't last forever. He soon found himself suffering in his own personal form of hell. One simple lie now seemed to be smoldering out of control, just waiting to burst into flames.

How many times had he tried to tell her the truth, only to find his tongue bound by fear? How could he come clean now and risk losing her just when he'd found out how she felt about him? She loved him, and he loved her. Everything should be perfect, and it would be, if it weren't for the black cloud that hung over his head.

He'd been looking for someone like Rachel his whole life. He just never realized it until now. The empty space in his soul and the yearning in his heart had just been filled. Finally, true happiness was within his grasp, and he wasn't about to let it slip away.

Lying in the darkness, Tristan realized he wasn't strong enough to reveal his secret. There was no doubt now what he had to do. He would simply bury the lie once and for all, no matter how much it tortured him. His secret would forever remain undisclosed.

Twenty-one

The phrase "time flies when you're having fun" had always struck Tristan as peculiar. That was until his time alone with Rachel had come to an end, and they were packing up the car that would take them back to the train station.

Over the last two days, Tristan was granted a glimpse of her childhood—a glimpse that included a walk through timeless memories, hilarious stories, and embarrassing moments. The tour of her past only made him love her that much more. He felt as though he'd known her his whole life.

The last few days together had united them. They had formed a bond of friendship, love, and, of course, trust. Tristan shared more than he'd anticipated, almost crossing the line several times. He freely disclosed his hopes for a bright future and his dreams of owning his own advertising company.

Although nothing more was said about her father's will or his stipulation, Tristan knew exactly what he needed to do. If he wanted to spend the rest of his life with Rachel, he would need to make some relatively mild modifications when compared to the reward he would gain in the end.

First, he needed to find a job. Any job would do, as long as he was making his own money. Money he could spend on Rachel, while at the same time, sending her the message that her wealth meant nothing to him.

Second, he would be baptized. The missionaries were eager and Tristan felt ready. With every lesson, Tristan's testimony of the gospel had grown stronger. The only thing holding him back from progressing was the little white lie that bound him to his own personal purgatory.

Tristan knew the battle between right and wrong raged inside him, but he seemed powerless to control it. If he told Rachel the truth, he risked losing her forever. If he kept his secret hidden, he risked never sharing an honest relationship with her.

With that in mind, Tristan thought about his future with Rachel. His third step was to ask her to marry him for time and all eternity.

Was that third step realistic? He'd come a long way since that first night he met Rachel. Nevertheless, he still felt unworthy to ask for her hand in marriage.

Rachel approached him right as he slammed the trunk closed. She looked up at him and smiled, snuggling into his arms.

"Who says we have get back on the train? I wish we could just drive and drive until we get lost," she sighed.

Tristan wrapped his arms more tightly around her shoulders. He rested his chin on top of her head and closed his eyes. He inhaled the alluring aroma of her shampoo. If it were up to him, he would leave everything and everyone behind and take her away to be his forever.

"I'm game, but I don't think Stewart would like it if you didn't go back to work."

"Maybe I'll get lucky, and *he* won't come back."

Tristan pulled away and looked down into Rachel's face. "Come back? I didn't realize he was gone."

"Yeah, he was so weird about it," she said, shaking her head.

"What do you mean by 'weird'?" he asked.

Rachel looked up into Tristan's perplexed face. He could see she was wondering why he even cared what Stewart was doing.

"Well, he was acting so secretive. He wouldn't tell me where he was going or why. All he said was he was flying out some-where to check into something. Come to think of it, 'investi-gate' was the way he put it. He said he would be back in a few days. Why, is there something wrong?"

"No, I was just curious," Tristan responded.

He could feel his face heating up with anger at the thought of Stewart digging into things that didn't have anything to do with him. His fingernails dug into the palms of his hands as they tightened into fists of fury.

"So you have no idea where he was going?"

"Are you okay, Tristan? You look really pale."

Tristan nodded his head, brushing off the sudden dose of anger, or maybe it was panic. "I'm fine, really," he reassured her. "Are you ready to go?"

"Unless you want to say good-bye to my mother again," she said, rolling her eyes.

Eleanor had already said good-bye three times, complete with hugs, kisses, and his solemn vow that he would visit again very soon. Actually, Tristan rather liked all of her overly zeal-ous traits and her determination to stay young and vibrant.

"I don't think I can handle another farewell hug. Or kiss, for that matter."

Laughing to himself, Tristan opened the car door for Rachel and then walked around the car, taking one last look at the amazing home. This was all way out of his league. He must be insane to want to try and fit into her world.

Shaking his head, Tristan slid into the seat next to Rachel, and the driver pulled out of the driveway. As Tristan struggled to keep up the conversation, he found his mind speculating on Stewart's whereabouts.

Was it coincidence that Stewart flew off to some mysterious destination to investigate something so top secret he couldn't even tell Rachel? Maybe he was jumping to conclusions, thinking the worst. Or perhaps he was right on the money and Stewart was in Cleveland snooping around and asking questions about him.

The anxiety was agonizing. He knew Stewart could very

well be uncovering the horrible truth at that very moment. He would most certainly expose Tristan for the lying, manipulating creature he was.

Keeping his eyes focused ahead, he inadvertently missed out on most of the conversation.

"Tristan," Rachel called out loudly.

Tristan jerked his head in her direction, feeling the strain of her probing eyes. "What?"

"You seem like you're a million miles away. Is everything all right?"

"I'm sorry." He kissed her hand in an apologetic gesture. "I guess I'm letting my mind wander a bit."

"Anything I should be worried about?"

Noticing the uneasiness in her face, he could sense she was letting doubt creep in. "Rachel, I love you. My mind is set on that."

"You just look so upset about something. I wish you'd talk to me."

"I was thinking about Stewart actually."

"Stewart? Why?"

"I'm worried he's going to start trouble between us. You know how he is. He's so possessive of you, not that I blame him, really. The poor guy is so lovesick, it's pathetic."

"Tristan, get to the point," Rachel demanded.

"Oh, right. Well, I think he's gone off somewhere to plot against us."

"Plot against us? Stewart may be a little competitive, but he's not vindictive," she rebuked. "Besides, he was the one that broke up with me in the first place."

"He broke up with you?"

"Don't sound so surprised. You're giving me a complex."

"I'm sorry. It's just that he's been so determined to get you back."

"Yeah, well, he found out the grass wasn't greener on the other side."

"Rachel, you're making me squirm over here."

"I know. It's kind of fun to watch," she giggled.

"Ugh!"

"Okay, I'll tell you, but it's really not that interesting. Our fathers were old friends, so it didn't seem strange when we started to date." Rachel looked over at Tristan. "Are you sure you want to know all this?" she asked.

"Keep going," he encouraged.

"Well, we dated for almost a year. Then one day he pulls me into my office and tells me that he's met someone else. I found out later they'd been dating behind my back for a few months, and Lynnette was, well, kind of plain. I know it sounds funny, but I think I would have been less hurt if she'd been beautiful.

"Anyway, her family is also in the medical-supply business and our biggest competitor. Right off the bat, her father asked Stewart to come work for him as the vice president of his company. I'm still not sure in what order that happened. I guess it doesn't really matter now."

"So Daddy's Little Angel finally found a man, and Daddy was prepared to make it permanent. Huh, go figure," Tristan growled, hearing the hurt in Rachel's voice.

"Something like that," she agreed, perking up a little. "To make a long story short, Stewart went to work for Lynnette's father and broke things off with me."

"After a few months, out of the blue, he starts calling me again, asking if I wanted to get together with him. When I asked about Lynnette, Stewart just said it didn't work out. Come to find out, her father never put him on as vice president of the company. It was more like vice president of the mail-room." Rachel laughed at the thought. "Somehow he talked my father into hiring him back."

"And you? Did you want him back as well?" Tristan pried.

"Haven't you been paying attention? Just who do you think is chasing whom?"

"That explains a lot," Tristan mused.

The light was shinning on so many different things all at once, and it was making his head spin. It definitely explained

Rachel's low self-esteem and her reluctance to let anyone close to her.

"I assumed Stewart was a snotty little rich kid. He's not?"

"Not even close," Rachel said. "His father and mother run a small catering business out of their home, barely enough to pay the mortgage. My father put Stewart on as a favor to his dad. Otherwise, Stewart would still be a bag boy at Walgreens."

Well, well, well. The tables have certainly turned, Tristan thought. Perhaps he wasn't the only one after Rachel's money. All along, it had been a competition over the money, not Rachel. If Tristan hadn't been guilty of the same act, he would have been furious.

"So Stew thought he would make it big if he married this other girl, only to find out it was really a step down." Tristan chuckled, shaking his head at the irony. "Who's the gold digger now?" he mumbled under his breath.

"Well, now you know the whole story."

Reaching over, Tristan rubbed his knuckles softly down the side of her cheek. "I can't say I'm not glad he broke up with you. But I am sorry he hurt you."

Not only did Stewart break her heart, but it had always been about the money, never about Rachel. How could he have missed it? The threats, the intimidation—it was all so clear to him now.

✶ ✶ ✶

Standing in the middle of Penn Station, Tristan wrapped his arms around Rachel. They embraced in a long, meaningful kiss. He released her lips but kept his arms tightly around her.

Affectionately caressing his back with her hands, Rachel snuggled her head into his shoulder. Tristan could sense she felt the same way about their parting. In her arms there was a security he'd never experienced before. It was like nothing else mattered.

Finally releasing her from his arms, he looked into her eyes with a deep, sincere stare. "I love you," he whispered.

"And I love you."

Standing motionless as he watched her walk toward a cab to take her home, Tristan could hardly wait to see her again. Everything was perfect.

＊ ＊ ＊

Slamming the door shut, Tristan dumped his bag on the living room floor. He collapsed on the couch and rested his feet on the coffee table. Cole sat across the room slumped over, his cell phone in one hand.

"I just spent the last two days in heaven," Tristan announced proudly. He sat up and rested his elbows on his knees, ignoring Cole's unpleasant stare. "She loves me Cole! Can you believe it? Me! *She* loves *me!* Wow, I never knew how great those words could make you feel." He rubbed his hands through his hair, still unable to comprehend that she wanted him.

"Um . . . Tristan, I need to talk to you for a minute," Cole said softly. "It's about your dad."

Jumping up from the couch, Tristan headed for the kitchen. "Whatever it is, I don't want to hear it. I'm in too good of a mood," he said. He grabbed a soda from the fridge and popped open the top. When he returned, he noticed Cole's face was paler than usual. He wasn't smiling like he usually did when Tristan made a crack about his father. Instead, he held a blank stare.

"Okay, what is it this time?" Tristan asked. "Does he want money again?" Tristan stood a few feet in front of Cole, still trying to figure out why he looked so upset. "Did he get thrown in jail again?"

"Tristan, your father . . . "

"What?"

"He had a heart attack."

"But he's okay, right?"

Cole's eyes filled with tears as he shook his head. "He didn't make it, Tristan."

"Didn't . . . make . . . it?"

Tristan felt his whole body suddenly go numb, and he fell back on the couch. His eyes searched out Cole's, pleading for him to tell him it was all a horrible joke. But there was only sadness in Cole's face.

"He's . . . dead?" Tristan gasped.

Cole nodded his head again. He stood and walked over to the couch and sat down next to his friend. He put one hand on Tristan's back to comfort him.

"I'm sorry," Cole whispered.

"When?"

"Last night. My dad called. He said . . . he said the neighbor found him." Cole carefully took the can of soda from Tristan's trembling hand and sat it down on the coffee table.

Tristan sat very still, trying to comprehend what was happening. He knew he was sitting there listening to Cole, but at the same time, it all seemed like a dream. His ears began to ring slightly. He wasn't sure if he wanted to pass out or throw up. The tears began to well up in his eyes, and a sorrowful ache collected in the middle of his chest.

"I can't believe it," Tristan said. His breathing became heavy and tears streamed down his face. He quickly wiped them away. "I didn't think I would react this way. I always thought I would be happy when he was finally gone."

"Tristan, he's your father. Of course you're going to react this way."

"Yeah, I guess." Tristan inhaled deeply and shook off the devastation. The hate soon returned. He refused to shed another tear for the man who cared more about his whisky than his own son. "I better see if I can find my sister," he said.

"Do you know where she is?"

"Not really. I've got an old number I can try, and I'll need to arrange some kind of burial." He stood up from the couch, swaying from the woozy feeling in his head. "I'm not even sure what he wanted," he said. "We never even talked about the small stuff, let alone anything important."

"I'll call the airline and book us on the next flight out," Cole said, interrupting Tristan's thoughts.

"Yeah, right, we'll need to fly home. Okay . . . well . . . I guess I'll go pack . . . again."

Tristan went to his bedroom, sat on the edge of the bed, and ran his hands over his burning face. He took a long, deep breath to calm his nerves and restore brain activity. With his mother out of the picture and no word from his sister, there was no family left for him.

His father had been an only child. He had lost his parents in a tragic car accident ten years ago. The only other family was his father's aunt, who was probably dead, for all Tristan knew. She lived somewhere in the northwest—or maybe it was the southwest—he couldn't be sure.

There was no one to call, no one that cared. There would be exactly eight people at the funeral: himself, Austin, Austin's parents, Cole and his parents, and the pastor. His father had no friends, no colleagues, not even a dog. *Unless the drunks at the bar were considered friends*, Tristan thought bitterly.

Would the pastor want him to speak, to say something wonderful about his father? What could he say? That the man was mean, arrogant, selfish, and lazy? That should leave the pastor speechless.

As he unpacked his clothes and repacked some clean ones, he thought of someone he needed to call. The one person he wanted to talk to more than anyone. Rachel.

The phone rang twice, and then he heard her voice bubbling over with enthusiasm on the other end. "Tristan, I wasn't expecting you to call so soon. Not that I mind, I was—"

"Hey Rachel, I need to leave town for a few days," Tristan interrupted.

"Why? Where are you going?"

"I need to go home. My father passed away last night." His tone was flat and uncaring, and he was left wondering why his emotions were so conflicting.

"Oh, Tristan, I'm so sorry," Rachel said. "Is there anything I can do? Do you want me to come with you?"

"You need to be at work. I'll be fine, really. I'll go take care of this and be back before you can miss me."

"That's not possible. I miss you already."

"I miss you too. It's just something I need to do by myself. Do you understand?"

"I do. I just wish I could be there for you."

"I need you more than you know, but I'll need you even more when I get back."

"I'll be here."

"Do you promise?"

"Of course," Rachel said with confusion in her voice.

"Will you say it?" Tristan continued. "I need to hear it."

"I promise, Tristan," Rachel said. "I'll be here when you get back."

"You don't know how that comforts me. You mean the world to me, Rachel. I don't know how I could live without you in my life. You are like air to me."

"I feel the same way about you, Tristan."

"I love you, Rachel."

"I love you too."

Tristan hung up the phone just as Cole and Austin came in. "Ready?" Cole asked, holding a large brown suitcase in his hand.

Nodding his head, Tristan picked his bag up off the bed and followed them out the door. He was about to face his biggest challenge yet—burying his father and laying to rest all of his anger and resentment.

Twenty-two

Taking significantly small steps, each one awakening a painful memory, Tristan slowly walked across the grounds of the Cleveland Cemetery. He was dressed in his best pair of black slacks and a black silk button-up shirt. His feet felt overwhelmingly heavy, as if they were dragging the weight of twenty-five years behind him.

Emotions he'd once locked away now came rushing to the surface. At that moment, he was pleased his father was dead. There would be no more disappointing looks. No more belittling remarks. No more useless attempts to gain his approval.

Tristan abruptly stopped a few feet from the grave site. The cemetery was deserted. The mortician had brought his father's body up a little earlier, anticipating the arrival of friends and family.

Taking another step, he could see the blue casket sitting on metal posts above the hole in the ground. Flowers lay on top of the casket and several bouquets surrounded the site. They were all compliments of Cole and Austin's parents. If it had been up to Tristan, he would have sat a bottle of whisky on top of the coffin and called it good.

Tristan chuckled when he saw the dozen or more folding chairs that were lined up in front of the grave. It gave the impression of a professional and honorable burial, one which his father was not worthy of.

Pushing the hesitation aside, Tristan walked to the side of the casket. It wasn't the most elaborate one available, but it was what he could afford on the eighteen-month payment plan they'd put him on. It figured his father would leave him in debt. *Even after he's dead, he expects me to support him*, Tristan thought. He swallowed an obscene word before it had a chance to escape his lips.

Sitting down in one of the chairs near the casket, he leaned up, placing his elbows on his knees. He was totally alone. Not even Cole and Austin had arrived. He stared at the casket as reality finally sank in. His father was really gone—his life was over.

"I can't believe I'm sitting here," Tristan said, his voice unsteady and weak.

As he thought about the past and his childhood, his hostility grew stronger. He could feel the years of abuse working their way to the surface.

"You deserved to die alone! Do you know that?" Tristan shouted. "You never cared about anyone but yourself!" His tone became rigid as his mind conjured up the images of his abuse-filled childhood.

Breathing deeply, he found it difficult to hold back his burning resentment. What he couldn't tell his father in life, he would now tell him in death.

"I worked so hard to please you. I wanted you to be proud of me, but nothing I did was ever good enough for you; nothing, because no matter what I did, Mom wasn't coming back."

Tristan wrestled to move the words past his lips. For years his anger had been festering like an unhealed wound. Now, unable to evade the deep infestation any longer, Tristan released the bitter monster from within.

"I hate you!" he cried, as the tears began to collect in his eyes. "I hate you for never allowing me to be a kid! For showing up drunk to every school activity! For criticizing everything I ever did and for the unjustified abuse! You were never a father! You were some embarrassing bum I had to support!"

Stopping for a moment to take a breath, he walked closer to the casket. The adrenaline surged through him, and his body began to tremble.

"And most of all, I hate you for holding me responsible for Mom's decision! It wasn't my fault Mom left!" He tightened his fists, confronting his father with all the things that had tormented his existence.

"Do you hear me, you son of a—!"

Falling to his knees, Tristan's unrestrained sobs broke the surface, sending tears of anger, hurt, and sorrow streaming down his face.

"It wasn't my fault! I didn't make her leave! I was just a kid, and yet you condemned me to a life of guilt! How could you do that to your own son?"

Out of the gloomy mist that seemed to engulf him, a friendly hand reached out and gently touched his shoulder.

"It's all right, Tristan," Cole said.

Pulling himself off the ground, Tristan instantly reached out and grabbed Cole. He collapsed in his friend's arms and released his unexpected grief.

★ ★ ★

Tristan reached for another box from the top shelf above his father's bed. This one was crammed to the top with papers. He'd been going through boxes and boxes of old pictures, newspaper clippings of various events, and other miscellaneous items.

The funeral services had finished around ten o'clock that morning, and Tristan was anxious to get things straightened up and moved out of the old double-wide mobile home. He was looking forward to closing the door and walking away—once and for all.

It wasn't too difficult, considering his father owned very little. The furniture was old and worthless. He'd already packed up his clothes to donate to Goodwill. Now the only thing left to do was go through the boxes to determine if any of them contained anything worth keeping.

So far he'd thrown out or burned everything, including old bills, bank statements, and letters from his sister, Kathy. Tristan was ready to leave it all behind.

After Kathy had left home, she wrote once a week. She let them know everything about her life—where she was and how she was doing. Eventually, the letters died off and she didn't bother with so much as a phone call. Tristan knew in his heart that she hated their father as much as he did, but it still devastated him to lose her the same way he'd lost his mother.

Tristan had tried his best to find her. The only phone number he knew of had been disconnected, and there was no forwarding address. It was as if she had vanished from the face of the earth. Perhaps that was what she wanted.

With a sigh, Tristan sat back down on the bed and brushed some dust off the top of a small box. At one point it had some writing on the top of it, but the blue pen was now faded and hard to read. Tristan opened the flaps and began to pick through the old papers that had been jammed tightly into the box.

Partway through, Tristan inspected the papers more closely. He instantly recognized the aged drawings right away. The colorful pictures were produced inside a school classroom when he was just a kid. There were also old report cards, some awards he'd received through the years, and photos of his high school and college graduations. His father had kept everything.

Tristan looked over the pile in disbelief. He'd just assumed his father threw everything out. His father never commented on anything he ever did, let alone praised him for his accomplishments. Still, here was everything he'd ever done, right down to the Father's Day card Tristan had hand-crafted for him when he was nine.

As Tristan placed all the papers back into the box, he thought about the good times he and his father had shared. He hadn't thought about those memories in years. There were just a few memories, but they still hung around in the back of his mind. They were memories Tristan had thought would never surface again.

There was one last place to go through—the drawer of his father's nightstand. Tristan knew his father kept important things in that drawer, because it was the one place in the entire house that was off-limits to him. He'd always wondered what secrets were kept inside that tiny compartment. Whatever they were, they must have meant a lot to his father. Now with his father gone, Tristan could finally investigate the mystery.

Reaching over, he tugged on the handle. The drawer made a funny squeaking noise as it opened. Tristan looked around the room, almost feeling a sense a betrayal. Inside the drawer was a large yellow envelope that took up every space across the bottom of the tiny drawer.

He pulled out the envelope and inspected it carefully. The tape on the outside was old and no longer held the flap shut. Tristan opened the top and looked inside. There was an old folded-up piece of paper and a smaller white envelope. He reached in and pulled out the piece of paper, gently unfolding it.

The fading lined paper looked worn, like it had been read over and over again. Tristan skimmed through the barely legible print. Halfway down the page, tears began to flood his eyes.

It was a letter, written on Father's Day of 1994, by Tristan Taylor. He was only ten years old at the time. It was a letter of praise and recognition. He had told his father in writing how much he loved and appreciated him.

Tristan recalled the day he handed his father the letter. He wanted his father to take him in his arms and tell him how much he loved him. He wanted it more than anything in the world. Instead, his father thanked him while stuffing the letter into his shirt pocket before walking away. Tristan remembered how devastated he was. He vowed never to tell his father that he loved him again, and he never did.

Wiping the tears from his eyes, Tristan put the letter beside him on the bed and pulled out the small envelope. The envelope was addressed to him. There was no return address, and the stamp had never been used. For whatever reason, it had never been sent.

Inside the envelope, he found another letter. Taking a deep breath, he exhaled slowly and unfolded the paper. His rapidly beating heart thumped hard against his chest when he saw his name at the top, and the tears fell from his eyes all over again.

> Dear Tristan,
>
> I don't know where to begin. Expressing myself has never been one of my strong points. Let's face it, I don't have many. But you, my son, are my one strong point. You are everything I wish I could be——compassionate, loyal, and hard-working. I am so proud of the man you've become. I wish I could take credit for that, but it was not because of me.
>
> When your mother deserted us, I lost my soul. She was my one true love, and when she left, she took my heart with her. When you find that one true love, hang on to it with all your might, because it may not come around again. Something I took for granted. Well, I'll stop rambling now and just tell you that I love you. I know I haven't been the kind of father you deserved, but I tried my best. I hope one day you can find it in your heart to forgive me.
>
> Love,
> Dad

Tristan sat staring at the letter with tears streaming down his face. "Why couldn't you have said that before?" Tristan sobbed. So many times he'd wanted to hear those words. So many times he'd wanted to feel his father's love for him. Now all he had was a piece of paper full of scribbled words.

He replaced both letters into the large envelope and set it in the box with the rest of the papers he planned on keeping. Releasing a heavy sigh, he secured the top of the box with some tape, sealing all of his anger and resentment inside.

Tristan finally understood how much his father suffered from losing his mother. Perhaps he never meant to turn mean and abusive, but living without her had altered him forever.

The letter sent a swarm of thoughts about his own life plummeting through his head. The concept that he was more like his father than he realized suddenly sunk deep into his soul.

Lying back on the bed, he stared at a small crack in the ceiling. He was becoming just like his father—resenting everyone around him for having more and angry at the world for the life he was harshly thrown into.

There was a slight hesitation when his mind wandered to Rachel. In the beginning, he hadn't cared who he hurt, just as long as he got what he wanted. But something had changed. She had ignited a spark in him. His way of thinking, his objectives, even his faith had been transformed.

The room seemed to get colder as the reality of his deception sliced through his heart. "What have I done?" he whispered. There was no other way to cleanse his conscience of the tortuous guilt he'd carried around for far too long—it was time for Rachel to know the truth.

Getting to his feet, Tristan shoved the small brown box under one arm and started for the front door. He paused to take one last look around at the empty space he'd once called home. The musty smell of stale cigarette smoke and beer filled the air, the odor of the life he was leaving behind. Saying good-bye was harder than Tristan expected, but the pain was insignificant compared to the good-bye that was still to come.

Driving to the cemetery was not as difficult as it had been earlier that day. Tristan's emotions were now level and clear. He knew exactly what he needed to do to set his mind free.

Getting down on to his knees, Tristan gently ran his hand

across the top of the temporary gravestone. "Dad," he said softly. "I'm sorry about earlier. I was angry. Well, mostly hurt, but I'm ready to leave it all behind and move on with my life. You see, I met a girl in New York. Rachel is so wonderful, Dad. I know you'd like her. She's opened my eyes and awakened something in me that I never thought existed. She is my one true love and, if she'll still have me, I'm going to marry her."

Pulling himself to his feet, Tristan looked down at the fresh grave. He fought back the tears, finally coming to terms with his true emotions.

"I love you, Dad," he said sincerely. "I forgive you, so you can rest in peace."

✯ ✯ ✯

When Tristan walked into the airport to meet Cole and Austin, he felt a sense of release from the burdens he'd carried with him for most of his life. It was a self-proclaimed freedom that sent his soul soaring. Letting go of his anger and resentment had caused him to see himself in a new light.

Cole was the first to meet him at the terminal. Cole walked toward him with a peculiar look on his face, one that Tristan couldn't quite make out, but it sent a cold chill down his spine.

"Dude, what's wrong?" Tristan asked.

"It's Stewart," Cole said heavily. "I just found out from my father that someone has been snooping around, asking a lot of questions. From his description, I would bet my life it was Stewart."

Gritting his teeth in anger, Tristan clutched his fists tightly together. "Yeah, it's Stewart all right," he said.

"You don't seem surprised?"

"Rachel said he'd left town to investigate something. I kind of already had a feeling what he was up to."

"What are you going to do?"

"Try and beat him to Rachel," Tristan said with urgency. "She needs to hear the truth from me."

Twenty-three

When the elevator doors parted, Tristan bolted down the hallway, eager to get to Rachel and tell her the truth.

Stopping in front of the closed door, he took a deep breath and then gave it a soft tap. At Rachel's voice beckoning him, he turned the knob and pushed it open. What he saw next brought his heart to an abrupt halt.

Rachel sat behind her desk with tears streaming down her sickly, pale face. Stewart stood next to her, a comforting hand around her shoulder.

The comprehension that he was too late cut so deeply that Tristan had to gasp for air. He ignored Stewart's boastful expression and focused on Rachel. Her eyes were red and swollen and her bottom lip quivered. She stared at him, speechless, almost begging for him to deny the accusations that had been brought against him.

The hurt in her eyes tortured him terribly. Tristan felt the excruciating pain rip through his chest like thousands of sharp needles extracting the blood until his heart was an empty vessel.

Tristan just stood there, immobilized by his agony. He'd just lost his father and had forever buried the man he once was. Now his future hung in the balance with his past jeopardizing the only thing he had left to live for.

Watching her every move and reading every facial expression, Tristan tried to see into her thoughts. Rachel stood from the chair and balanced herself against the desk with one hand. Stewart grabbed her by the arm to assist her. His touch sent a vibe of jealousy and hatred gushing through Tristan's bloodstream.

"Rachel, I can take care of him," Stewart said, smirking over her head.

Shaking her head, Rachel slowly walked over to Tristan's frozen statue. She stood close, coming face to face with him. She kept quiet for a moment, her eyes focused on his. He could almost hear her mind's plea for truth and her broken heart's demand for justice.

"Tell me!" she hissed through clenched teeth. "I want to hear it from you!"

Her hostility bit at his tortured mind, leaving little hope of reconciliation.

Opening his mouth, the truth came gushing out like hot lava, burning his throat and scorching what was left of his heart.

"Rachel, I've tried to tell you a thousand times," he began.

"Liar!" Stewart shouted.

"You're not a member of the Church?" she asked.

"No."

"You lied to me?"

"Yes," he said, keeping his eyes locked with hers. "Rachel, I—"

"Was it about the money? About getting my father's inheritance?"

"At first, but now—"

Rachel reached and slapped Tristan across the face. He kept his eyes to the floor for a few seconds. The sting to his face was less painful than the blow to his heart.

"You're despicable!" she roared. "I never want to see you again!"

Rachel started for the door, and Stewart came around the desk to confront him.

"Rachel, I love you," Tristan declared.

"Yeah, right," Stewart snickered, folding his arms.

Stopping at the door, Rachel took a deep breath. She kept her back toward him, almost as if she were afraid to look at him for fear she might be lured back into his trap.

"I . . . don't . . . believe you," she said, emphasizing each word like it was a struggle to decipher the truth from the lie.

When she left the room, Tristan stood, still frozen to the floor. "Well, consider this game over," Stewart mocked. "I guess I win!" he boasted.

Tristan turned to Stewart. He should have been infuriated with him, outraged that he destroyed his life. Instead, Tristan was filled with gratitude. He was unexpectedly thankful that Stewart would be there for Rachel, to help pick up the pieces of her broken heart. Even if Stewart wanted the money more than he wanted her, she would not be alone, and right now that was all Tristan had to hold on to.

"Don't hurt her, Stewart," Tristan said in a calm, even tone. "Even if it's just about the money. Don't hurt her. She doesn't deserve that."

"You have it all wrong, buddy." Stewart smirked again. "I care for Rachel. The money's just an added bonus. Now that you're out of the picture, I get both."

"Money isn't the key to happiness. I used to think that way, but I was wrong." He placed his hand on Stewart's shoulder, causing his former enemy jump. "Don't you see, Stewart? Rachel is much more valuable. She is more precious than gold or silver. Those things are temporal, but Rachel can be with you forever. At least I used to think so." Tristan sighed and shook his head. He dropped his hand from Stewart's shoulder and headed for the door.

"Well, at least you put up a good fight."

Shaking his head in disappointment, Tristan left the office and boarded the elevator, anxious to escape this horrible nightmare once and for all.

Heading back to his apartment, he stared at the lights in the subway tunnel as they flew by, trying to collect his thoughts before explaining things to Cole and Austin.

His body felt numb, like he was going through the motions, but he wasn't really there. It was as if he were caught in one of those hideous soap operas where lies are revealed, lives are destroyed, and the villain ends up with the girl. But there was no chance to change things, because he'd been written out of the script.

Tristan opened the door to his apartment and took a few steps inside. Every muscle in his body hurt. He felt like he'd just been beaten up in a fight, only in his case, his heart and soul bore the bruises instead of his face and body.

"Hey, how did things go?" Cole asked. He was the first one out of his chair to meet Tristan at the door. Austin stayed silent and watched from a distance.

"It's over," Tristan announced without feeling. "We can go back home. There's nothing left for us here."

"Tristan, I'm so sorry, man." Cole placed his hand on Tristan's shoulder.

"Yeah," Austin agreed, coming over to meet the two of them. "Is there anything we can do?"

"No. I'm just sorry I blew the plan," Tristan said. "I'll go pack so we can get out of this miserable city."

"Um, actually Tristan, I found out this morning I landed that job over at Ridges," Cole said. "But, you know, we'll stick by you no matter what. If you still want to leave, we'll be right behind you."

"Oh, you . . . got the job. That's really great," Tristan grunted, trying his best to sound upbeat, but finding it came out more like tragic disappointment. "No . . . no, we should definitely stay now. After all, this is what we came here for, right?"

"Will you stay with us?" Austin asked.

"Of course I'll stay," he huffed. "You're my best friends. Besides, someone's got to keep the two of you out of trouble."

"You'll find a job, Tristan," Cole reassured him. "It's just a matter of time."

"I think I'll just go lie down for a while. You know, collect my thoughts," Tristan said.

"That's a good idea. Let us know if we can get you anything," Cole said with a concerned tone.

As he walked away, Cole and Austin shot each other a worried look. They could see there had been an instant change in Tristan. He was emotionless and cold, like there was nothing left inside. Rachel had shattered not only his heart but also his soul, leaving him an empty shell.

Tristan quickly undressed and crawled into bed, enjoying the warm, comfortable feeling of his fleece blankets as he threw them on top of him. It was a safety zone from the harsh reality, one he didn't intend on leaving any time soon.

Pulling the covers up over his head and curling up into a ball, he secured himself from the outside world. Right then and there, Tristan decided this was his new home. It was the next best thing to death itself.

Twenty-four

"Time to get up, sunshine!" Cole squealed in a high-pitched voice. "It's a beautiful day!"

Cole yanked opened the mini blinds covering Tristan's bedroom window as Austin pulled the covers from his motionless body.

"Come on, Tristan, we're taking you out to lunch today," Austin pleaded.

"Leave me alone," Tristan sulked, reaching for the covers. He hated the sun—it reminded him of Rachel's bright, enthusiastic face. He hated the warmth on his skin—it only reminded him of her soft touch. His only sanctuary was his dark, cold room where he could hibernate, shutting out the rest of the world so he could endure his state of misery alone.

"Tristan, you've been in bed for two weeks," Cole hissed. "You can't go on like this. It's unhealthy."

Finding his blankets, Tristan ripped them from Austin's fingers and hurled them back over his head. "Says who?" he asked, his voice muffled by the covers.

Both Cole and Austin jumped in the middle of the bed and began to shake the bed. "We do!" they yelled in unison.

"And we're not going to let you curl up and die a disgraceful and painful death!" Cole wailed.

"You can't help me! Just go away and leave me alone!"

Tristan argued. "I'll get up tomorrow."

"We're not the only ones worried about you. Bishop Anderson called today. He said you missed your appointment with him, and he wants you to call him. I didn't even realize you were talking to him. What's that all about anyway?" asked Cole, trying to get Tristan talking.

"That doesn't matter anymore either."

"Come on, Tristan," Austin said. "No girl is worth this."

The covers suddenly flew off, and Tristan sat straight up in bed. His hair was a ratted mess, and his bloodshot eyes were wide with fury as he glared up at Austin.

"Rachel was not just some girl!" he yelled. His face was growing as red as his eyes. "Don't you get it? I don't care if I live or die! Without her, there's just no point! So get out of my room and leave me alone!"

He threw the covers over his head again, hoping he'd gotten through to them. "We'll leave you alone," said Cole. "For now."

☆ ☆ ☆

The weeks slipped by while Tristan fought to gain some perspective on his life. Cole was right. He couldn't just stay in bed forever, although the idea was tempting.

Every thought he had was about Rachel. Every dream and every nightmare revolved around her. She consumed every space in his mind, making it impossible to try to forget her. Instead, he let the memories torture him. His memories were painful reminders of how he'd destroyed her life.

Wearing nothing but his red silk boxers and a white tank top, Tristan walked to the kitchen. He shivered as his bare feet touched the cold tile. The smell of rain filled the apartment, filling his head with another agonizing memory of Rachel.

Nonetheless, he was grateful the sky was covered in dark gray clouds. They hid the bright, hopeful rays of the sun. The downpour sounded like hard, wet pebbles against the rooftop. The gloom of the day matched his mood, making it easier to get out of bed.

After pouring a bowl of cereal, he went to the living room and turned on the television. He flopped down on the couch and crossed his ankles as he placed them on the coffee table.

Flipping through the channels, he came to the program he was looking for. Soap operas were his newfound salvation. Watching the bizarre circumstances of the imaginary characters made his chaotic life seem less appalling.

It had been six weeks, two days, and three hours since his heart had been crushed into pieces and scooped out of his chest. He'd kept precise track of every day he'd been without Rachel.

Although his life had ended, everyone else around him kept moving forward. Cole's job was going great. It was what he'd been searching for. His second week working there, he met a girl and was now enjoying an honest relationship. Austin was promoted to sous chef at Bubba's, and strangely enough, was still seeing Marley. Tristan had given up trying to figure that one out.

For Tristan, one day flooded into the next without distinction. Days were something he had to get through in order to finally escape to his dark, secluded room, or as Cole liked to call it, "Tristan's chicken coop." He thought Tristan was acting like a coward by hiding away from the world to avoid hard times.

"Oh, come on, Joel!" Tristan shouted at the television. "You know she doesn't love Kirby. Fight for her! She loves you!" Placing his empty bowl on the coffee table, he clicked off the show. "What an idiot," he grumbled under his breath.

Out of the silence of the room, soft, incriminating whispers spoke up. _You're the idiot,_ they alleged. _You're spineless and deplorable. You should have fought for her._

Tristan realized it was his own delusional mind condemning him. Nevertheless, he verbally acknowledged the accusations, surrendering to the ridicule. "I _am_ an idiot!" Tristan yelled back into the silence, "for ever thinking I had a chance with her! I don't deserve her!"

The voices rang out inside his mind until he could take it no longer. "Leave me alone!" he growled.

Racing back to the safety of his chicken coop, he collapsed on the bed. He hated the hopelessness he'd been sucked into. It was like falling through a bottomless black hole, spiraling out of control without knowing if or when you would hit rock bottom.

Tristan placed his pillow over his head to drown out the torment that plagued his mind. Even worse than dwelling on his own misery was the realization of how much pain he'd caused Rachel, which was something he wondered if he would ever be able to live with.

✳ ✳ ✳

"Tristan," Cole called from what seemed like a million miles away. "Tristan, wake up!"

Rolling away from the annoying sound, Tristan stuffed a pillow over his head and groaned miserably, "Go away."

Cole pulled the pillow out of Tristan's hands and used it to smack him over the head.

"Knock it off!" Tristan bellowed. He sat up just in time to take another two whacks to the head. "What's your problem?"

"You want to know what my problem is?" Cole hissed, still holding the pillow in a threatening manner.

"Yeah!"

"*You're* my problem!" Cole shouted, and then he came down with one blow of the pillow after another. The constant beating finally forced Tristan from the bed. He stood on the opposite side, glaring at Cole with irritable confusion.

"Okay, I'm up! Is that what you wanted?" Tristan asked.

"It's a start."

Cole lowered the pillow, but Tristan could see by his stance that he was furious with him.

"What did I do?"

"Like you have to ask?"

"Come on, Cole. You know it hasn't been easy for me. Just give me some time."

"No! No more time, Tristan. Do you even know what day it is?"

"Tuesday?" Tristan asked, placing the palm of his hand against his sweaty forehead. He wondered what absurd thought was going through Cole's mind.

"Wrong! It's Friday!" Cole shouted across the bed. Throwing down the pillow, Cole folded his arms and walked around the bed to confront him. "And it's not just Friday. It's August nineteenth!"

"Cole, what in the world are you blabbering about?" Tristan took a few steps back, feeling a tiny bit apprehensive of Cole's sudden outburst.

"Not only have you been a catastrophic basket case, moping around the apartment day after day feeling sorry for yourself, which is really pathetic I might add, but you forgot one important factor."

"What are you talking about?" Tristan urged in a strained voice.

"In exactly two months from today, Rachel will turn twenty-five."

"So?"

"So, get off you lazy, good-for-nothing butt, and go rescue the girl of your dreams from losing her father's inheritance!"

"Did you forget one small detail? She *hates* me!" Tristan roared. He swiftly darted around Cole and leaped for his bed. Cole caught Tristan in mid-flight and wrapped his arms around his waist.

Cole tackled him to the floor. The blow to the hardwood floor knocked the wind out of both of them and only aggravated Tristan that much more. Cole had no right to butt into his affairs! If Tristan wanted to throw himself a pity party, he had every right.

The harder Tristan struggled to break free, the more Cole fought to restrain him.

"She *doesn't* hate you!" Cole wheezed, finally managing to secure Tristan in a headlock. "You need to go talk to her!"

"No!" Tristan panted from within the clutch of Cole's arms. "I'm not going to hurt her anymore!"

"You stubborn, hard-headed, dim-witted jerk!"

Tristan pried Cole's fingers apart and finally broke free. He crawled to the other side of the room and leaned against the wall.

"Now I see why they call that a choke-hold." Tristan coughed.

"Tristan, have you heard anything I've said?"

"Sure, I'm stubborn, hard-headed, and a major jerk. I couldn't agree with you more. Tell me something I don't already know."

Tristan pulled his knees up and rested his arms across them. He relaxed his head against the wall and stared up at the ceiling.

"How about I remind you who you really are?"

"Please don't. I'm quite aware of the monster I've become," Tristan said. "I should've listened to you, Cole, but regrets don't mean squat."

"That's what I'm talking about."

"Regrets?"

"No, the fact that you didn't listen to me." Cole walked over and squatted down in front of Tristan. "For as long as I've known you, you have never followed the rules. Not once. When others went right, you went left. If you were told you couldn't do something, you set out to prove them wrong. I've never known you to give up on anything. You used to fight and fight until you came out on top."

"Not this time."

"Why, because you got caught up in a lie?"

"No!"

"Because you found something that, for once, meant more to you than money?"

"No!"

"Then what is it, Tristan? Which excuse are you going to use this time?"

"I'm scared!" Tristan blurted out. He stared into Cole's eyes, angry at him for forcing him to admit it.

"Scared of what? Allowing yourself to finally be happy?"

"No!"

"Scared of the money then? Or perhaps it's—"

"I'm terrified of being rejected, of losing her all over again. And most of all, I'm scared to death to look into her eyes and see the hurt that I caused." He focused on Cole, who seemed surprised at first, but then smiled. "What, you don't think I get scared?"

"No, no, I know you do. I just never thought I'd hear you admit it." He plopped down on the floor next to Tristan and crossed his legs. "So you're going to let your fears control you?"

"Like a marionette."

"Wow."

"What?"

"She's changed you more than I thought."

"I wish she could see that."

"You need to tell her."

"She won't believe me. I've lied and deceived her. Why should she believe anything I say now?"

"Because the truth is, you love her. That kind of truth can dispute any lie." Cole stood up from the floor and patted Tristan on the shoulder. "Don't give up so easily, Tristan. I've seen you fight harder for a cab."

Cole walked to the door and then paused. He looked back at Tristan, who was sitting despondently, an emotionless ruin of the free-spirited friend he once knew.

"Hey, Tristan, just one more thing, and I don't mean any disrespect when I say this," Cole said. "You postponed making amends with your father until it was too late. Don't make that mistake with Rachel. The only thing worse than living with regret is being haunted by the what ifs. Living with the unknown can be much worse than rejection."

The words "what if" rang out in Tristan's mind long after Cole left the room, sending Tristan's thoughts into a whirlwind. That tiny phrase insinuated a life of speculation and wonder. It implied an alternate future, a destination into the unknown. It was that little voice inside his head that mocked him, reminding Tristan of what could have been.

Tristan wasn't looking forward to a life of speculation. After all, Cole had a valid point. Tristan never gave up on anything so easily, not even the biggest of challenges.

When he was accepted into Ohio State, he had little money for tuition, but determination burned deep within him. Working full-time at nights and going to school during the day took its toll on him. Nevertheless, he worked hard to get through the four years of school and graduated at the top of his class.

Tristan had always figured his fear of failure had come from his childhood. His mother and father had failed him as parents, and his father had failed as a caregiver and provider. From his parents to his career, his whole life had consisted of one letdown after another.

A life of disappointment was the driving factor behind his determination to prove to himself, as well as others, that he could succeed.

So why now? Why was Rachel different from all his other challenges? Where was the strength he'd relied on so many times before? He couldn't help but wonder whether it was fear or ego keeping him away. He'd never been the type to go crawling back on his hands and knees to seek forgiveness.

Pulling himself from his frozen state on the floor, Tristan moved to the bed and sat down, running his hands through his hair. Breathing deeply, he tried to sort out the erratic thoughts that were running wildly through his head.

Glancing over to the nightstand, he noticed the Book of Mormon lying where he'd left it the night before last. He took it in his hand and cradled it like it was made of gold.

Besides hiding in bed, reading had been his only other escape from the torment of losing Rachel. Although he'd missed his appointments with the missionaries, the stories in the Book of Mormon made his spirit swell inside him. It was a sensation that comforted him and gave him hope for the future.

Opening the book somewhere in the middle, he flipped through the pages, convinced he would find the guidance he was seeking, when he came across a scripture that put everything into perspective, and he knew just what he had to do. It was Alma 38:11: "See that ye are not lifted up unto pride; yea, see that ye do not boast in your own wisdom, nor of your much strength."

Twenty-five

The elevator ascended a little more quickly than he would have liked, and Tristan tried to concentrate on the reasons he was there. Instead, his mind kept wandering to the worst case scenario.

Sure, there was a good possibility Rachel would slap him across the face again, appalled that he would have the gall to show up after what he'd done. Furthermore, it was likely that he would resemble something of a blubbering idiot in a speedy attempt to explain himself before she had security throw him out.

The odds were stacked against him, but his determination had been restored, making the ride to the fourteenth floor a little more bearable.

The elevator came to a halt, and the doors opened, leaving Tristan no other choice but to exit. It was after seven, and the office staff had left for the day. However, Tristan knew Rachel well enough to know she would still be there, working late as usual.

Looking down the short corridor, he could see a tiny speck of light shining from the open door. For the first time since he'd left his apartment, self-doubt crept into his mind.

"What if, Tristan," he whispered, reminding himself of the torturous life he would lead if he didn't walk in there and tell her exactly how he felt.

Taking a deep breath and exhaling slowly, he inched his way down the hall. Perspiration collected on his forehead, and he quickly wiped it away with his hand. The air suddenly seemed extremely hot and muggy, making it that much harder to breathe.

He wished now that he'd made a different choice in apparel. His navy blue fleece pullover stuck to his damp skin, and his blue jeans felt like hot packs against his thighs.

When he reached Rachel's office, he peeked inside the door into the room, spotting her sitting at her desk. Her long, wavy brown hair hung down around her shoulders, and she pushed it out of her face every now and then. She was dressed more casually than usual.

With her pale complexion and the dark circles under her worn eyes, he could see that she had been suffering from lack of sleep, just as he had. Regardless, she was every bit as beautiful. It was the face that had never left his mind, and his heart nearly jumped out of his chest just seeing her again.

Deciding against announcing his arrival, Tristan walked in, watching her every move. He cleared his throat and attempted to speak.

"Uh . . . Rachel? Can I talk to you for a minute?" he stuttered, sounding pathetically weak and helpless.

Looking up from her stack of papers, her eyes met his, and it was as if the last two months never existed. Her eyes gleamed, and her face lit up with joy. She eagerly raced to be in his arms.

At least, that's what Tristan imagined.

In reality, Rachel merely stared at him with an expression devoid of anger or surprise. It was the look of someone who had just found something that had been missing for a long time. It seemed to be relief. Although Tristan could still see the hurt underneath, he was grateful the anger had vanished.

Without speaking, she nodded her head for him to come in. Tristan closed the door and forced his feet to move across the room to a chair in front of her desk.

He sat on the edge of the chair and looked into her eyes, searching for the words he'd rehearsed.

"Rachel, I . . . I just want to explain some things to you, and then I'll leave, and you'll never have to see me again," he began.

He felt awkward and uneasy, but he kept his eyes locked with hers in an attempt to make her understand that everything he was about to say was the truth.

"When I came to New York, I thought it was a second chance for me. I yearned for success, I wanted money . . . I was out to prove I wasn't a failure. When things didn't turn around for me, I became desperate and impulsive. When I saw you in the restaurant and learned of your circumstances, I lost all perspective on right and wrong. I only thought of myself and getting what I thought I deserved."

Taking another couple of deep breaths, he broke eye contact and looked at the floor, too ashamed to hold up his head. "The plan seemed perfect. Marry the girl, take the money, and live comfortably for the rest of my life." It sounded cold and heartless saying it out loud.

Swallowing the lump in his throat, Tristan looked back up into her tear-filled eyes, feeling her agony burn inside his chest.

"But something happened along the way. Something unexpected, something I didn't plan on. It was so powerful that not even money could hold a candle to it. I fell in love with you."

Watching Rachel wipe the tears from her face was tearing his heart into pieces. He'd caused her so much pain already. But he had to go on. She had to know everything.

"I owe you so much, Rachel. You have no idea how you've changed my life. You've opened my eyes to things I never would have found on my own. You taught me the principles of charity and compassion. You taught me the true meaning of gratitude. Most of all, you introduced me to the gospel."

"The gospel?" she questioned. "But I thought you lied about—"

"In the beginning, it was about playing the part like an actor reading his script. I worked hard to convince you I was someone I wasn't. But the more I read, the more intrigued I became. As I read the Book of Mormon, I felt like my soul was bursting into flames. It filled my heart with peace. I know that book is true. I can't explain how, I just know. So you see, I really owe you my life. You helped me discover the missing pieces. You helped me find . . . myself."

Keeping her eyes on the floor, Rachel couldn't control the tears streaming down her cheeks or the unrestrained sobs that came from deep within her chest.

"I'm . . . sorry," Tristan said softly, feeling the tears finally working their way into his own eyes. "For everything."

Tristan stood to leave, listening to her heartbreaking sobs echo through his head—just another painful reminder of the anguish he'd inflicted. She couldn't possibly hate him any more than he hated himself at that moment.

"You've given me so much, and yet I leave you with nothing but sorrow. I hope one day you can forgive me," he said. "I do love you, Rachel. More than anything in the world. That part was never a lie."

Between her tears and the anguish that tore at his heart, he couldn't stand to be in the same room with her any longer. He walked toward the door without looking back; he took his regrets with him and left the "what ifs" behind.

Just before Tristan made it to the door, Stewart came rushing in from the dark hallway. His eyes blazed with anger when he came face to face with Tristan.

"You have some nerve showing up here!" Stewart seethed. "You have five minutes to vacate the building before I call security and have you thrown out."

"Don't bother, Stewart. I was just leaving," Tristan replied.

"Wait," Rachel whimpered in a voice so low Tristan turned around to make sure the sound had come from her. "Stewart, I want to talk to Tristan alone."

"What? Why? Hasn't he done enough damage already?"

"Stewart, please," she said. She rose from her chair and circled the desk to stand next to Stewart.

"No! I'm not leaving you alone with this lying sack of . . ."

"Enough!" Tristan barged in. "This isn't about you or me anymore, Stewart. Don't you get it? We've hurt the one person we both care about the most. Rachel is not some trophy to be won over in a wrestling match. It's over between you and me. It's about Rachel and what she wants."

"You think you can come in here with your sweet talk and just expect her to forgive you?" Stewart said, incredulous. "You're crazy if you think she's going to—"

"Stewart!" Rachel interrupted. "Who I forgive, or don't forgive, is none of your business. This is between me and Tristan. Please leave. Now."

Smiling on the inside, Tristan moved out of the way and held his arm out in the direction of the door. Stewart gave Rachel one last look before heading for the door. He slammed it shut, leaving them alone once again.

"I can't blame him, you know?" Tristan remarked.

"For what? Pouting like a spoiled child?" Rachel asked.

"Well, when I said you were no trophy, I didn't mean you weren't still the ultimate prize. Any man would have to be out of his mind to let you go."

"Is that why you came back, to claim your prize?" Rachel asked, sounding annoyed and bitter.

Tristan shook his head and walked a little closer to her. "You're not mine to claim," he said. "You never were. Something acquired through dishonesty isn't ever really yours."

He looked into Rachel's eyes, watching her reaction to his noble confession. He felt liberated by setting free the lies that had bound him for the last several months.

She kept her eyes locked with his, keeping her defenses on guard. "You lied to me, deceived me."

"Yes," Tristan answered.

"You hurt me."

"I know." Tristan ran his hand through his hair and sighed

heavily. "That thought alone has tortured me more than you'll ever know. But I had to come back to explain things. You deserved to know the whole truth. So many times I'd tried to tell you, but I was a selfish coward. I didn't want to lose you. But no more lies, Rachel. No more deceit. Whatever you decide, I will accept."

Turning away from him, Rachel folded her arms across her chest. "I don't know how to trust you again." She sighed and turned back to face him.

"I know I don't deserve it," Tristan said, "but if I did have a second chance, I would spend every minute working to earn that trust back."

He walked over and took Rachel's hand, gently cradling it inside of both of his. When she didn't pull away, Tristan continued, staring deeply into her eyes.

"You're the best thing that has ever happened to me," he whispered.

"Tristan, I . . ." she began, looking down at the floor.

He took one finger and lifted her chin. "Do you still love me?" he asked.

A small teardrop hung in the corner of her eye. Tristan reached up and wiped it away, running his fingers tenderly down the side of her face while he waited for an answer.

Rachel closed her eyes and took a deep breath. Tristan was patient, though he could feel his knees shaking beneath him in anticipation.

Feeling her hand crunched tightly around his, he watched as she opened her eyes. "I love you," she whispered, her face suddenly becoming free of burden, "and I don't want to lose you again."

Letting out the breath he'd been holding, Tristan cupped his hand around the side of her face. Bending down, he sealed her lips to his with an unbreakable force. It was a kiss without secrets, without lies, and without a hidden agenda.

Parting lips, Tristan grabbed her around the waist and crushed her against him, lifting her off the floor. He could feel her warm breath against his neck and her beating heart against his chest. Her presence gave him the reassurance he needed.

The gleam in her eyes had returned, and the smile on her face was like seeing the sun for the first time in months.

"What now?" Tristan asked.

"Lunch. I'm starving!" Rachel grinned. "I think I've finally gotten my appetite back."

"You too, huh?" Tristan joked. "I've been living on cereal and Diet Coke."

As Rachel walked to the door, Tristan came up behind her and wrapped his arms around her waist. "Or, we *could* order in," he joked.

"As nice as that sounds," she agreed, turning around to capture his lips once more, "you still owe me, remember?"

"I thought I followed through with the picnic basket."

"The idea was to be taken out."

"Okay, but I still get to choose the restaurant."

"I should have known you weren't really a Mormon," she said.

"How? I was a great actor."

"Toga party?"

"Okay, Stewart got me on that one." They both broke out in laughter at the memory.

"You did look kind of sexy in that bed sheet though."

"Oh that's nothing. Wait until you see my Halloween costume."

"That ought to be interesting." Rachel grinned again.

Tristan held her hands in his and looked into her eyes. He had one more thing to ask her. Something he'd been waiting to ask her for a long time.

"Rachel, there is one more thing," he said. "I know I've still got a ways to go, and I don't know how long it will take me to get there." Tristan sighed, trying to find the words he wanted to say. "I know you may risk the chance of losing your inheritance if you wait for me. But I'm kind of hoping you will. I mean . . ."

"What, Tristan?" Rachel asked.

Tristan took her hand in his and looked into her eyes. "Will you marry me, Rachel?"

Tears filled her eyes and a smile slowly came across her face. "Yes! Yes, I'll marry you!" she exclaimed.

She lunged for him, almost knocking him over. She wrapped her arms around his neck and crushed her lips against his. Tristan held her face in his hands and lovingly kissed her back.

When Rachel pulled back, Tristan gazed into her eyes, wondering if she really comprehended the sacrifice he was asking her to make.

"Rachel, do you understand what I'm asking of you?" Tristan asked.

"Well, I think you just asked me to marry you," Rachel said with a confused stare.

"But I'm not ready to take you to the temple. If you wait for me, you'll lose your inheritance."

A grin appeared on her face. "We don't need to wait," she said.

"But I haven't even been baptized," Tristan insisted. "Do they let you go to the temple anyway?"

"No, you need to be baptized first."

"Okay, then. Like I was saying—"

"We can be married civilly, collect the inheritance, and then be sealed in the temple a year later," Rachel explained.

"You can do that?"

Rachel laughed. "You can do that."

"Then what are we waiting for?"

Tristan scooped Rachel up in his arms and kissed her lips. He was eager to start their life together, and he was happy to finally be free of lies. Tristan was ready to live his life to the fullest.

Twenty-six

The darkness of the bedroom disappeared, and the sun cast its early morning gleam over the city across the river. Tristan stood quietly by his bedroom window, mesmerized by the orange and yellow glow.

Cracking the window, Tristan inhaled deeply, letting his lungs expand with the crisp morning air. The colorful leaves of the treetops glistened when the sun finally appeared.

Tristan reflected on his past and looked forward to his future. He recalled the path that had led him to this point. For so long, he had been lost in a haze of selfishness, unaware of anyone else around him. Now here he stood with a new understanding.

Austin and Marley had been officially dating for three weeks. Not only had Austin dropped ten pounds, but he was also meeting regularly with the missionaries. His progress was a little slower than Tristan's, and he still had plenty of questions, but he was otherwise well on his way.

A soft breeze flowed through opened window and flushed over his face. Although he'd stood in that very spot several times before while contemplating the meaning of life, things were simply not the same on this particular Saturday morning. The old window hadn't changed, nor had the busy street below. He was the one that was different.

After breaking free from the chains of deception came a period of self-discovery. Tristan finally realized the meaning of life and where he was going. He'd uncovered the truth, and he had gained a testimony of the gospel.

Taking the missionary discussions enlightened his mind and captured his heart. With the help of the missionaries, the Spirit confirmed what Tristan already knew to be true. He was now ready to embrace the next step in his spiritual progression. He was ready to be baptized.

Walking back over to the bed, Tristan let out a sigh. Not everyone was as excited as he was about his baptism. His confrontation with Cole two nights ago still lurked in the back of his mind.

After his last meeting with the missionaries, Tristan decided it was time to tell Cole about his plans.

"I knew this would happen!" Cole erupted. "I told you not to read their poisonous book! It's corrupted your mind!"

"Cole, would you just listen to me for a minute?" Tristan pleaded.

Cole flopped down on the couch and folded his arms. The scowl on his face and his body language told Tristan explaining things would not be easy.

Tristan sat down and leaned forward in the chair. He kept his eyes focused on Cole, feeling a little like a criminal defending his actions.

"Look, Cole, I know you don't agree with my decision to be baptized, and I'm not asking for your blessing. Nevertheless, I am asking you to do two things for me," Tristan said.

"What? Help you choose the proper attire for your ceremonial dunking?"

"No, they've already told me what I need to wear."

"That figures."

Tristan ignored him and went on. "First, I want you to just listen to me while I explain to you why I want to be baptized."

"Fine, explain away!"

"I've always believed in God and in a life after death, but I wanted to know more. Reading the Book of Mormon was like being on *Jeopardy*. I received the answers before I could ask the questions. I had the most amazing feeling of understanding, and I knew that it was all true. I knew it because when I prayed about it, my chest felt like it was on fire. I received my confirmation through the Holy Ghost."

"Are you sure it wasn't just bad food?" Cole grunted.

"I'll tell you what I am sure about. I'm sure that God the Father and his son Jesus Christ appeared to Joseph Smith. I'm sure that Joseph Smith restored the Church upon the earth, and I'm absolutely sure I'm doing the right thing."

Tristan breathed heavily and ran his hand through his hair. "Cole, I'm not asking you to believe what I believe. We all have our free agency. What I'm asking is for you to believe in me and trust in my decision."

"I feel like I'm losing my best friend, and to be honest, it scares me," Cole confessed.

"It's true I'm not the same person that I was six months ago, but I'd like to think I've changed for the better. You and Austin have always been like brothers to me. That will never change. I guess what I'm asking is for you to accept me for who I am and stay my brother."

"I don't like it. I think you're wrong about this church," Cole said. "However, as your brother, I will respect your decision."

"That means a lot to me," Tristan responded with optimism. "Now for my other request," Tristan said, letting out a long breath. "We've been through a lot together. You've always been there for me and have supported me in everything I did— crazy or not. So, it would mean the world to me if you would come to my baptism."

Cole let out a heavy sigh and hesitated. Seconds ticked by while he contemplated Tristan's request. He finally looked over at Tristan and cracked a smile.

"I'll be there," he said. "How could I miss an opportunity to see someone hold you under water?" They both laughed, releasing the tension between them.

"Thanks Cole. You have no idea how much this means to me."

Although Tristan knew Cole might never believe in the Church, he knew they would always be best friends.

✦ ✦ ✦

Taking the two small steps, Tristan entered the warm water of the baptismal font. Just hours before, he was filled with so many emotions, from fear and anxiety to skepticism. Now the only emotion he felt was overwhelming joy.

His spirit seemed to be singing out with delight, rejoicing at the choice he made. His heart pounded with excitement, and his mind was full of gratitude for the gift he was about to receive.

Standing next to Tristan was Elder Scott Finlayson, one of the missionaries who had taught him the gospel. Tristan looked into his smiling face and felt comforted. He took a moment to look out over the several faces that were also smiling back at him.

Sitting in the front row were the people that meant the most to Tristan. Those he loved, those who had helped him progress spiritually, and those who had been with him through thick and thin.

Focusing his eyes on Rachel, Tristan gave her a warm smile. Her face was full of pleasure and love. It only took Tristan one glance to find reassurance.

"Are you ready, Brother Taylor," Elder Finlayson asked.

Tristan hadn't realized he was taking so long. He turned to Elder Robertson and nodded.

Taking Tristan by the left wrist, Elder Finlayson gave Tristan a wink and raised his right arm. After a short prayer, Tristan took a deep breath and was lowered into the water. His mind was free and his heart was full as the warm water engulfed his entire body.

In an instant, everything Tristan had been working for came into focus. When he emerged from the water, he could feel the burdens of his corrupted past lifted from his shoulders. He was refreshed with confidence, knowing he now stood spotless in front of his Heavenly Father.

Tristan turned to look at the friendly faces watching him closely. Next to a glowing Rachel sat Marley, her face lit with a smile. Austin was next to her with an expression that Tristan could only assume was curious fascination.

Finally, there was Cole. His face was tight and unhappy. Tristan grinned at him, breaking down the displeased look. Cole let out a sigh and nodded, returning Tristan's smile. At that moment, Tristan knew Cole had given him his blessing.

After Tristan left the water to change out of his white clothes, he felt as though he might burst at the seams. He never knew this kind of joy existed. The gratifying feeling of self-worth was undeniable.

Over the last six months, Tristan had found the love of his life and the truthfulness of the gospel. But in all reality he'd found much more than that—he'd found himself in the process.

Discussion Questions

1. How does dishonesty bind us from enjoying a happy life?
2. How did the visit to the Children's Hospital Carnival change Tristan's perspectives?
3. How did Tristan's views on The Church of Jesus Christ of Latter-day Saints change?
4. How was Tristan able to deal with his unwanted thoughts?
5. How did Tristan's childhood affect him as an adult?
6. What part of the Book of Mormon had the biggest impact on Tristan? Why?

About the Author

Linda was born and raised in Providence, Utah. She attended Cache County schools and graduated from Mountain Crest High School in 1988. She married the love of her life on November 28, 1987. Their marriage was later solemnized in the Logan Temple on June 3, 1989. They have five wonderful children, including a set of twins.

Linda and her family moved to Ogden, Utah, in 1994, where she continued her education at Certified Careers Institute. She graduated in 1995 with a degree in data entry. She has also taken classes in poetry and creative writing.

The Chadwicks moved back to Cache Valley in 1997 and have made their home in Providence. Linda is currently employed at the Cache Valley Youth Center, where she has worked as a cook for the last seven years.

Linda is a member of the Providence Third Ward and has had many callings in the Primary. When she's not attached to her computer writing, she enjoys camping, boating, and otherwise spending time with her family.

0 26575 54174 8